GIRLS FROM DA HOOD
2

GIRLS FROM DA HOOD 2

KASHAMBA WILLIAMS, JOY & NIKKI TURNER

GIRLS FROM DA HOOD 2

Urban Books
6 Vanderbilt Parkway
Dix Hills, NY 11746

ISBN 0-7394-6104-4

Printed in the United States of America

Chocolate Girl

By

KaShamba Williams

URBAN BOOKS PRESENTS

Chapter One

At age eighteen, Africa, a.k.a. Chocolate, came home from shopping in Manhattan's garment district as she normally did on Saturdays to purchase her knock-off designer gear and handbags, only to find a meal in the microwave and a note on the fridge from her mother. It read:

Dear Africa,

You fuckin' slut! How could you fuck my husband and walk around like you ain't done shit to me? I took care of your ugly ass when your father left us to rot. Dorsey didn't do nothing but help you, but I guess that wasn't enough. You wanted to fuck him too. You couldn't find your own piece of dick to fuck? Well, I'll tell you what, since your pussy is grown, let that mothafucka take care of you. Dorsey and I have moved on. Here are some words of advice to live by: Never fuck a man that belongs to your mother. You nasty tramp!

P.S. The rent and the light bill is paid until the end of the month. After that, you're on your own.

Metta

P.S.S. Slut, don't you ever call me Mommy again!

Africa Evans was the offspring of a young love gone awry. Her parents, Metta and Carlton, were married at the age of 18, fresh out of high school. By the time both of them turned 19, they parted ways, Metta was left with a bun in the oven.

If asked, Metta would claim Carlton to be the low down dirty dog of their duo, but Carlton would suggest the opposite. After they split, Metta went off to live in a poverty-stricken area in Brooklyn, New York—Sutter Gardens housing complex. The only possessions she had were the clothes on her back and baby Africa in her stomach.

She raised Africa with the help of the WIC program, welfare assistance and occasional help from her 33-year-old sugar daddy, Dorsey, whom she later married.

Growing up in Sutter Garden projects was lonely for Africa. The girls in the projects teased her so much because of her government name and her skin color that she was nicknamed Chocolate. Africa's low self-esteem coupled with her finger-spaced gap teeth, raccoon rings around her dark eyes, and charcoal skin didn't suit the bubble ass and perfectly matching wide spread hips. If he were to get a glimpse of her backside, a man would damn sure say, "She's phat as a mothafucka!" and women would be envious. However, once they took one look at her face . . . men would back the fuck up and say, "Damn, she ugly, but she got a bangin'-ass body. I'd still hit that, but only with the lights off." For women, it would erase all envy. But Africa had a common beauty, which is commonly overlooked.

Boyfriends were very scarce for Africa, although she fantasized about every cute guy in school and in the neighborhood, pretending that she was someone's girl. Dorsey, her mother's husband, however, was her reality. He was the dark secret on which some light was shed.

Africa balled up the note her mother had written and cried that night more than she ever had in her life. She never imagined that Dorsey would be the one to tell her mother about their secret love affair. Sex between them was blazin'. Why would either of them tell and ruin it? Africa often thought they'd get caught in the act. She also knew it would hurt like a two-edge sword if her mother double-backed on them.

Dorsey was gentle and sweet with her. Every stroke was a lasting one. With him, she never had to worry about being teased, for he always complimented her on the small things—her nails, her genuine smile, her fragrance. It was those little things that helped her build her extremely low self-esteem.

Too many days and nights Africa suffered verbal abuse from her mother. "Your father sure did mark your ugly ass!"

"Momma, that's not nice. You really hurt my feelings when you say those words to me."

"Come 'ere child." She would pull Africa to the bathroom mirror and make her look at herself. "Tell me what you see! How can I be hurting your feelings when what I'm telling you is the truth?"

When Africa's eyes met the mirrored image of herself, she screamed, "I hate myself! I hate myself!" over and over again; leaving a teardrop trail behind her. These were feelings she exposed on the inside of her home. She would never reveal to anyone that she had low self-esteem, but most knew it by the way her head hung low.

Her mother never ran behind to comfort her. She was still very bitter with Carlton after all those years for leaving her to be a single mother, taking all her animosity out on her daughter. Unfortunately, she couldn't get past her rubble or clean it up because the truth remained—Africa was the rubble of life that collapsed around her, and even though Dorsey came into her life, her heart had Carlton stamped on it. Dorsey became her security and she would never let that go.

It was Africa, at the age of sixteen, who came on to him the night of their first rendezvous while her mother worked the nightshift.

"Dorsey, would you mind putting this lotion on my back? My skin is dry back there," she called out to him from the confines of her bedroom.

Perhaps Dorsey should of said, "No," but he didn't. Instead, he went to look after her as he always did. He proceeded inside the room where she was resting her naked body, her breasts softly cushioned by a pillow, waiting for him. The baby oil was to the left of the bed with the towel beside it. Dorsey ran his lips across his gold-trimmed front teeth and closed his eyes. For a brief moment, he thought about turning around, but that changed when Africa parted her legs for him to see the plump, hairy pussy mound that he thought was winking at him. Instead of leaving, he closed the door behind him, locking it for their safety.

Africa silently and patiently waited for him to massage her down. Dorsey rubbed his hands together to stimulate his circulation, and bent down to pour some of the baby oil in his palms, never saying a word to her.

Dorsey was smooth, warm spoken and kind, never leading on young girls unless they pushed up on him. He was your typical sugar daddy, turned on by firm-bodied young girls. That's what had attracted him to Metta.

It was only a matter of time before Africa put her sweet chocolate juices on him. She had been watching his bronzed body far too long. When he gave Africa friendly hugs, they were welcoming. She romanticized how it would be if he made love to her to spite her mother. Would it be soft and gentle, or rough and hard? Either way, she wanted to find out for self-seeking reasons.

"Get the small of my back," she instructed, betraying her mother with pleasure, wanting him to nibble on her ass or suck her clit from the back as she had fantasized many times before while watching porn movies to bring her to climax.

Dorsey followed as instructed, massaging her backside in outward circular motions. When he reached her mountain-high ass cheeks, he slowly made love to them with his hands, opening her legs wider for his tongue to rest in between them.

Africa had sex partners in the past, but they were young and immature. Most laughed as they fucked her, just trying to get a nut off. So, when Dorsey placed his pointy tongue (while she raised her ass up in his face), and started to eat the shit out of her pussy with his tongue tickling her clit with it's back and forth movement, she loved it.

The baby oil spilled onto the floor when Dorsey kicked it over as he repositioned his body up on the bed to raise her ass closer to his face. She felt so soft and tasted like chocolate cream to him as he slurped away, trying to bring her to climax. Africa moaned, calling out his name in pleasure. "Dorsey, Dorsey, eat this pussy, daddy. Eat it!" That intensified the slurping to sucking. He began tongue kissing her clit, dodging his tongue in and out of her dark juice canal. She started going crazy over his mouth action.

She wanted to fuck badly and he knew it. But after Dorsey bought her to climax, he picked up the towel, wiped off his face and left her room to go into his and her mother's bedroom. He wanted the fullness of her body, but it felt so wrong.

He knew how his wife treated her like an unwanted child. Often he'd find himself feeling sorry for Africa because of the way Metta continued to call her unattractive. That's why he began to tell her she was beautiful no matter what her mother would say. He'd take her in front of the same mirror Metta did and make her repeat these words:

"I love myself, and I don't care what others think of me. I am not unattractive. I am beautiful and worthy to be loved."

Butterflies filled her stomach each time he made her repeat each sentence. In time, those harsh words her mother constantly poured into her spirit turned into vengeance inside of her. It was payback time!

Africa went running behind him, titties bouncing and ass steady jiggling like Smucker's jelly. "What's wrong? I won't tell. Please come back!" She yearned for him.

"I know you won't, but that's all for now. There will be a next time . . . if you want it to be," he responded, raping her body with his eyes.

"But I want it now. Can't you tell?" She slid two fingers inside of her hotness, pulled them out and placed them in his mouth. "You like the way it tastes, don't you?" Any trick to get him to penetrate her.

Dorsey closed his mouth on her fingers and swallowed to give his taste buds the full effect of her nectar. Africa placed her hand on his crotch and felt the hardness of his stiff member. How disrespectful she was, in her mother's room about to fuck the brains out of her mother's husband, and she didn't flinch about it one bit. Her mother deserved to suffer every hurtful feeling that her daughter felt when she verbally abused her.

"Not like this." He breathed out heavily, unbuttoning his shirt. She began assisting him. Her body was shuddering for more. She wanted to know what it felt like for him to be inside of her, mounting her. When his pants dropped, she pushed his chest back with her foot and his body landed on the bed, ready for her to joyride on his veined brickness.

Shaking her breasts in his direction, she wanted his mouth to catch hold of one of her firm nipples. He palmed them then began licking each nipple, side to side.

Africa wanted to suck his dick like she had done many other boys in the projects, but fought the temptation and gripped it to sit on. The moment she

7

wrapped her pussy lips around his penis, she yelled out in pleasure, "No wonder my mom married you. This dick is gold." Her 16-year-old hips were working the hell out of this 46-year-old man who'd watched her grow from a baby to a young woman. She was double pumping, squeezing her muscles tight on him, not an ounce of guilt about boning him on the same sheets her mother did. Revenge is bittersweet!

"Fuck me like you always wanted this pussy!" She stroked harder. "I see how you look at my body."

Dorsey's face began to distort. He couldn't take much more from this dominant, deep-pussy young girl. It didn't go unnoticed by Africa, who began to slow-wind him. She dared not to let him cum in her—this time. She wanted to taste the essence of his sweetness in her mouth. When she sensed he was about to cum, she hopped off of him pronto and slid her mouth over his dick, into the deepness of her throat.

"Good God a'mighty!" Dorsey screamed. Africa took him beyond ecstasy with her good neck pussy (head). Dorsey skeeted cum in her windpipe, causing her to lose her breath for a second until she swallowed.

He couldn't believe how experienced his stepdaughter was. Her pussy grip felt better than his wife's did, and many times after that, he longed for Africa's golden center at the risk of losing his marriage. He fell in love with her touch and the way she could make him feel. Even though he continuously encouraged her self-esteem, it was the sex that made him keep coming back. It was a rare occasion if he had sex with his wife. Making love to her wasn't the same anymore. She couldn't clench him like Africa could.

He knew why he was always attracted to younger women. It was the firm breasts and ass, and the tightness in the love canal that he yearned for. When he did make love to Metta, it felt sloppy and unpleasing. But he also knew he was playing in a dangerous zone, mounting someone under age.

However, they would continue their affair secretly for the next two years. That's when Dorsey's guilty conscience from "bending over" his stepdaughter began to haunt him in his sleep. Metta's suspicions arose on several occasions due to little things—Africa's panties in her room, cum stains on the sheets that they hadn't sexed on, and the way Africa was all touchy-feely when they were in the same room. Dorsey noticed how openly his stepdaughter started to behave, and before he found himself behind bars, he broke down to his wife, finally confessing to her what they'd done, blaming Chocolate for coming on to him.

Dorsey told Metta he understood if she left him. However, she chose to stand by her man and blamed her slutty daughter (as the neighborhood boys called her) for being so frisky. While Metta was hurt, she acknowledged her husband's apology, and flipped out on her daughter, leaving her to fend for herself. By this time, Africa was 18 years old anyway; Metta was so angry that she didn't give a fuck what happened to her.

"What the fuck am I gonna do now?" Chocolate asked, digging deep into her face with her nails to pop a pimple on her forehead. Dorsey had been her provider. He took care of her. All she had to do was have passable grades in school and come home and fuck him like he loved to get fucked and sucked. When she graduated from Franklin K. Lane High School, the sex sessions increased, and so did the amount of money. Now she would have to get a job to pay the rent and the bills if she planned to keep the apartment. Besides, who would care for her now? She was still the unattractive girl from the projects that people frowned their nose upon.

For this reason, she took on a job at White Castle as a cashier. At least this way she could cut the cost of food because she could eat there and save that money for other needs. She had no choice but to take care of herself.

Her plan to maintain the apartment only lasted for thirty days until housing informed her that her mother had terminated the lease and she had to vacate the premises—immediately! With nowhere to go, Africa found herself up shit's creek with oozes of it coming down like diarrhea.

She was happy after staying two weeks in a dingy motel that her father Carlton, whom she barely knew, came to offer his assistance one day when she was at work.

White Castle was packed with customers and the drive-thru was full with cars. Africa was doing her best to take her customers' orders quickly, to get them in and out. When Carlton stepped up to the register, she had no idea who he was.

"Yes, can I take your order?"

"I'll have five burgers with a side of fries, and here's my address and telephone number . . . use it." He began reaching for his wallet to pull out his money.

"Excuse me, sir?" Africa was startled.

"Listen, I'm Carlton, your father. I heard I could find you here. Now, let me get my order, and you get in contact with me so I can help you."

Dorsey had been watching from a distance. He had finally persuaded Carlton to check up on his daughter. It hadn't been his intention to leave Africa out there like that, but Metta demanded it. The least he could do was contact her father so she could sleep peacefully at night—not in the prostitute-infested motel that he'd watch her go in. He didn't want her to become victim of

10

that type of life. He wasn't completely unsympathetic. Plus, he felt the blame for stopping her cash flow, leading to her current living conditions. He knew her father through other associates, and thought this was an opportune time for him to make good with his own flesh and blood.

With the food order packed, Africa stepped out from behind the counter to question her father. The grimace on her face, with her curled lip, was an indication that she wasn't sure about him. She always wondered if she'd ever meet her father. If this was really him, she didn't want to miss the possibility of getting to know him. But when she searched the crevasses in his face, she knew he had to be. She was his twin.

"Are you really my dad?"

"Yes, I am. I was married to your mother when I was young. I ain't know what the hell I was getting into, before you start yabbing off at the mouth like your mother. And yes, I ran off like a man with no responsibilities. I wasn't ready for no family."

Africa giggled at his openness. "Why should I believe you, though?"

"Either you do or you don't. I don't give a shit. I've lived this long without you. I don't have time to play games with you."

That sure wasn't the response Africa thought she was going to receive. "Well, what the fuck you come for then?" Her voice rose, exposing her unhappiness.

"Because your step-pop said you live with prostitutes in a motel, that's why."

Africa paused. "You know Dorsey?" she asked with a sparkle in her eyes.

"I know that old mothafucka. He always did like young girls . . . He ain't never touch you, did he?"

"I'll ask the questions. You ain't been 'round long enough," she said to avoid his question.

"So, you can come live with me if you want to. I have a nice three-bedroom house in Rockaway, Queens. I also own a little flower shop out there. You can work in there. It's your decision." This was the best he could offer her; a clean bed and a job where she didn't have to slave as much.

"That's okay. I'm doing fine at White Castle," she thanked him.

Carlton started to walk away. "Well, never say I didn't offer."

"Hold a minute." She debated whether to accept his invitation. She was tired of living at the motel, and he was right; prostitutes worked on the hour, selling cunt. "Can I take you up on living with you?" If he wasn't her father, although he appeared to be, from the same finger-space gap in his teeth and other physical traits, at least he was nice enough to offer her a place to rest her head. She had an older man before. What difference would it make if he came on to her? She was into older men.

Chapter Two

"Welcome to White Castle. May I take your order?" Africa asked her customer with her head plunged low. Instilled with a complex from her mother, she purposely avoided direct eye contact with people.

"Only if you can look me directly in the face instead of acting like you can see me from the floor," the customer addressed her.

She lifted her head up and half smiled. She knew that voice was familiar, although she struggled a bit with her memory, trying to place the face.

"Hey, girl, stop acting like you don't know nobody," the pretty brown-skinned woman in her twenties with long, curly, sewn-in hair shot at her.

"Fire, is that you?" Africa asked, very surprised. She hadn't seen her in years.

"Yeah, it's me, girl."

Fire was her cousin on her mother's side. Metta had two sisters, one named Adrianne, who she didn't fool with behind some drama over Dorsey. Adrianne disagreed with her sister's relationship with Dorsey. She knew of him, and knew he was poison for getting with Metta, who was barely of age. By no means did she believe that he would settle down with her when he ran so many others.

Adrianne had two daughters, Fire and Marcy. When Africa was younger, they had many sleepovers at her aunt's house, but when Adrianne decided to move to Miami, they came to an end.

Her other sister, Jaletta, was a victim of rape and murder at the young age of 26, leaving her son Zulu behind with his heroin and crack dealing father. Zulu soon learned the trade. Africa hadn't seen him in years, but the years they shared growing up, they cherished. Zulu fought many battles with schoolmates and kids in the hood for calling his little cousin names.

"When did you come back? I thought y'all were living down in Miami."

"Chile, I've been back. We tore them damn strip clubs down in MIA. Bitches down there know about Fire and Marcy. We won't no mothafuckin' joke!"

"Is that right?" Africa asked, impressed by Fire's candidness.

"Yeah, girl. Since we been back up here, Marcy and I copped a crib in Marcus Garvey projects," she said, brooding in a harmonic tone.

"What about Aunt Adrianne?" Africa asked of the aunt that she remembered as kind and loving—the opposite of her mother.

"Mom's still in Miami. She said she was never coming back to NY."

"Damn! It's like that? I can't believe y'all been chillin' in Brooklyn all this time." She put her head back down somberly. "Y'all couldn't look your cousin up?"

"Don't even try that, girl! We went by your old crib in Sutter Gardens when we first came back. Some Cuban family was living up in there."

"Yeah, I moved in with my dad about a year ago."

"Your dad? When the hell did he come back around?" Fire asked Africa.

"I know, right. He showed up at the Castle one day, telling me, 'I'm Carlton, your father,' and I went with it. Turns out he was really telling the truth. He took me in when my mom up and left. It's a long story. One day I'll share it with you."

"Whaaat? Where did Aunt Metta go?" Fire was eager for the answers.

14

"I don't know, and I don't give a flying fuck!"

Fire studied Africa's face, noticing the pain that came across it in a flash. She felt sorry for her because she knew it was far more to the story. "Look, cuz, here's my number. Give me a call when you're ready. You can come hang out with Marcy and me in Marcus Garvey. It's mad niggas over there too. You do get dick, don't you?"

"Not like I used to," she mumbled, eyeing the telephone number.

"Give me a hug, girl. I need to get up outta here." Fire held her arms out, and Africa leaned over the counter to hug her.

"Tell Marcy I said what's up."

"You tell her. You got the number, and if you don't use it, I'll be back over here to bust your ass, trust," Fire added, swaying her hips toward the exit.

That night, Africa lay in her bedroom thinking about her run-in with Fire. She was debating on calling them. Yes, this was her family, but those were the ones who always hurt her emotionally—most of them, anyway. She wondered if Fire and Marcy would be included in the number. Or would they help her out of her slump? She hadn't seen them since they were kids and was skeptical, since people tend to change over the course of time. But did they change for better or for worse? Regardless of what she thought, she knew hanging out with them couldn't be any worse than sitting at home alone. She pulled the number from her nightstand and proceeded to dial Fire's number.

"Hello," a voice answered, and Africa recognized her cousin Marcy's babyish voice.

"Marcy, hey, girl. This is Africa. What the hell it be like? Long time, no see."

"Heeey, cuz!" Marcy sounded ecstatic, shouting happily the way they used to when they were little girls.

15

"Fire told me she ran into you down at shit burgers." She joked.

"Watch your mouth." Africa laughed. "Shit burgers put money in my pockets."

"So can many other things. It depends on what you're into." Marcy hypothesized, trying to get a feel where Africa was at mentally.

"Well, it's only work for me. I ain't into nothing else. My life right now is boring as hell. Got any ideas for excitement?" she pleaded with her.

"Shit, if I lived in Rockaway like you do, I'd be tucked away with one of those fine-ass Puerto Rican, Rico Suave-type pussy-eating mo-fuckas out there."

"Mmm," Africa sighed. She hadn't found one man out there that could put it on her like Dorsey, and she didn't want to waste her time with the boys her age again. Her intentions were to find an older man who could teach her some new tricks, not to play games with boys who needed to be taught how to be men. She wanted a man that was already groomed. They handled her better.

Marcy assumed that Africa didn't have a man when she sighed heavily. "Uh-huh, let me find out you ain't getting no dick. You're too old to be masturbating when it's plenty of pipes hanging in between niggas' legs that are ready and willing and ain't ashamed to say it . . . they want pussy!"

"Yeah, well, I'm good with my three fingers. Those bitches do a great job when it's time for me to let off," Africa confessed. "Besides, I'm into mature, older men."

"Damn, girl! You like suga daddies, huh? Ain't nothing wrong with that. Come on over to BK. One of these old heads would love to eat your ass out."

"You are still crazy as a mothafucka, girl. Where's Fire?"

"She's in the bedroom with her man, getting her back twisted out probably. Hold on." Marcy moved the receiver from her mouth to call Fire to the phone.

Africa waited for a few minutes for Fire to pick up. Marcy had put the phone down, but returned when Fire never responded.

"I told you she was getting her freak on. Anyway, here's the address." She gave it to Africa then asked, "When you gon' come over?"

"Probably tomorrow when I get off of work. Will y'all be home?"

"Hell, we're always here. Don't nobody work in this bitch. We're entrepre-negros!"

"Bye, crazy ass. I'll catch you tomorrow," Africa replied, disconnecting the call.

Africa was bored out of her mind living with Carlton. Their father and daughter relationship was nothing more than a "hi" and "bye" one. Carlton didn't make her pay any bills. He felt he owed her that much for being out of her life for so long and never paying child support a day in her life.

However, what he perceived to be mending a broken relationship was not, according to Africa. She wanted a loving relationship with her father, but Carlton avoided her as if she had a plague. That began the downward spiral of their attempt to form a bond.

Chapter Three

The following day after work, Africa went to visit her cousins as promised. The projects where they lived weren't too different from any other projects in Brooklyn, except Marcus Garvey houses weren't high rises. They were more like three-floor low-budget townhouses.

Africa suspected that Fire's house was the official hangout for everyone when Marcy told her that nobody had a job. She wasn't trying to fall into the same category; she was gonna keep her job no matter what, even if the house was jumpin' and she didn't wanna go home. How else would she contribute to the party if she didn't have a job? She didn't want to fall completely under.

When Africa knocked on the door, she was greeted with an open invitation.

"What's up, cuz? Come the fuck on in!" Fire greeted her. "Everybody, this is my li'l cuz Africa, a.k.a. Chocolate. That's what the fuck y'all can call her, and y'all betta treat her like she's blood, because if you don't, I'll fuck up every one of you bitches in this place." It was no doubt that Fire ran the house.

They were overjoyed to see her. She learned that with them it didn't matter what she looked like or what she wore; they loved and accepted her for who she was.

After the first visit, you couldn't pay Africa to keep her from Fire's crib. She quickly became a regular over there, showing up faithfully every day after work for five months straight. Yet even with all the time she spent over there, she never pushed up on any of the men that frequented the house. Although she had a silent crush on Rock, who was the older hustlin' partner of Talib, Fire's man. Rock spoke, was friendly and all, but he never came onto her, and she didn't want to embarrass herself by playing him too close at first.

One evening, Africa, Fire, Marcy and a mutual friend, Anne, were sitting around playing cards, sippin' on Alize, when they heard the echoing sounds of men talking trash outside the door. Fire went to the door.

"This ain't nobody but Talib an' nem making all that damn noise," Fire assured them, putting the spades game on hold.

"Who's them?" Anne asked. She didn't want to be bothered with her ex-man, Junior, if he was with them.

"Rock and Junior, your boo-boo," Fire teased, knowing that with the mention of his name, Anne's heart fluttered.

Fire had been involved with Talib for two years. When she met him, he'd just come home from Riker's Island. Talib was a former hustler turned Muslim. She took to him because she saw he was trying to live righteous, yet he did have faults as did everyone else. Talib and Fire played matchmaker last summer, hooking Anne up with Junior. It turned out to be a disastrous relationship. They went at each other like cats and dogs after Junior hit. They had fistfights in Fire's apartment over half of the time they were there together.

"That ain't my damn boo-boo. Matter of fact, I'm out. I'm not try'na be around his ass. I don't feel like fighting tonight or dealing with his stupid ass." Anne had become that frustrated and was getting up to leave.

"Sit your ass down, Anne. Ain't no nigga gonna run you out of my house. You are family," Fire insisted.

"Yeah, girl, if anything, this time we'll jump his ass," Marcy added. She was the sneakiest of the two, always creepin' off with a nigga.

Africa chose to keep her mouth shut. She knew damn well she wasn't getting into Anne's squabble if it jumped off. Fire and Marcy were the fighters.

The three men came marching in the door, wild and out of control. They had smoked out, and the smell in their clothing followed them inside. The women proceeded to play spades, but paused when Junior started to make Anne jealous with sexual advances aimed at Africa. Even though they didn't fuck around anymore, he knew how to make Anne's hair stand up on her arms.

"Chocolate," Junior called to her, snapping her out of her gridlocked trance on Rock.

"Yeah?" she replied, forcing herself to look away from the object of her secret admiration.

"How come you never bring some burgers over this bitch? You get them shits for free, don't you?"

"If we're about to close, I can get them free, but I mainly work day shift. I have to pay for them. I mean, it's a discounted price, but still that's coming out of my pocket."

"Check it, can a brother come through late-night when you're working to eat your burger and buns?" Junior asked flirtatiously, only to irritate Anne.

"I don't work nights like that," Africa replied, ignoring his childish behavior.

"Pay that cornball no attention, Chocolate. He's goin' through an Anne relapse. Nigga want attention, that's all, and he's trying to make her jealous by pushing up on you," Marcy explained to her, lighting up a cigarette. Her gold rings sparkled with the lighter flame.

"Oh yeah. Well, that shit sound good during warm-up, Marcy, but at game time, Anne and I know what it's really hittin' for," Junior came back, finally provoking the reaction out of Anne that he was longing for.

"Kiss my ass, nigga," she cursed him out. This was not going to be her night.

The argument caught Rock's attention and for once, he united with Africa's constant stares, wanting Junior and Anne to shut the fuck up and have a peaceful evening, if only for one night. Africa used this opportunity to really examine him. He was 5 feet 8 inches, 200 pounds of flesh with a demanding presence for his age. She could tell he was the eldest of the three. Maybe it was the maturity he possessed or the full mustache and beard that covered his face that made him more of a man in her mind. He had to be in his late thirties, so what the hell was he hanging around those young knuckleheads for?

At home, Africa fantasized about Rock as she had about Dorsey. *Rock is a real man*, Africa always thought; a man she wanted to make her own. Yet how could her flight of the imagination ever come true when she turned to mush every time she looked at him? She couldn't force a word out of her mouth. She wasn't even sure if he even noticed her. She began to wonder if she had only imagined it. Just then, when her doubt began to get the best of her, he looked again. For two seconds, she froze like a piece of ice, not moving or breathing, her heart racing a million miles a minute. Then she forced herself to look at the cards she was holding in her sweaty hands.

"Junior, don't come up in here startin' that bullshit. Talib, tell your boy something." Fire asked for her man's assistance before she started telling her guests to get the fuck out.

"Me? What about your girl? She's the one snappin' and shit. I ain't said shit to her," Junior replied in his own defense. He chugged down some beer and placed the bottle on the table.

"All right, all right, we're going in the back to fuck with the X-Box," Talib said, ushering the men to Fire's bedroom.

"Chocolate," Fire called, but she was wrapped up in watching Rock walk away.

Marcy peeped Chocolate, snapping her fingers in her face, getting her attention for Fire. "Snap out of it wit' ya hot ass! Damn! The nigga ain't goin' nowhere."

"I was asking if you were staying over tonight. If not, I'll get Junior to carry you on home."

"Oh, I'm staying . . . if your guests are," Africa replied, and Anne handed her a cell phone.

"Here, call your dad."

"For what? I'm a grown-ass woman. I don't have to check in with a damn soul!"

"All right then, bitch, it's a wrap! You can sleep on the pull-out bed." Fire commended her for boldness.

Africa tried to pull Fire to the side. "What's up with Rock? He got a woman?" she asked quietly, knowing if Rock was in the room she wouldn't be talking like that.

"Check Chocolate out, y'all. I think we're corrupting her," Fire announced to Marcy and Anne. "As far as I know, he fucks with plenty of bitches, but he doesn't have one main chick. He's always bragging about pimpin' hoes for they shit."

"He ain't really no pimp, but he doing something illegal to get money," Marcy interjected. "I know a little some'in about that nigga, but that's about it. I had an occurrence or two with him on a business level."

"Yeah, every time I see this nigga he's wearing some new hot shit, and I know he ain't got no job," Anne sided with Marcy.

"Did y'all peep the way he was looking at me?" Africa was looking for a little self-fulfillment.

"Don't fuck with him, Chocolate," Fire said, not looking at her.

"Why? What do you mean, Fire?" Africa asked, stunned, like her dreams of being with him were shattered by her cousin.

"I mean exactly what I said. Don't fuck with Rock. He ain't shit and he'll end up hurting you. He's older, more advanced and more experienced than you. The nigga is way outta your league." Although Fire was telling her for her own good, Africa could only think that Fire didn't know who she really was and how she was turned on by older men. She was too far gone and weak to resist the urges in her hot spot to not fuck with Rock. Still, she was crushed knowing that Fire held the power to keep them apart.

Fire read between the lines and reached across the table, taking Africa by the hands. "Listen, Chocolate, I ain't telling you what to do. I ain't your mother. I'm just warning you of what you'll be in for if you decide to fuck with that nigga. I don't think nothing good will come out of it, but who I am? I want you to trust me on this, but really, it's your go," she said warmly.

"Listen to Fire, girl. She's usually on point when it comes to men. She done fucked with enough men in MIA to know how to weed and seed the good and bad ones. Me personally, I know he ain't shit, but the ball is in your court. Fuck it. I'm trying to tell you about him, but it seems to me you ready to play regardless of what we say."

Marcy was trying to school her, but Africa wasn't even listening to them. She didn't read between the lines. Rock had her at "hello," and she knew if he gave her the time of day, she'd be all over his good-looking ass.

The men were relaxing in Fire's bedroom while the women continued to play cards in the living room. Talib and Junior were playing Def Jam Vendetta: Fight for New York on Fire's X-Box. Rock was leaning against the bedroom window rolling a blunt.

It was Rock and Talib who were fresh out of prison. That's where the two met and became close friends. Rock had only been out of jail for six months, and in that time, he held one job for two weeks, and he only took that job to keep his parole officer off his ass. Rock was a resourceful dude. He wasn't hustling drugs with Talib, he was hustling side goods like boxes of toilet paper, paper towels, cleaning supplies and other industrial products. He had a woman on the inside, working for a janitorial service, that was hitting him off with goods. If she were to get busted, he'd move on to another hustle—whatever, he could hustle out of the next victim.

In his previous years, Rock had been a big-time cocaine dealer in Brooklyn until it landed him in Elmira Correctional Facility in upstate New York. The only thing he had to show for his glory days was a two-bedroom apartment in Jersey City. He tried to maintain his expensive habit and addiction for clothing and jewelry, but the funds weren't adding up.

He wanted to get money using his old tricks, but the problem was, he was scared—not scared to sell drugs, but was scared of getting caught. The five years he did were a real kick in the ass, and he never wanted to experience being shackled again. Jail wasn't a spot he wanted to frequent, so to avoid that, his new hustle was catering to unattractive women with money or goods that could help support him. Despite the illusion Rock was under that he was pimpin', he was really only whoring for a buck like strippers who would go too far in the VIP room to get cash.

"Junior, why you keep messing with Anne? I'm starting to think you really do want her back. You had

24

your fun with her. Let her go, pimpin'," Rock said before licking the blunt to seal it with his juicy lips.

"Mind your business, dawg. Worry about black-ass Chocolate. We peeped you putting your mack stare down at her, ya fake-ass pimp, you," Junior retorted with bloodshot eyes.

"Man, I ain't said nothin' to shorty. You were the one talking 'bout eating her out, you nasty bastard." Rock lit up the blunt and inhaled with force.

"You did say that, though, Junior," Talib said, laughing with Rock.

"It sounded good, but y'all know I didn't mean that shit. Rock wasn't bullshittin', though. He was serious with his," Junior made his point.

"You damn right I meant it. She's a catch in my book. Bitch got a job and no responsibilities. I've been listening to her conversations with the girls." Rock admitted his true intentions of going after Africa.

"I knew it," Junior hollered. "You like that ugly bitch."

"Hold on, playa," Rock said. "A true nigga loves women and what they can do for him. Tricks like you love 'em for what they can do *to* you. You're after the pussy. Nigga, I'm after the paycheck! Feel me, pimpin'?"

Junior argued his position. "Nigga, that bitch work at White Castle's. All she can do for you is pay a mothafuckin' beeper bill. You was feelin' that broad. That's why you kept staring at her."

"Okay, boss. Just know that all are potential subjects, but sometimes I like to test my power of persuasion over them. You know? I call it keeping my tools sharp." Rock blew tree smoke in Junior's direction.

"So, how you think you did, pimpin'? Is the power of persuasion working properly?" Talib joined in sarcastically.

25

"Bitch, I got A-plus. That chick had an orgasm when I looked at her ugly ass. She's property if I want her. My game is that tight."

"I see," Talib pondered. "So, you think you got this chick in the bag?" He paused the game to look at Rock, hoping they weren't loud enough for the women to hear them.

"Mafucka, what part of the game did you miss? Nigga, I'm that one! This ain't no game. I'm real with my shit," Rock said, bragging on himself. "Nigga, how else do you think I got the name Rock? My shit is solid like that, pimpin'."

Talib reached for the blunt that Rock passed, challenging his game. "Dawg, I don't think you can get her. I think your pimp skills are suspect at best."

Rock put it out there for him to come up on some quick cash. "How much money are you willing to invest in your big mouth?"

"Bet fifty dollars, nigga," Talib quickly mouthed.

"Nah, bet a hundred." Junior upped the bet.

"Come on, y'all bitch-tossin'. Bet a thou' a piece, niggas, and pay my cell for the next six months," Rock suggested. He knew he would come out the winner on this bet.

"And if you lose?" Talib asked, rubbing two fingers across his upper lip and his nostrils.

"I'll hit both of you niggas off with a grand a piece."

"Cool, but what exactly are we betting?" Talib wanted to clarify it before he gave the final say so.

"That I can hit it and get at least the bitch's pay for a two-week pay period."

"And we're not talking about robbing and raping her for it, nigga!" Junior was putting him to the test because Rock was known to pull a fast one.

"Fuck, nigga. That ain't even my style." Rock frowned.

"How do you know when she gets paid?" Talib asked.

"Man, I've been paying attention. On Fridays when she comes over with a bag full of shit, that's her pay week. On her off days, she comes in bummin' shit. Feel me?"

"Damn, nigga!" Junior had to laugh. Rock had been clockin' her.

"All I need to know is how much time do I have to get this done?"

"You've got until Monday. Today is Friday. You have two days to get it done. Don't let it backfire on yo' ass!" Talib set the limits.

"A'ight, I only have one request."

"What's that?" Talib raised his wife-beater tee to show off his six pack of abs. He played the weight room close when he was in prison.

"Let me chill over here for the weekend to get it done."

Talib quickly agreed. It was no way in hell Rock could mastermind his plan in Fire's house, especially with Marcy around.

"So, Monday morning you gotta walk out of here with her money, and she gotta be all right with it," Talib instructed before the bet between them was misinterpreted.

"I'll have it done. Don't fret, nigga, provided that Fire and Marcy aren't in my face cock-blockin'," Rock replied, knowing Fire wouldn't willingly allow him to run game on her cousin like he did to her sister.

He got Marcy pissy drunk one night after they had been out all day, hustlin' cell phones. Celebrating the $2000 they made, both of them were up for a drinky-drink or two. Rock purchased two gallons of Yukon Jack

27

and two gallons of Armadale vodka. After five glasses of Yukon, Marcy was blacked out! Being the nice guy that he was, Rock told Fire he would look after Marcy when Talib and her stepped out to get something to eat. Soon as they left, Rock went to her bed, undressed her, fondled her, and then penetrated her. He left big passion marks all over her neck and her thighs so she could freak out the next morning.

When Marcy saw herself the next day, she was shocked. The last thing she remembered was celebrating with Rock. She knew it was his freaky ass that did this to her, but she was ashamed for letting herself get so drunk that she didn't remember what she'd done. When she accused Rock, he said she was out of her mind to think he would do something like that, but in fact, Marcy was something extra he had tasted. He would tease her with, "You give good love. Come on, girl, gimme that!" making reference to taking her unwillingly. This let her know it was him.

"A'ight, Junior will give Anne a ride home and I'll keep Fire out of the way. You'll just have to work around Marcy," Talib reckoned with him.

"Man, hell no! I'm not driving that bitch Anne nowhere. Let that wack bitch walk home!" Junior protested, still holding a grudge from the little spat they just had.

"You wanna win this bet or not?" Talib assured him.

"Yeah man, but—"

"Then drive the chick home. I ain't asking you to fuck her tonight. Just give the bitch a ride home," Talib reasoned, restarting the game.

"A'ight, I'll do it, but when you lose, Rock, I want my money, and I don't wanna hear you talkin' that pimp shit no more." He was sick of hearing that shit and hoped one day it would sneak up on Rock, and a female would reverse game on him.

Rock wasn't paying either one of them any mind. He was devising a plan to win the bet. He figured sex would come easy; she wanted him and he already knew that. It was the money part that he hadn't mastered, but Rock was capable of turning out an experienced woman, so Chocolate would be child's play. In his mind, he'd already won the grand prize.

"Let's hurry up and smoke the last three blunts so I can get to work," Rock announced like a winner.

Poor Africa had no idea Rock wanted to run game on her. She was in search of love.

Chapter Four

After the card and weed session, Junior went into the kitchen and offered Anne a ride home. She was prepared to curse his ass out again, but the thought of catching a bus back to Bushwick on the other side of Brooklyn wasn't too appealing. She accepted his offer reluctantly.

"I hope this is not on some bullshit, Junior. And before we leave, let's get this straight—You ain't getting' no pussy!" Anne proclaimed, trying to stand her ground. Junior brushed her off, knowing if he wanted to hit, he could. If she wasn't trying to fuck, she would've never accepted the ride home with him. So, the possibility was there.

Rock headed to the door with Anne and Junior. Africa had the saddest look on her face until Rock let Talib know he'd be right back.

Once he got outside, Rock went up the street to locate a dude named Moon. He knew Marcy had the hots for Moon. Being a man, Moon didn't turn down a shot at some easy pussy. Rock talked him into checking for Marcy on a booty call by promising him she was drunk and would be with it. His advice proved to be correct. Only fifteen minutes after Rock schooled him, Marcy was preparing herself to meet with Moon in his building.

Rock trotted over to the bodega to put together a rush job seductive kit. When he got back to Fire's apartment, everything was on schedule. Talib and Fire were in their bedroom with the door locked, probably ass naked by now. Africa was sitting alone in the living room on the pull-out couch, watching TV, curled up with a thin sheet. Marcy was on her way out the door, with her jacket half on, moving as fast as she could to get that booty call.

"Where are you off to in such a hurry?" Rock teased Marcy, already knowing the answer.

"I . . . uh . . . I got some business to take care of. Now, move outta my way, nigga!" Marcy replied, not wanting her business out there. "I knew you two were up to something. Don't fuck over my li'l cousin. I'm telling you, Africa, whatever you do, don't drink wit' this nigga! I mean that."

"Have a good time, Marcy. Shit over here is in control!" Rock held the door open for her and commenced to let his games begin with Africa.

"Shit, everybody's leaving. I might as well take my ass home." He played it off, making brief eye contact with Africa before turning and heading back to the front door.

She darn near panicked. She assumed that if Marcy was bouncing to get her groove on, she'd be left alone to kick it with him. But here he was on his way out the door, and she couldn't think of one clever thing to say to get him to stay.

"Rock, you don't have to go. You can chill and keep me company," Africa said with hopeful eyes.

Rock stood there holding his small brown grocery bag, appearing indecisive, before he drew his attention to her. "It's up to you, Chocolate. Are you sure you want me to stay? I'm not trying to impose on you."

"You can chill. I'd like that. I mean, that's if you want . . ." she said shyly and uncertain.

"Bottom line, do you wanna hang out with me or do you want me to take my ass home?" he said, punking her after she exposed her weakness for him.

"I really want you to stay, Rock," she admitted quickly before he left her alone.

Rock walked over and sat on the couch across from her. He stared at her silently until she had the guts to give him direct eye contact. Once she did, she smiled and turned away.

"What are you watching?" he asked to strike up conversation.

"Nothing. I'm channel surfing. Here, you can turn to what you want," she said handing him the remote.

"That's not what I want to turn on. I'd rather turn you on, but for now, I'll accept that remote you've got."

Africa immediately covered her mouth with her hand, hiding the sight of her gap. Rock skipped through six or seven channels before turning off the TV.

"Fuck TV. I'd rather talk to you." He began his *mind games*.

"That's cool. I watch enough—"

"Not to cut you off, but you have the most sexiest lips I've ever seen. Why do you always cover them when you smile? If it's 'cause of your gap, I find women with gaps sexy as hell . . . in more ways than one. I know your man loves sucking on them lips."

Africa's bottom lip fell to her chin. "I don't have a man." She made sure he saw her smiling even wider, thinking that she was full of sex appeal and more than willing to let Rock suck on them.

"Why me, Chocolate? Why?"

"Excuse me?" she quizzed, not knowing what the hell he was talking about.

"I'm easy when it comes to beautiful women. You don't have to run game on me. I know you have a man."

"No, really, I don't have a man!"

"Well, it doesn't matter. It's not like I'd have a chance with you." Rock appeared to be sulking.

A chance? Nigga, I'd marry you yesterday. Africa quivered at the thought. Rock had her that intrigued with his hypocritical ways that she wasn't up on.

"But you do have a chance," she whispered softly. "I've been trying to get next to you since I started coming around. I know you probably look at me as a young girl, but believe me, I don't mess with dudes my age. I'm into older men."

"If I had a chance," he said, "I'd be sitting over there next to you, holding your hand and whispering in your cute little ears."

She was biting his bait, responding by removing a pillow from the pull-out couch, tossing it to the floor to make room for him. "So, now what's stopping you?" She got bold with hers.

Rock eased over and pulled his legs up on the bed after removing his Rockport soft walking shoes. He took Africa's hand and gently massaged between her fingers. She knew at any given moment she would drop them drawers for him, one-night stand or not. But to her, it wouldn't really be a one-night stand since she'd known him for months now.

"Chocolate, why don't you have a man?"

She could smell the strawberry crème candy he was seductively sucking on, rolling his tongue like an expert. "I haven't found the right man yet. The guys my age play too many games." The truth was, she hadn't found anyone who could compare to Dorsey. That's why she didn't have any luck. She kept comparing them to a man she had in the past, setting her standards for another man from her last man. That always proved to fuck up her relationships.

"What are you looking for in a man? I may be qualified for the job," he probed.

"I'm really simple." She began to pour out her feelings. "I want an honest, loving man with a good sense of humor. One that's understanding and will hold it down for me. Of course, hittin' me off with some good wood and a few dollars here and there is warranted too."

Rock thought *Get real*, but replied, "What about a good kisser?"

"Yes . . ." she whimpered as he took her lower lip in his, sucking it softly. He worked his tongue around her lips before she opened her mouth fully to let him in to moist-dance tongues with him.

This was life, Africa thought as she enjoyed the feel of his lips on hers, his tongue exploring the inner depths of her mouth, the passion of his hands caressing the back of her neck. Then suddenly, it ended. Rock released her with a frown on his face. He began sniffing up in the air and under his arms.

"What's that smell?" He was all game. Africa was ignorant to the fact.

"I don't smell anything. What's it smell like?" She was surely embarrassed, but she was only concerned with getting her lips back on his.

"It smells like musk, like sweat," he said, pushing fast forward on the game he was playing.

Africa quickly drew back. She knew it had to be her. After all, she came straight from work and hadn't freshened up at all.

"Sorry, Rock. I came here from work." She was more ashamed than when a young boy from the Sutter Projects asked her if he could put his dick between the gap in her teeth.

"Don't worry about it, baby girl. We're human. We all sweat. You can easily handle that. It's your cousin's crib. Go take a shower."

"You mean right now?"

"Yeah, right now." He chin-checked her to see if she would follow his command.

"But I don't want to leave you out here." She really hoped this wasn't game, and that when she came out of the shower, he would still be waiting for her.

"Don't worry about me. I'll be cool. I ain't gon' leave."

"Okay, I don't think Fire would mind."

"Fire is handling her business . . . Are you ready to handle yours? And, after that kiss you put on me I wouldn't leave the crib without you, if it were on fire. Now take care of that and get back to Daddy!"

In the rush of the wind, Africa dashed to the bathroom to freshen herself up for Rock. She picked a towel, washcloth and a long white T-shirt to change into out of Marcy's closet. Every movement was in a dream-like state. All she could think about was the kiss Rock placed on her. She had quickly gotten past him telling her she smelled a little stale, since he was so kind about it. If it had been one of the young boys, they would have clowned her and broadcasted it in the hood.

While undressing, she noticed the moisture in her panties. Rock had her wanting him, as did her stepfather, Dorsey. They possessed the same presence to her, which pleased her lustful whispers.

Africa adjusted the water temperature before she stepped in the shower. With the white terry washcloth that looked as if it came directly from a motel room, she washed, digging deep into the lips of her private spot to get it squeaky clean. She wanted to tone down the itching between her legs so it could last, not cum too quickly.

While washing, Africa heard the bathroom door open. "Who's that?" To her surprise, it was Rock.

"It's me, Rock. I gotta take a leak real quick, if you don't mind."

"No, go ahead." This would be a way for her to check out his genitals and see what the nigga was working

35

with. She prepared to watch over him like a spotter in the gym, but as soon as she heard the stream of urine hit the toilet water, the lights went out.

"Why you turn the lights off? You gon' piss all over the seat," she stated in disappointment.

"So you wouldn't keep staring at my wood," he answered, laughing. When the urine flow stopped, instead of zipping up his pants, Rock dropped them to the floor and joined her in the shower.

Africa felt his naked body pressing against hers from behind. She tensed for a second, out of surprise and shock, but soon relaxed. This was the first time she'd actually taken a shower with a man. She leaned her back against his solid frame as he wrapped his strong arms around her. She felt the warmth of his mouth on the side of her neck as he gently kissed her, pushing all her fire buttons.

Rock began to grind his erect penis against her soft ass cheeks while he used the lather from the soap to wash her breasts and rock-hard nipples. Africa felt her fingers digging into her own furry mound. She was so turned on by his touch. Rock turned her around to face him and made himself believe that he was kissing Halle Berry when he palmed her face for an intimate kiss. Africa could feel his manhood pressed against her stomach right above the 'V' of her womanhood. She wanted to touch him with her mouth, but was afraid that he would call her a slut like her mother had, so she settled for making slow, circular licks around his nipples.

Rock pulled her small wrist and guided her hand down to where her mind wanted her mouth to go. She wrapped her fingers around it, enjoying the way he felt in her hand. Before she realized it, she'd bent his wood downward, forcing the tip to slip inside her creamy center. Rock allowed her to wrap her moistness around, even assisting her hips by lifting them up for him to get completely inside. He grinded deep, hitting her side walls, and couldn't believe how good the pussy was—it was tight, right and better than any woman he had been with since he'd been home!

By this time, she was pinned against the shower wall, and both of them were trying to see who could pump the hardest. Panting like a dog in heat, Rock stopped and released himself. At first, Africa thought he was doing what Dorsey had done many times, stop to let his nut pour out on her body, but Rock hadn't. He left Africa in the shower, stepping out of it, using her towel to dry off.

"What's wrong? Did I do something wrong? I didn't mean to if I did," she apologized, holding onto his bulky shoulders.

"Nah, you don't have to be sorry. It's my fault. I should be apologizing."

"For what? What happened? I thought you were enjoying this as much as I was." She didn't want it to end like this.

"I'ma be real, I'm only taking advantage of you. You were an easy catch, and I thought with my other head."

Africa was oblivious to his truth. She didn't care if he was trying to abuse her body. She had longed to be his target.

"I'm glad you're being real, but I don't care. All I know is I wanted you from day one. Now that I've finally gotten close to you, it don't matter if you only want to fuck. I can deal with that."

Rock couldn't believe how naïve Africa was. Here she was holding some of the best pussy around—she could sell and package that shit for cash—but she wanted to give the pussy away for free. She was definitely a catch for him to run with. Were women that damn slow, not to know they possessed the gold medal no matter what their facial appearance presented?

He tested her vow. "Do you really want it like this? I mean, I can make it really special."

"Special how?" She knew he wasn't in no love at first sight, but he sure kissed and touched her like he was in love. Or was it her illusion?

"We can discuss this in the living room after you put your T-shirt on. I'll be waiting for you." He left her confused and unsatisfied.

Damn! I can't even give the pussy away to him. She berated herself, pulling the tight-fitting white T-shirt over her head.

Africa walked into the living room and found the room lit with small scented candles on the card table. Rock was sitting bare-chested on one side of the pull-out bed, holding a small paper plate full of Hershey kisses. Africa was so enticed she didn't even wonder where he got the chocolate or candles. She was wide open.

"What's all of this?" she asked, standing beside the bed, watching the glow from the candle dance and flicker across his chest.

"It's your special night, baby girl. Lay back and enjoy your time. Shit like this only happens once in a while. Let's make it memorable."

Rock spent about fifteen minutes romancing her, saying the sweetest and most touching things to her, seducing her soul, and feeding her Hershey kisses. Africa was head of her world, queen of the Nile. The feeling that filled her body had to be love.

Rock asked her, "Chocolate, are you ready to give yourself to me unselfishly?"

She nodded without words. Admiring his lower half, she wondered how she withstood his package of meat.

When he climbed on her and started to make love again, it didn't matter if it was too much. Pain is love!

In the mix of things, Africa's T-shirt ended on the floor, leaving her completely naked, exposing her beautiful, curvaceous mold. Rock produced a small bear-shaped jar of honey to pour between her legs. She moaned as the warm globs touched her skin. He began to coat his lips with her moisture and the natural essence of honey. It felt amazing to her. The combination of bliss mixed with pain after he licked her down to pump his hardness in her, caused her to mumble sweet nothings.

After the love session ended, Africa rested her head against Rock's chest, listening to his heartbeat, wanting this moment never to end. This was a moment she wanted to savor.

"Rock, are you sleeping?"

"No, what's up?"

"I wanted to thank you for being so gentle with me."

He embraced her, thinking he had her where he wanted her. "That was nothing. Wait until we get to my crib."

Africa was flattered. She'd never been invited over a man's house. They always met her in dark alleyways or places that didn't have much traffic coming through, and here Rock was telling her he wanted her to come over.

"For real?"

"Matter of fact, it would be the shit if you could move in with me, but you're probably not ready for that." He planted his seed of hope.

Move in with him. She pondered the thought for a few seconds. *Why not?* He was right. It would be the shit if she made that move.

"Oh, I'm ready for that, believe me!" She was much too willing without even consulting with anybody about this.

"Well, it's not that simple, Chocolate. I've got other issues I don't want to get you involved with."

"Like what?"

"I have slight money problems. I don't even have enough to cover my rent this month. How can I move you in then turn around and get evicted, leaving you out there like that?"

Africa sighed. "How much you short? I can help if we're gonna be a couple."

"Baby, I can't take your money like that."

"Rock, don't be filled with so much pride. We all have our down times. Money isn't the issue. It's about us being together. I know we haven't been kicking it for that long, but I feel like I've known you for years."

"Damn, baby, I feel the same way . . . How much can you spare, though?" He aimed specifically at her cash flow.

"I just cashed my check. It was a little over three hundred. I wasn't gonna use it for anything in particular. Now, if you need more than that, I need to withdraw some funds from my savings account."

Rock's greed kicked into full gear and his wheels started turning.

"That would only cover a portion of the rent. I'm still five hundred short. If we go to the bank tomorrow to get the rest, we can get you moved as early as Monday."

"Hell yeah! I'm with that. I'm even with moving in as early as tomorrow. I don't want to spend another day without you."

It was settled. The next morning, they left bright and early, leaving Fire and Talib in dead man zone. They took a cab to the bank, where she withdrew $1000, handing over $500 to Rock. She still had a healthy balance because she'd been saving up her money from her Dorsey days and from her paycheck.

They went window shopping, and Rock even convinced her to try on a few engagement rings, gassin' her up. The entire day was spent on quality time together. He held her hand in public, kissed and hugged her, showing open affection. Africa couldn't believe her luck in getting with this man. He had to be feeling her, showing affection like this. In her mind, it was established. Rock was her man. Fuck what everybody else thought of him!

When their day was over and they finally parted ways, they'd made arrangements to meet up at Fire's apartment then rendezvous back to Rock's place. Africa went home to pack her things and Rock went to pay his rent. He was bullshitting that he was behind. That shit wasn't true.

Later that evening, Africa showed up at Fire's crib with two rolling bags and a carry-on bag like she was going on a trip. She explained her plans to Fire, Marcy and Talib. Fire's insides were turning, but she looked away cynically and kept her comments to herself. Talib was wondering if he'd lost the bet, but his uncertainties were clear when Africa told them she let Rock borrow $850 for his rent and utilities.

"Mothafucka!" Talib yelled out. "That nigga won the bet."

That comment went flying above Africa's head, but it smacked Fire and Marcy dead in the forehead. Fire was going to confront her man about it later.

"That's a lot of money to be giving a nigga you just gave the pussy to last night. I heard you two nasty buzzards sounding like y'all was making a porno." Fire knew that Africa didn't have a clue who she was fucking with, and smelled the smoke that was under her feet.

Africa quickly covered her wide-ass smile. Talib knew he was out some cash.

Chapter Five

Fire's house was in havoc for days after Africa spilled the beans about her and Rock. It seemed that everybody was beefing with each other. Anne was still going a hundreds miles a minute, arguing with Junior. Marcy was cussing Africa out because she knew Rock was playing her. Fire was hot with Talib for participating in the fiasco to lure money from her cousin, but none of them were tripping out on Rock . . . because he was nowhere to be found.

They joined for a gathering as usual, and Fire called over a good friend of hers, Nay-Nay, and her crew to come party with them. Talib had invited his uncles, Foots and Stoney, who in the past enjoyed sniffing coke, but had now escalated to cooking that shit up, hence calling it crack cocaine that they loved to smoke. The house on any night was a smoke-out, loud-cursing, card-playing, drug-passing party zone. The walls were painted ancient white with serious smoke stains residing on them. There were a few holes in the wall from Junior and Anne's brutish fights. Limited ambitions obviously had taken over this crib from the many destructive personalities.

Nay-Nay was originally from the same hood, but when her dad moved up in the dope game, he moved his family up out the hood and to the 'burbs. She only came back to the hood to kick it with Fire from time to time. This time, though, the other girls tagged along with her—Kendra, La-La and Harmony. Two of them seemed cool, but they didn't know what was up with the wanna be down chick.

"Nay-Nay, can I talk to you for a moment?" Fire pulled her up from the card table. "What's up with your little friend? I mean Kendra and La-La seemed chill, but home girl over there," she said, pointing to Harmony on the living room couch talking with Foots and Stoney, "she's trying too damn hard, okay!"

"Relax, she's cool. That ho's probably on a dream," Nay-Nay calmed her, trying to talk loudly over the sounds of "Dreams" by The Game that deafeningly blazed throughout the crib.

Foots and Stoney eased their way back to one of the bedrooms. Fire and Talib knew what that meant—pipe time. The rest of the group were heavily involved in the spades game and didn't even notice Harmony slip away to the bedroom to meet up with them. They just figured she was going to the bathroom.

Talib called Rock on the phone and told him to steer clear of them until he could make peace. He couldn't really be mad at Rock because the conception of the idea began with him, but Rock took it too far by taking Africa for that amount. However, he justified his actions by pointing out one thing.

"You can't tell a playa to pimp a ho halfway. That's like telling a surgeon to fix your heart halfway. I'm a professional—it's all or nothin'.'"

Talib reminded Fire that she schooled her cousin about fuckin' with him. But before he let Rock know it was cool for him to pass back through, he made him promise to apologize to Africa for the damage that he caused.

◆◆◆

Two weeks after Rock was MIA, Africa and Fire were sitting around the crib watching Marcus Houston on BET music videos.

"Didn't that young boy get thick?" Fire nudged Africa, who was sitting in her misery beyond depression that Rock pulled a number on her. "He's always been cute to me. He grew up, that's all."

Just as she finished her sentence, Talib, Junior and Rock strolled in. It seemed like months since Africa had last seen her so-called soul mate, yet she could still feel his touch as if it were a second ago. The sight of him made her cheery, but angry that he kept her waiting. In a flash, she gained a firm grasp on the phrase, "It's a thin line between love and hate." She hated him for the embarrassment she had to face, but she also longed for him for giving her the most meaningful, loving night of her life. He had put that hummingbird on her ass and had her singing for days, "Rooock." She sang even after she learned that his M.O. was using women for money.

The fellas greeted Fire and Africa, who greeted them in return. Rock avoided looking at them. Africa stared, waiting for him to utter a word, but eventually turned back to watch the videos when he failed to even glance in her direction. She wanted to ask him so many questions like, "What happened? Why did you do that shit to me?" And most importantly, "Why didn't you come back to get me as promised?" But she bit her tongue and sat quietly.

Casual conversation began flowing, but the tension was still thick. They were all waiting on Africa to open her mouth to dig in his ass. Everybody knew this was the first time she'd seen him since he dipped out on her.

Africa had grown irritated by the way Rock nonchalantly carried on like he hadn't shitted on her. Just when she almost brought herself to say something to him, Marcy and Anne walked through, carrying grocery bags. They went straight into the kitchen to put the bags down and came storming back in the living room with grills on their faces.

"Hell no! Y'all didn't let this dirty bastard back up in here," Anne shouted, referring to Rock.

"Nigga, if you ain't up outta here by the time I get my shit, I'm cuttin' ya funky ass, word up!" Marcy said, digging into her purse for her box cutter. He had played her family one too many times.

"Marcy, chill the fuck out. You ain't cutting no damn body. The same goes for you, Anne. I told him he could chill back over here. Whatever happened between him and Chocolate, that's their business," Fire stated, trying to prevent Marcy from cutting Rock the fuck up. She knew Marcy was spitting blood over this shit.

"Chocolate, curse that bitch-made nigga out. In fact, I'll let you borrow my shit. Cut him the fuck in pieces," Marcy supported, hyped up.

"No, Marcy. I can deal with this my way. Thanks, cuz."

"Uh-huh, bitch, your way is *no way*. Don't be scared of that no good dirty dog."

"That's not my name, shorty," Rock interjected. "If you're gonna keep using it in vain, get it tattooed on ya ass. Girl, gimme that! You know you want to." The men started laughing.

"Y'all think this shit is funny? You lucky it wasn't me, asshole," Anne shared with them.

"Word up, you would've gotten some hot grits thrown on ya ass had it been me," Marcy added.

"Both of y'all need to stop frontin' and mind your business," Talib spoke up on his boy's side.

"Chocolate is our business, and ain't nobody frontin' over here, nigga! Like I said, that nigga betta be glad it wasn't me."

"So you saying if a guy shit on you, Marcy, you're going to do what?" Talib asked, baiting her.

"Hot grits, bitch! That's what!" Marcy stood up and gave Anne a high-five.

"Anne, sit the fuck down! Junior used to treat you like shit on a stick, throwing your ass all around!"

46

"Yeah, but the nigga got punched all up in his face every time he did some bullshit. You were there most times," Anne replied proudly. "You see the holes in the wall, nigga. That's from mothafucka!"

"Yeah, from him bangin' your head up against it. And your dumb ass would turn right around and give him the pussy again. Come to think of it, didn't you give him the pussy the same night Chocolate fucked Rock? You also gave the pussy to him again last night, didn't you? Am I lying?" Talib pulled her card in front of everyone, and Anne quickly shot an evil eye to Junior, who sat back puffing on his blunt, not saying a word, just smiling. They had vengeful sex as much as they fought.

"That's what I thought," Talib continued. "And don't let me get started on you, Marcy. You don't even want to go there."

"What, nigga? You don't know shit about me."

"Word? I know that dude Moon up the block been shittin' on you. That cat gave you a booty call like a slut and you fucked him, no questions asked. Now he won't even mumble 'Hi' to your ass, and you callin' that nigga like you all turned out and shit."

"I ain't been calling him! And that little-dick-havin' mothafucka can't turn a baby out," Marcy came back defensively, wondering how in the hell he knew about that since Fire didn't even know.

"Oh yeah? Then why were you at the nigga's doorstep ringing his bell when we pulled up on the block? Yo, and the nigga telling everybody that you burned him. You might wanna get that shit checked out." He shut her up with that, just as he did Anne. "That's what I thought."

"Stay the fuck out my biz-ness, bitch! That's what you need to do." Marcy was vexed.

"Then stay the fuck outta Chocolate and Rock's. If she got beef with him, let her handle it."

Africa sat there quiet, pretending to be disconnected from the theatrical scene jumping off in the living room.

"Chocolate!"

"Huh, Fire?"

"Do you want to blast on this nigga? If not, we'll leave this shit alone."

The stage was set and the spotlight was shining on Africa. The mic was hers for freestyling. However, she was so stunned that the floor was hers, all she could blurt out was, "Why me?" Her voice cracked like a dam, and out came the torrents of tears. Africa fell apart; Anne and Marcy started toward her to comfort her, but Fire stopped them.

"Let her get that shit out. This is the only way she can get it out of her system." She didn't want any of them holding her hand through this. Africa needed to stand up, be a woman and deal with this on her own, but what happened next, she damn sure didn't anticipate.

This nigga Rock was a piece of work. He got up from his seat and eased over to Africa, who was still seated on the couch. He kneeled in front of her, took one hand in his and lifted her face with his other hand. He wiped off one of her tears and put it on his tongue, closing his eyes temporarily as if the taste of her tears were like ecstasy.

"Chocolate, let's go for a walk outside so we can talk in private. This started between us. Let's keep it that way."

"She ain't goin' nowhere with your fake ass," Marcy began, but Fire cut in.

"Marcy, it's her call. Chocolate, do what you want to do. You know right from wrong, and you also know he ain't shit! Don't let the game fool you."

Africa sat for a few seconds, crying, still allowing Rock to hold her hand. While she wanted to be tough about it, it would be a straight-up lie if she acted like she didn't want to go, even though the dog had already bitten her. She felt there was good in him and all he needed was a good woman to bring it out.

"Come on," Africa said, encouraged. "Let's walk and talk. After all, it's about you and me and nobody else."

"Ya cousin is a weak bitch!" Anne couldn't believe Africa left out with Rock when he dissed her like that.

Africa and Rock walked side by side up Saratoga Avenue in silence. Anyone from the outside would assume they were a happy couple in love, but they'd be only half right. Only Africa had fallen for that "love at first sight" bullshit.

"Did you pay your rent, Rock?" she asked out of lack of anything better to say.

"Of course," he sounded flatly.

"Why didn't you come back to get me then?"

"Because I didn't want to. I was on another mission."

"Damn, Rock, are you that heartless? You acting like you don't give fuck about what you did to me. Our night together didn't mean shit to you?" She was on the verge of another tearful flow.

"Chocolate, I'm not gonna stand here and play remorseful, acting like I'm a good guy, 'cause I'm not. I survive by finding women to provide for me on their own free will. That's how I eat. I wasn't trying to hurt you; I was doing what I knew best to survive—dickin' you down and getting paid for doing it so well."

"So, when we made love . . . you were only hustlin' me?"

"What did it feel like? Did it feel like I was hustlin' you? Or did it feel like I made love to you?" This caused her to flashback to that passionate night, and the answer was evident. Those weren't the kisses of a hustler, the touches of a hustler, the tenderness of a hustler, nor the forte of a hustler to fall in love; no, it wasn't the work of a hustler.

"You don't have to answer that, girl. Your heart is telling you that on that night, we were one. I gave you my all and took all that you had to offer. It was a beautiful thing. Now, here's some truth for you . . . I hustled your ass the next day. But like I said, it wasn't personal. It was business. I had money on the line."

"So, you hustle women, out of all the hustles out there? Why don't you get a job or slang rocks? Didn't you used to be a dealer?"

"I'm an ex-con on parole. Who's gonna hire me? And the only reason I'm not slingin' is I don't have the start-up money."

"So, where does that leave us? Are you done with me? I mean, am I still moving in?"

"What do mean by that?" He pulled away from her.

"Can there ever be an us?"

"Damn, girl, I'm sittin' up here telling you how I roll and you still want to be wit' a nigga?" *This is lovely*, he thought. "Baby, you can do better than an old con like me. If you catch the right nigga your age, shit might work for you."

"But I don't fuck with clowns my age. I'm attracted to older men, always have been. I want to give it a shot with you—I ride, you ride. How does that sound? We can do this shit together."

"Baby girl, you are so genuine. If I decided to be with you, it still wouldn't work. I'd still be dealing with other women for cash, and you'd get your feelings hurt again and again. I know you think I'm that guy, but honestly speaking, I'm not that dude."

"What if you had enough money to start slangin' again?" She knew money motivated him. Any trick she could pull out the hat, she'd try.

"Excuse me?"

"I said what if you had the money to get rolling? You know, get a pack. Would you still need to mess with those other women?"

"Well, not really if the down payment was right."

"But if I gave you the money, could we make it happen?"

"Fuck yeah!" It was always about the dollar. However, he was far from being persuaded without holding the start-up money in his hands.

Those were the magic words she was waiting to hear. She would help him become financially secure and they would live it up. Rock would be her man, and that would be that.

Dorsey taught her early how to take care of and please a man. Rock couldn't be any different than him. This was an obstacle she'd be sure to straddle high over.

That night, she began reciting in the mirror again, "I love myself and I don't care what others think of me. I am not unattractive! I am beautiful and worthy to be loved!" This strengthened her every time.

Chapter Six

Unfortunately, Rock didn't follow through as planned, and Africa packed up her belongings from Fire's apartment and headed back to her father's house. She would lay in bed with sexy lingerie, touching herself to the memories of him, but it was nowhere near as good as the real thing. She was like a crack addict chasing that first high, always falling short. It was so bad, she was worse than men in jail dialing for pain when they knew their woman would reject the collect call.

Working at White Castle wasn't the same; neither was frequenting her cousins' home. The majority of her time was spent in hopes that Rock would show up and brighten her day. All she could talk about was Rock, and her cousins were plain sick of hearing about that no-good-ass nigga. Marcy was so fed up, she slipped Africa his cell phone number to get her to shut up.

"Here, bitch. Here's the nigga's cell. Call that mothafucka and sing the blues to him."

"Thank you, Marcy." Africa couldn't wait to hit the numbers on the phone pad.

"You know it's fucked up when a nigga don't even give you his number." Anne shook her head.

Africa ignored them. She was tired of having visions of Rock screwing other women, knowing she could do more for him, but this was about to change. She held his number in one hand, the phone in the other hand. It was time. She dialed his number and he picked up on the first ring.

"Yo, who this?" He thought it was a potential.

"Hey, sexy."

"Yeah, that's true, but I still don't know who this is, and I don't like playing the guessing game, so I'm 'bout to hang up."

"It's Chocolate." She used the nickname they called her. "You forgot about me already?"

He paused for a moment and said, "How'd you get this number, Chocolate?"

"Marcy gave it to me. Are you mad?"

"It's not that. I just like to give out my number myself." He was on the other end mumbling disrespectful things about Marcy.

"I can't hear you."

"It wasn't meant for you to hear. So, what's up? Is this a casual call, a booty call or do you want something specific?"

"I do want a booty call, but I'm calling to fulfill my promise to you."

"What promise might that be?"

"Remember I said I'd get that start-up money for you so we can live happily ever after? It's time, Rock. I got what you need."

"How much do you have?"

"How much do we need to run off together?"

"Chocolate, let's not play games. Tell me how much you have and where it's coming from?" he asked short-tempered. It wasn't time for playing when it came down to getting money.

"My dad left his safe open and went to work. There's a lot of money and jewelry in there."

"Damn, shorty, you gon' rob your father to be with me?" His neck raised back from the cell phone.

"Well, it ain't like we that close. Fuck him!"

"How much money is in there exactly?"

"I don't know, Rock. That's why I'm asking you. How much do you want me to take?"

"Shit, take it all—the jewelry too," he told her, and she fell silent on the other end.

"Chocolate, are you still there?"

"I'm here."

"Talk to me."

"I'll take it all, but all I'm saying is I'll need to live with you because when I take his shit, I won't be able to come back here no more. If you do what you did to me the last time, I'll be ass out."

"I already know that, but this time is different. We'll be partners from this point on. Partners in the game and . . . partners in life. Us against the world, if you're willing to ride."

"You mean that, Rock?" She exhaled, closing her eyes, interpreting what she perceived as a new beginning.

"Get a pen and paper so I can give you the information on how to get to my crib—our crib." The plea was simple. He had captured her mind again with his cunning tricks.

Africa jotted down the info quickly. "All right, I got it. I'm on my way, sweetheart."

"Chocolate, don't leave nothing behind." He gave her inspiration. "I'll see you when you get here." Like a sponge, she sucked all of this up.

She hung up and went to work. In her father's safe, there were four stacks of bills and a small box filled with jewels. She emptied the safe's contents into a duffel bag and closed it. She quickly packed her clothing and other personal belongings once again to take flight. In the middle of her heist, she felt a tinge of guilt sneaking up on her. Here she was stealing from her from her father, the one that took her in when she had nowhere else to go. She kept telling herself that he owed this to her for being out of her life for all those years. However, she also felt that she was doing him dirty as she did her mother. Who gave a fuck, though? They left her out there, so she left them hanging out there as well. In all truth, did either one of them care for her? Her sudden challenge became to hurt them both for the lack of love, the abuse and the abandonment.

Africa wanted one thing for her past—to be put to rest.

She took a train and decided the train was stopping too frequently, so she got off to catch a cab. She took the taxi all the way to Jersey City, where Rock resided. When the taxi came to a halt, she double-checked the address and thought she must've made a terrible mistake. Before releasing the driver of his duty, she asked him to hold tight for a few seconds.

The building appeared to be abandoned, with broken windows on the first floor. She pressed forward, entering the dark building, looking for the second floor bell that Rock told her to push. When she felt around for the bell, she heard the taxi driver blowing his horn, and hurried to push the button. Thinking there was no way that Rock lived in this building, she allowed a teardrop to fall. That fool had stood her up again. It was fucked up that he had her on a wild goose chase. Damn if she wasn't fed up with him, but when he came thumping down the stairwell with his pants past his ass and his boxers showing like a young boy, she lit up like a firecracker.

"Hold on, baby. I need to pay the driver." She excitedly ran out to pay the impatient man ready to get back to work.

Once she got back inside of the building, Rock signaled for her with a slight gesture of the hand. He was not about to assist with her bags. Africa happily jogged her way over to him.

Despite the appearance outside of the building, Rock's two-bedroom apartment was filled with luxuries. Africa was taken aback by how nice it was. The furniture and carpeting appeared so expensive, and she really wondered how he could afford it. She knew he hustled women, but it couldn't be for that much.

"Damn, you got here fast!"

"The train was taking too long, so I jumped off to catch the cab."

"I don't understand why you would do some dumb shit like that. That was a sucka move. Don't be so damn easy! Make a nigga miss you for a change. Don't sweat a mothafucka all the time!" To Africa, his stinging words felt like a slap in her face.

"But . . . I thought you wanted me here," she replied timidly after seeing a side of him that she wasn't familiar with and didn't know how to take.

"You thought? You thought? Didn't I specifically tell you to take the fuckin' train?" Rock said in a dangerously calm, restrained voice, which was scarier than if he was screaming.

"Yes, but—"

"But nothing, Chocolate. This shit ain't gon' work unless you are willing to fuckin' listen to my instructions. From this point on, I'll make all the decisions. If you can't roll with that, then take your little money and roll the fuck out." He had the door unlocked and jarred it open.

Africa walked to him with tears trailing down her cheeks. She gently grabbed his shirt, looking up into his eyes. "I don't wanna leave, Rock. I want to be with you. I'll be good and I'll listen. I'll never do that again."

"Can you listen, Chocolate?" He reached for her face and planted a soft kiss on her lips.

"Yes, baby." She kissed him back.

Rock closed and locked the door, and gripped her tight. "One thing you need to do is stop all this fuckin' cryin'. I'm sick of that shit every time you think I'm not feelin' you. Stop being a punk bitch! Now, grab the stuff you vicked from your pops and let's see what we've got."

He spread out all the money and the jewelry from the bag, while he sent Africa off to fix them a bite to eat. After inventory and estimating the return on the jewels, he came up with approximately $16,000. He showed his appreciation by showering her in the kitchen with hugs and kisses, which she relished. After that moment, she never gave thought to how her father would feel about being robbed by his own daughter. All that mattered to her was Rock.

"I'm going to change my clothes and take you shopping for some official outfits. I can't have my baby running around in some K-mart, Wal-mart shit. Only the second best for my baby. Garment district, here we come!"

Africa loosed on his hug. She could afford the garment district. She thought he was going to take her to Neiman Marcus or other expensive retail shops. She didn't sweat it, though. At least they were together.

Rock left her and proceeded to the bedroom, pulled out a small ladder, stepped up on it and reached to open a secret compartment using a magnetized key chain. Inside, there was a small safe, where he deposited all the money she brought along with her, with the exception of $200 for them to shop. He changed into a thin State Property jacket and filled the pockets with her father's jewelry.

They were ready to leave when the doorbell sounded. Rock appeared puzzled. He had shooed away his other female friends for a week or so. When he gazed in the peephole, he saw two detectives. Without a word of explanation, he grabbed Africa's arm and rushed into the bedroom.

"What the—?" she said before he covered her mouth.

"Shhh, it's the cops. Who did you tell you were coming over here?" he asked in a soft whisper.

"I only told Fire and Marcy, that's all."

"Damn! For now, we've got to get the fuck up outta here."

They climbed out of the kitchen window onto the fire escape, then down into a small courtyard. They cut through a few backyards until they ended up on the cross street. Rock walked into a tramp-infested motel called Midnight, where he checked them in under a fake name after giving the clerk a few extra dollars. He quickly got her settled in.

"I'll be right back," he told her, rushing to leave.

"Where are you going?"

"I'm going to see what the cops want. Now sit the fuck tight!"

"What do you think they want?"

"You already know what they want! Now, it sounds like you don't trust me. Why do you want to be with me if you can't trust me?"

"I'm sorry."

"Just trust me, don't be sorry!" For a minute, he thought he may not see her again so he left her with the jewelry. He didn't want to part with it, but he didn't want to get hemmed up with it either.

He left the motel and rushed back to his crib in time to see the cops snooping around his building. They stopped when they saw him approaching.

"Excuse me, sir. You wouldn't happen to be Rodney Greene, a.k.a. Rock, would you?" the black detective asked, exchanging glances with his partner.

"Depends on who wants to know."

"Police, nigger. Don't be a smart ass!" The white detective ran his fingers through his hair and his partner

58

cut his eyes at him. He absolutely hated when his partner called black people—niggers.

"Is this your jurisdiction, of-fi-cer? I would hate to file a formal complaint for harassment."

"This is the last damn time I'm going to ask you—Are you Rodney Greene?" The frustration was written all over the black cop's face.

"Yes, I am," Rock finally admitted before they felt like supercops and hauled him away in cuffs.

"Are you an acquaintance of Africa Evans?" The racist white officer read from his notepad.

"Yes, I know her. I didn't know her last name was Evans, though. Is she all right? What seems to be the problem, sir?" He acted concerned. He wondered how they tracked her down to his place so quickly.

Carlton knew it was his daughter that got him. When he came home, he went to make a deposit to his safe and found his belongings gone. He hit the redial button on the phone. It was a Jersey City number. He suspected she'd stolen the money with the help or encouragement of someone else—that someone being one of her cousins. However, when he arrived at Fire's, they directed him to the police and told him the address where Africa might have been. That's how the cops got the information.

"Have you seen her today?" the white cop asked.

"No, sir! My god, I hope she's all right!" Rock was putting on a great act.

"When was the last time you heard from her?"

"I don't remember. A few days ago, maybe."

"What if I told you that we know for a fact that she called you today?"

"I'd ask you, what's your point? It still doesn't change the fact that I haven't seen her today." Rock remained unworried by the cops.

"You know, guy, you're a real wise ass. How about we search your fucking apartment?" The tight-ass white cop joined in angrily, wanting a reason to knock him with his club.

"Do you have a warrant? I know my rights."

"No," tight-ass reluctantly answered. "But all we need is probable cause, dickhead, and the fact that Africa Evans called you today gives us reason enough! So, do you want to cooperate or what?"

He allowed the salt-and-pepper duo to walk through the apartment to verify that Africa wasn't there. On their way out, the black cop stopped in the doorway.

"You plan on going somewhere?"

"No, why'd you ask that?"

"Whose luggage was that in your bedroom?"

"My ex-girl. I'm putting her cheating ass out on the streets. You know the rule: the bitch is only leaving here with the shit she came with."

"Sure." The white cop walked out. "When she comes back, have her call me, please. We know you're harboring her somewhere, and when we catch up with her, we'll make sure your ass gets booked too."

When the police were gone, Rock breathed easy, thinking that was too close for comfort. He couldn't afford to catch an accomplice to a robbery charge while he was still on parole. He waited a while before returning back to Midnight, where he'd left Africa. He was 'noid, but it quickly faded. Jersey City police had too many unsolved murder cases to follow up on to stake them for a warrant. Africa wasn't a high risk.

Rock entered the room carefully, checking both views before entering. Africa jumped up off the bed.

"What happened?"

"Those pricks were looking for you. Why didn't you keep your mouth shut? Any other time you do! Why you gotta tell them bitches your every move as if you need approval before you do shit? Now the pigs are after you."

"They are?" Her shoulders fell heavily.

"We have to chill here. It's no way I'm letting you back in my crib. I ain't going back to jail for nobody, especially a thieving-ass bitch!"

Africa put her head down and closed her eyes. "What have I done?" she uttered. She knew she couldn't return to work or Fire's, for that matter. If they traced her back to Rock's, they had to know about her other hangouts.

Chapter Seven

A week later, Africa still hadn't faced the cops. She was too busy setting up shop with Rock. They had cashed in on the jewels and came off with $3000, although it was worth much more. It was definitely do or die now.

Even though the hotel occupants were mostly prostitutes and junkies, Rock had her believing she was in a mansion. As promised, he took Africa to buy some clothing. He picked out Apple Bottoms for her fat ass and Evisu outfits. He even picked out a Blackberry Nextel for her. She was wide open, just like the gap in her teeth.

Africa, who never sold drugs or knew about them like that, informed Rock that she had a cousin in Brooklyn who sold weight. She learned this from Fire. All she had to do was get the number from her, but she was hesitant to make that call from her phone. So, she stopped at a payphone in case Fire got slick and sent the police after her. After all, she did rat Africa out. She would never tell Rock that she called Fire, though. He was already leery about dealing with her cousin, who he wasn't familiar with. He knew plenty of dudes that sold weight, but he figured if this was her cousin like she said he was, they could get better rates.

"Who the fuck is this?" Fire yelled into the receiver.

"Damn, girl, is that any way to answer the phone?"

"Chocolate, where the fuck are you at? I told you not to fuck with that nigga. He got you all jammed up!"

"Fire, please, not now. I can't put this on him when I initiated it."

"You would never harm a fly, Chocolate. I don't believe that shit. Rock has been known to steal panties from a bitch!"

"You don't really know me. I'm not that innocent, Fire. I know I'm in some deep shit, but I need a favor, cousin. Please don't scold me."

"What is it? You know I'd do anything for you."

"I need Zulu's num—"

"What the fuck? This nigga got you really gassed! I don't believe this shit. When Marcy told you to come get dick from Marcus Garvey, she didn't mean for you to lose your goddamn mind over your first shot, damnit!"

Fire made her laugh. "It's good to me, Fire. I can't explain it. He makes me feel better than my last lover. And you know good lovers are hard to come by."

"Well, dayum! Why don't you try a new nigga or go creep back with your last man?"

"I'm not pretty like you, Fire. Niggas ain't feelin' me like that. All they want to do is fuck me and ditch me. It's only been two men that genuinely cared for me . . . one is Dorsey, and the other is Rock."

"First off, Rock fucks you and ditches you! Secondly, that nigga don't genuinely care about you! Now, I don't know nothin' about Dorsey, 'cause I never met him. Who's that?" she asked.

"You know Dorsey . . . my mom's husband . . . my stepfather."

Fire's mouth was left open in awe. "Girl, you as slimy as they come. You fucked your mom's husband? No wonder Aunt Metta left you out there. I don't blame her."

"Fire! How can you say that?"

"Bitch, 'cause it's true. You are out there, Chocolate, and don't be using that excuse about your looks. That shit wasn't cool. It's somebody for everybody out there. You just have to find them, or let them find you."

Fire made her feel shameful. "I know it was fucked up, but it sort of happened like that. Rock is the only man who comes close to him. You can say what you want about him, but that nigga is swift with his shit."

"Write this number down, bitch, 'cause you talkin' stupid. You gon' be behind bars fuckin' with this nigga." She knew there was no hope for Africa, and was tired of trying to convince her to leave Rock.

Marcy grabbed the phone from her. "When I see you, Chocolate, I'ma fuck you up for G.P., for being so stuck on that broke-ass nigga!"

Africa didn't respond. She ended the call.

✦✦✦

Africa gave Zulu a call on her new cell phone and explained to him what she was trying to do in a roundabout way. She asked to meet up with him in Jersey City. He hadn't seen her since she was in high school, when she lived in Sutter Gardens. He wasn't a big fan on chillin' over the 'get high' houses. Usually he had one of his men sell out of one or near one. This was the case with Fire's and Marcy's house. He stayed away and let his man handle the business in Marcus Garvey. However, he did speak with Fire and Marcy occasionally. But this call from Africa shocked him, especially since it was about business. He didn't know she got down like that.

Africa and Rock were waiting in front of the motel when a cream-colored Benz SUV pulled up, sitting on 24-inch Oasis spinning rims and a sound system that echoed and pounded in bass for the block. Zulu jumped out wearing a black hoody. Swinging on his neck was a diamond encrusted platinum chain holding a ZU platinum pendant that was also flooded in diamonds. There was no mistaking him—Zulu was that nigga! He hugged Africa affectionately.

"Chocolate girl, what the hell you out here try'na do, little cuz?" He was still quite surprised by her call, but very happy to see her.

Trying to sound like a down bitch, she replied, "Trying to get that money like you, Zu. I've been hearing about you."

"Does Fire know what you out here try'na do?"

"Fire is not my mother; she's my older cousin. This ain't about her. Besides, who you think gave me your digits?"

Zulu checked Rock out from head to toe. "Who's this sucka-type nigga?" Rock was lined against the motel wall like a fiend waiting his turn in line to cop.

"I'm sorry, this is my husband, Rock." She wondered if Rock heard him. She didn't want any drama, and neither did Rock when it came to Zulu.

"You the nigga corrupting my li'l cousin?"

"Nah, playa, you got it wrong. She's corrupting me just like she's about to corrupt you." Zulu had to laugh at Rock's coward ass. He read all through him.

"So, what do you want to cop?" he asked Rock, assuming Africa made the call for her man.

"We're trying to get a quarter key of cooked-up coke."

"That's gon' run you about . . . nine grand," he informed them.

Africa and Rock exchanged looks, trying to get their figures together.

"Zu, this is me, baby. We family." Rock's quick negotiating lessons helped. "I'm not asking for nothing free, but I don't expect to be robbed by my own flesh and blood." She was prepped well.

Zulu laughed. "A'ight, Chocolate girl, you drive a hard bargain. You better be glad I love you, girl. Now, I'll give it to you for six grand, but you're gonna have to cook it yourself."

She looked at Rock, who dipped his head.

"Deal," she agreed.

"Anyway, how's Aunt Metta doing?"

"I guess she's good, but I'm not trying to talk about her. When can we get that?"

"I'll be back tonight," Zulu said before hopping back in his SUV and mashing out.

That's how the drug sales began. Rock said he wasn't getting involved with drugs, but this deal was too good for him to pass it up. Africa was already stationed at a hotspot—Midnight motel. They were running through product so fast that Zulu started giving them double for what they paid. They would just pay him back when they were done.

This was the life for Africa. She never had a taste of being a drug dealer or a wifey. Not only was she basking in the warmth and love from Rock, for once, she felt like the Queen of Africa. Then without warning, the sun became eclipsed by the thick, dark clouds of an oncoming storm. The rain fell, the thunder roared and the lightening crackled across the raging sky. Africa's world took a 180-degree turn for the worse.

Rock started growing restless and wanted out of this. He started staying back at his apartment every night, leaving Africa at the motel alone while he crept with other women. He had her thinking it was her fault that she wasn't pleasing him right. She would buy porn movies, hoping it would help enhance the freak in her. She was willing to try anything new, regardless of how degrading or humiliating it was. Whatever it took to keep her man out of another woman's face, she was with it. But all her efforts were a waste. Rock kept her at the Midnight motel and out of his place. He would show up with lipstick on his collar, condoms in his pants pockets, his skin scented by another woman's perfume. The only thing he didn't return with was an excuse or an explanation. He was also spending money faster than they were making it. It got to the point where they were no longer able to pay up front for their product; everything Zulu gave them was on consignment. They owed him more than $24,000, and that's when shit went terribly wrong. When Rock showed up, Africa knew he'd fucked up again. She'd seen that look on him too many times.

"What's wrong, baby?"

"It's gone, baby, all gone."

"What's gone, Rock?"

"The drugs—all of it—the kilo." He made Africa's heart fall to her stomach. It was Rock that pursued this, but now that it began, Africa didn't want it to stop.

"How, Rock?" She sat confused.

"Somebody stole it out of my crib," he replied, and without him saying it, Africa knew that 'someone' was a woman; a woman he was fucking. What she didn't know was that the night before, Rock went to a club, met a scheming-ass chick named Unique passing through from Virginia. He took her back to his place for a night of pleasure. After he hit Unique off, he fell asleep, thinking she'd fallen asleep too. However, she hadn't. This is how she made her bread and butter—casin' a nigga. She grabbed the money, all $11,000 of it, and a brick of coke after performing a brief search to find it. In the morning, the broad was gone and so was his shit, and he didn't even know if Unique was her real name. The playa himself got played!

"What are we gonna do now?" She was scared for Rock, not necessarily for herself. She knew Zulu wouldn't hurt her. But at the same time, she knew Zulu wasn't to be played with when it came to his money.

"Just call your cousin and tell him we need some more," he tried to convince her like it was all good.

"What?" she asked, stunned. "What about his twenty-four grand, Rock? What am I supposed to tell him about his money? He's gonna want his loot!"

"Tell him shit went wrong. Damn! Shit, niggas take losses in the game. He knows that. Fuck! Tell him he'll get paid or tell him take it as an L!"

"But Rock, I think—"

"Shut the fuck up!" he shouted. "I ain't try'na go through this shit with you. Just do as I told you and call your bitch-ass cousin."

Terror-stricken Africa grabbed her cell phone to call Zulu. She was hoping he didn't answer. It would give her some time to talk some sense into Rock.

"What's poppin', li'l cuz?"

Africa had to make up some bullshit excuse about how they didn't get back what they thought they would because they cooked up a bad batch. Zulu was a wise hustler. He saw right through her charade.

"Chocolate, put Rock on the phone right now." She could tell by the tone of his voice, he was about to blow his top.

"Yeah, this is Rock. What up?" he answered like he wasn't backing down.

"My fuckin' money, nigga! Where is it?"

"Didn't your cousin just explain to you what happened? Yo, just send us more work and we'll handle that."

"Listen, you bitch-made nigga. You must think yo' shit is sweet. Yo, I've heard how you been playin' my cuz. I'm coming to see you, nigga, on account of two things: my money and to beat yo' ass. You won't be able to hide behind my cousin for too long, coward, you feel me?"

"Fuck you, nigga. You feel me?" Rock squirmed a bit.

Africa grabbed for the falling phone Rock had dropped. "Zulu, please don't—"

"Chocolate, fall back. I ain't tryin' to hear that. I love you to death, but that is a dead nigga. I gotta teach your man a lesson," he promised her and hung up.

That night, Africa slept in the Midnight motel in Rock's arms and cried for him. She knew her cousin was serious, and felt partially responsible because she'd introduced them. Now things had gotten out of control. Around four in the morning, they were abruptly disturbed by three men who stood at the foot of the bed. The entrance was simple to get open—one slide of a credit card is all it took. As for the security lock, it had been broken. Maintenance repairs were nonexistent; Midnight staff members ignored them.

When the lights came on, both Rock and Africa were speechless. Africa was holding tight to Rock, thinking of something to say. There stood Zulu and two of his goons. However, when the goons pried Rock from her, she knew it was out of her hands.

"Get that chump up!" Zulu demanded, smacking him across the face with his pistol. Rock's face was immediately covered with blood. All that talk about "I'ma lova not a fighter" must've been true because he didn't even try to defend himself. He cried like a bitch.

Africa screamed, jumping out of the bed with her ass cheeks bare. All that was running through her mind was that they were going to kill him before she could help. One of the goons gripped her and took her back over to the bed.

"Zulu, Zulu, noooo! Please don't do this," she begged for her man's life.

"Chocolate, I already told you that I'm not tryin' to hear that shit. It's learn-a-lesson time for this bitch!"

69

"Zu, I'll get you the money. You don't have to do this, man," Rock said through bloody, split lips.

"Oh, now you're actin' like the true bitch you are. What happened to that tough talk, nigga? Didn't you say *fuck me?*" Zulu smacked Rock with the gun a few more times, breaking Rock's nose and opening a huge gash over his eye.

"Oh God!" Africa cried out.

"Here's what's gonna happen. You owe me twenty-four grand, so I'ma take two toes for every six thousand you owe me. That's eight toes, niggas!" Zulu wasn't playing with him. "Cousin, you learn a lesson from this too. This will teach you to stop fuckin' with fuck-type niggas!" Rock's feet started dancing to avoid the gun aiming directly at them.

"This ain't gon' work. Tie that nigga up. I wanna make sure I get my target right," Zulu demanded of his goons.

After Rock was tied and Africa had pissed on herself, Zulu cocked his silenced gun and blew off three of Rock's toes on his right foot. He spared the other five after the fluid leakage became massive. Rock's head was tilted back and blood spewed from his feet as he screamed in pure agony.

Africa gained a newfound strength, getting away from the goon's grip to assist her man. She held Rock for dear life, wrapping the sheets around his toes so he didn't lose too much blood. In the process, she pleaded to Zulu, "Don't kill him, Zu. He's all that I have." Luckily for Rock, Zulu always had a soft spot for family. And when it came to Chocolate, he knew how tormented she had been by others growing up. He really didn't want to add to her anguish.

"A'ight, ya'll, that's enough. Fall back," he ordered and walked over calmly to Rock, squatting down to his level. "Listen, fucka. My cousin saved yo' ass. I'm gonna let this shit slide as a gift to her. But that's my word, if we ever cross paths again, even by accident, I'ma body you! You betta hide from me for the rest of your fuckin' life, you got that?"

Rock was in so much pain he couldn't even nod.

"You betta, nigga!" And with that, Zulu and the goons left the room, passing by the prostitutes peeking from the windows, afraid to come out of their rooms.

Africa swiftly triple-wrapped Rock's right foot in a sheet and rushed him to the hospital in a cab with his bits and pieces of toes in a pillowcase, hoping they could be reattached. She knew she couldn't stay with him at the hospital because of the nosy-ass nurses and cops that would be out to question him about his injuries, so she left him there, returning back to her motel room to clean up.

Africa didn't know what to do as she gathered up her towels and washcloths to clean the splattered blood off the walls. This had been one hella chapter of her life. She went from bad to worse, to an even worse direction in her life. Was Rock that bad a man? Dorsey never took her through any of this shit. Their relationship was simple— sneaking, fucking, and money exchanging, that's all. Rock had her ass wayward. She had to admit he was worse than the boys her age. At least she knew they either wanted a blowjob or a quick fuck. They taunted her openly, and never showed affection to her. Rock taunted her, but it wasn't about her looks. It was only when she asked too many questions or didn't listen.

Still, she couldn't forget how he made her feel about her looks. In fact, he was the first man to ever tell her that her gap was sexy and that her beauty lay within: "Stop covering your mouth every time you smile, Chocolate. Beauty is only skin-deep. Stop being ashamed

71

of yourself. I think a woman with a gap is sexy, baby. That shit turns me on."

She remembered that night, and many other nights with him. He said the same thing on the night she joined Rock and another woman for a threesome. He had her licking the ass and pussy of another woman (a prostitute at that) named Tee-Tee, who plenty of men had stuck dick in, while he watched in delight. It was whatever to satisfy him. She would never tell anyone that, though. This was their little secret, and she was good for keeping them. If Dorsey hadn't ever told her mother about their affair, she would have gone to the grave with it.

When her crying finally ended and the room was cleaned, she was getting dressed and retrieving the last bit of money they had. It wasn't much, only $3500, but it was a start. She thought about leaving Rock, turning herself in to the police and trying to put her life into perspective, but that wasn't happening. Her strength came with the only words she was instilled with to make her feel better about herself.

"I love myself and I don't care what others think of me. I am not unattractive. I am beautiful and worthy to be loved."

◆ ◆ ◆

It had been a few days since Africa checked on Rock. She knew she couldn't go up to the hospital, and when she called up there, a woman would answer the phone. She figured it was another one of his women, and let well enough be. When he came home, she would see how he made out, but until then she was straightening out her life.

She moved out of the room at Midnight motel to another unit that was set up like an efficiency apartment. It was only slightly larger than the room she'd left. She couldn't stand the memories that were in the last room. After paying the crooked clerk for a weekly stay, she pondered in her room about her future plans. How could she get her life back on track? Had she gone too far, or was there still time?

Trying to put the chapter of her life to a close, she walked over to Rock's apartment, not even sure if he was there. If he was, he hadn't let her know. She tried his bell, but no answer. Maybe he couldn't get to the door with his missing toes the way he had before.

She proceeded to the back of the building to the fire escape. She climbed each metal step carefully. When she got to the second floor and peered through Rock's window, a woman was in the kitchen, barely dressed, cooking food. Africa tapped lightly on the glass, surprising the woman that she'd met before. This was the same woman Rock introduced to her as his sister, but judging from the way she was dressed, she couldn't have been kin to him.

"Huh?"

"Open the window," Africa demanded of the woman.

"Rock said if you came by not to let you in. I figured that was you ringing the bell."

Africa couldn't believe her ears. "Open this fuckin' window, bitch!" When the chick waved the spatula that she was flipping pancakes with as if to say "No," Africa used her might and kicked the glass in. She was getting in there whether they wanted her or not. The woman moved back, leaving the stove on.

Africa didn't fully understand what was going on. All that she sacrificed for him, and he would out her like this. She was down to barely nothing and had the police looking for her. How could he dismiss her again? She went into the bedroom to find him.

"Rock! Why are you doing this? I just saved your fuckin' life!" Africa was staring at him in his weakened state. His right foot was propped up on pillows, tightly mummy wrapped. His head was bandaged, and the rings around his eyes were blacker than hers.

"It's over, Chocolate," he mouthed out of fat lips. "Look at me. You did this shit to me."

"How can you blame this on me?"

"Because you fucked it up!"

By this time, the woman had returned to the kitchen because the smoke detector had alerted them.

Africa sat at the foot of the bed. "No, Rock, you fucked it up. Not me!"

"Just get the fuck outta here, Chocolate."

"After all we been through you gonna do me like this?"

"What have we been through? You ain't been through shit. I was the one beaten half to death. Look at my fuckin' toes. My shits are missing behind your ugly ass."

The pit in Africa's stomach hit rock bottom. This was the first time she'd ever heard him call her ugly. She heard a giggle come from the kitchen. An instant flash of her mother and the mirror came to her. *Look at yourself. What do you see? How can I hurt your feelings when you know I'm telling truth—you is ugly!*

Africa swallowed hard, "You think I'm ugly, Rock? So, all this time you've been lying to me?"

"I hope that nigga wasn't telling you, you was pretty." The woman returned and cracked up with laughter.

Africa was starting to lose her patience with the woman, but demanded answers from Rock.

"You know what, Chocolate? I didn't mean that. You know I was only playin' wit' you. But what could you possibly do for me now? You broke, wanted by the police—there's nothing in it for me anymore. The sex, well, we've explored damn near all we can explore. There isn't one hole on you that I haven't fucked. I've watched you with other women and other men. I turned your ass into a try-sexual. There's nothing left for us to do. You're used up, baby."

Africa felt shameful that she allowed him to do her like this.

"Let's not make this an ugly situation, Chocolate. Why don't you just go back home?"

"Home? Go home? I don't have a home to go to, Rock, remember?"

"I didn't tell you to fuck that up. You called me on that one. That was a plan you concocted by yourself. I helped by getting the shit sold and helping you spend the cash."

The waterfall began. Africa was so distraught. This was all her fault. She politely got off the bed, coming face to face with Rock's acquaintance. She took the plate the woman was holding and mashed it in her face.

"I bet you don't think that's funny, bitch!" Africa screamed her and left through the front door.

"I love myself and I don't care what others think of me. I am not unattractive. I am beautiful and worthy to be loved," she chanted, attempting to stop the pain that was in her chest after Rock fed her insecurities.

Chapter Eight

Africa was sent running back to Brooklyn, right to Fire's apartment, with her tail tucked between her legs. She had nowhere to go. Fire and Marcy welcomed her without judgment or a single "I told you so." Zulu had already put them down on the story so they didn't need to hear it from Africa.

"Bitch, you gonna pass the weed or do we have to get high off a contact?" Marcy asked Africa, who was begging for the blunt. "You starting to become a weed head. I remember when you was scared to blow. Now you blow any goddamn thing."

"Fuck you, Marcy! You ain't far from sucking on anything ya'self. I seen half the niggas you've fucked with." Africa had changed from the shy, non-confrontational woman they were used to. She may have had low self-esteem, but her mouth had gotten real foul and her heart was getting larger.

"You went there with me? I've been waiting to beat ya ass for a minute anyway."

"Fight for what?" Fire intervened. "Marcy, you mad because Rock kept Chocolate around longer than he did you."

That comment shocked the shit out of Africa.

"Mad for what? Me and that nigga never had a relationship! If you want to get technical, I don't even remember doin' the dude. So, why would you say some shit like that, Fire?"

"Because the nigga played both of you, and y'all up here arguing about him!"

"Well, when a woman is loose with it . . ." Africa remarked, but stopped in view of the fact that she was loose with him as well.

"Yeah, I was letting him taste my puddin' at one time, until I found out he was eating off somebody else's plate, but that was before Chocolate was in the picture. But bitch, you knew what you were doing. At least I wasn't paying to get fucked by him—you were and still would, slut!"

"Why do I have to be a slut, though?" Africa asked.

"You're right. You ain't even worthy to be called a slut. Especially since you was hittin' off ya mom's dude."

Africa's neck yanked in Fire's direction.

"Fuck, Chocolate, you the only one can keep that shit to ya'self. Mo-fuckas need to know this kind of information. If you'll fuck your own mother's man, you will beyond a doubt fuck your cousin's man."

"So this is what it means to kick a bitch when she's down? I thought y'all were true," Africa complained.

"And bitch, we thought you were true too. But we see with a dick in your mouth, you ain't shit!" Marcy still wanted to rumble. She was angry at Africa for being so fucking stuck on stupid over Rock.

"Marcy, chill the fuck out! Y'all ain't gon' fight over this bullshit. We family no matter what!" Fire concluded.

"Bitch, you robbed your family members, sold drugs, sold pussy, and ate pussy for that nigga. And he ain't do shit for you! You ain't got shit to show for none of your dedication to him. Even a prostitute has something to show for selling her ass!" Marcy continued.

"I don't know about you, but where I'm from, you get it how you get it." Africa had to bring her back down.

"And how the fuck did you think we was getting it in MIA?" Fire chimed in. "We did that, but we ain't let a mothafucka turn us out. I only licked pussy 'cause I wanted to. Here Rock was bragging to Talib that he was making you do that shit for him. Those bitches you were eatin' out were probably infected and shit. You let that nigga really fuck up your rep."

"I'm surprised he ain't start making you put a needle in ya shit. That's how far gone you are. You carry your heart in ya pussy, dumb bitch!" Marcy said.

"The dick must've been good to you, like it is to me, Marcy. You the one carrying on about it. You mad that he cut you out? Did you want to join us in a threesome? You want me to eat your pussy out? Is that what you want? 'Cause you sound like you hella jealous from this side of the room." Africa boldly got up out of her seat. She wasn't going to hurt a fly, though.

"You probably could eat a mean pussy with that hole between your teeth, bitch, but I'll pass. And for the record, I wouldn't fuck you with a dead man's dick! I ain't like you and Fire. I love me some dick! I could be left on a deserted island with nothing but pussy and not get turned on!"

"Marcy, what the fuck did I say? I'll handle this shit!" Fire knew things would never be the same between them. "Africa, I'ma help you find a spot to rest your head at, all right."

Africa had no choice but to run with it.

Fire did as promised and helped her find a place to stay. She knew sooner or later if she let Africa stay at her apartment, the police would come. Africa moved in with Fire's friend Indie and her daughter Kitty, who was 18 years old.

Not only did Fire find her shelter, but she also talked with Carlton, asking him to drop the charges against Africa, which he did. His only request was that Africa never showed her face to him. He was disgraced.

This was a milestone for Africa. Things began to get better, even with the odds against her.

✦✦✦

On spurts, Africa would call Rock. Fortunately for her, he didn't answer the calls. He would never show his face at Fire's anymore, so meeting him over there wasn't an option. Instead of sulking about it, she began to spend more time with Kitty, who was close to her age. They smoked weed together, talked about men, sexual experiences, and stuff like that. Kitty was well shaped, a dark cutie with short, wet-and-go hair. She was a true chocolate dime piece, and it was evident from the way the young men pursued her. With Kitty around, there weren't enough young men to go around for Africa. But she wasn't interested in them anyway. They couldn't satisfy the taste for "real" grown men that she had. They could only appetize her—she needed a full meal.

One night, Africa and Kitty were getting high in Brownsville, where they were staying, and Kitty revealed a little too much information to her.

"Hey, Chocolate, you ever got your pussy ate out?"

"Girl, I was getting my pussy ate out since I was sixteen years old. Why'd you ask that?" This was nothing to her. Her experiences with Dorsey, Rock and others moved her into the advanced sexual group.

"Because the other night, my new friend Marshall ate me out for the first time and—"

"And what?"

"That shit didn't feel right. I don't like that shit, and I don't see what all the hype is about."

"Kitty, that nigga just didn't know what the fuck he was doing, that's all. I promise you, ain't nothin' like getting a good facial," she joked, opening up her legs and pretending to be holding a man's head in place.

Kitty laughed. "Oh, you real nasty."

"You ever gave him brain?"

"Sucked his dick, you mean? Waxed his balls?" Kitty shared her terminology.

"Yeah, polished his pistol, smoked his blunt, gave him neck pussy, whateva you want to call it."

"Nah, I never sucked a dick in my life." She was tripping over Africa's sexual experience.

"Well, that's why Marshall ain't tongue-lashin' your kitty-cat properly. One hand washes the other. If you suck that knob good, he'll suck you good."

"Girl, I ain't know you was a freak like that!"

"It's plenty you don't know about me."

"Can I ask you a personal question, Chocolate?"

"What did you call the first one—a common one?"

"No, seriously. Have you ever felt unwanted, unattractive and alone?"

"Shoot, that's the story of my life, but I deal with it. Why?"

"Sometimes Marshall makes me feel like I'm less than. He's always comparing me to other girls he's been with, like I'm not good enough for him. He's good for saying he's gon' trap me with a baby and nobody else gon' want me 'cause I'll gain all this weight when I get pregnant and be all fat and outta shape. He makes me feel ashamed of my body. Do you think I'm fat and nasty?"

As often as Africa heard negative comments about herself, Kitty was much too pretty and nowhere near fat to let Marshall tear her down.

"Kitty, repeat after me . . . I love myself and I don't care what others think of me. I am not unattractive. I am beautiful and worthy to be loved."

Kitty smiled and hugged Africa. It was a Kodak moment. "You are so sweet, Africa. So, what are you doing tomorrow? Do you want to go shopping—my treat? School is only half a day. I can meet you back at the house around two."

"Sure, but when did you get a job?"

"I don't need a job to have paper."

"You ain't got no money, girl."

"Oh, you don't know? I got paid from an automobile accident three months ago. I got plenty of loot."

"Word? How much?" Rock had corrupted Africa so much that she was ready to get Kitty for all she had, even after the moment of bonding.

"I won fifty thousand and my mom got paid a hundred fifty grand for her injuries. I only got like thirty thousand left, though."

The numbers started dancing in Africa's head. Instantly, Rock's face popped in her mind.

"Now, do you wanna go shopping or not?"

"Hell yeah!" If only Africa could only figure out how to maneuver some extra cash from Kitty. This surely would be her passport back into Rock's world. It was only the money that caused him to turn on her like that.

✦ ✦ ✦

The next morning, when Kitty was rushing, getting ready for school, going through her beauty rituals, Africa was going through her purse. She stole her wallet, along with her ID and her bank book. Kitty rushed off to school without bothering to check her bag, assuming everything was intact. Africa hurried to pack all she could carry up out of there. She figured Rock would know a way to easily get the money out the bank without getting caught.

That was a long-ass train ride, Africa thought as she exited the station. She arrived at Rock's place and proudly walked to his front door, ringing the bell. He answered the door wearing only a robe and stepped outside with her, closing the door behind him. Africa noticed that his health had absolutely gotten better. Losing a few toes hadn't stopped him. He had sweat glistening on his forehead and he smelled like he'd been interrupted in the middle of a fuck session.

"Please tell me what the fuck you're doing here," Rocked demanded in a hushed voice.

"You need to stop acting like you ain't happy to see me." Africa wrapped her arms around his waist, pulling him near to her. Rock pushed her away.

"Stop playing, Chocolate! What do you want?"

"I want you, Daddy. I want us to be together again. I forgive you for the last time."

"I already told you, if there's nothing in it for me, what's the purpose?"

"Well, my money is right and I'm back. I know how captivated you are when it comes to money, nigga. You just like a gold-diggin' bitch that's been exposed to a nigga wit' a knot of money. Your sensors go off! So, tell that bitch in there she has to go."

Rock smiled. "All right, listen. The broad in here is trickin' me out for five hundred, so you gotta be cool. Whatever I say, you just smile and agree. Then I'll ask my company to leave. If you say anything outta your mouth, you'll fuck up my dough. You feel me?"

"I got you," she replied, knowing she had put herself back in the furnace.

They walked into of his apartment to his bedroom, where a Haitian woman in her early fifties was getting dressed. She looked a bit mangled, sweaty, well fucked, with her hair out of whack.

"Conda, this is my cousin, Africa. We gotta take care of some family business. Please excuse us."

"I was getting ready to leave anyway. I have a meeting in an hour." She signaled him with her eyes to his bedroom mantle, where the money was waiting for him.

"You can see yourself out. And call me when you need to see me again."

"Oh, you know I will." She blew a kiss to him.

Africa wasn't fazed. She knew how Rock operated. He could still woo the fuck out of a woman.

When the woman left, Rock went to business. "Where's the money?" Africa pulled out Kitty's bank book and tossed it to Rock. "What the fuck is this?" he asked, looking at Africa with a twisted face. She had to explain to him what she'd done. If they were going to move on it, they had to do it before the close of the business day.

"So, how do you get the money out?" Rock didn't have the answer at first.

"I was hoping you could figure that out. You the fuckin' mastermind behind stealin'. Damn!"

It took only a few moments before Rock's mind kicked into full gear. He rushed on the phone to call his Aunt Zetty. She was a white collar crime expert: credit card fraud, check fraud, embezzling, tax evasion, insurance fraud, money laundering and most importantly, identity thief. She was about her business.

"Zetty, baby, I need your help like now!"

"Is this my favorite-ass scheming nephew?"

"Yes, baby, but I ain't got time for small talk. I'm pressed for time. You got a line where we can talk freely?" He was concerned that her phone might have been tapped. She was into so much shit that the Feds stayed on her ass.

"We're good. What you need?"

Rock explained the situation and told her about the material they had to work with. Zetty gave him a crash course in making a fake ID and withdrawing the money from an account that belonged to someone else.

"Thanks, Zetty. I'll send you my appreciation after I pull this one off."

"Nephew, please, you don't never pay up. I need you to do one thing, though."

"Anything, you name it."

"Don't go in the bank yourself. Have one of your little bitches do it in case shit goes wrong. It ain't nothing like serving federal time. You'll do that for me?"

"Yes, ma'am."

"Call me and let me know how shit went. Don't keep a bitch in suspense."

After talking with Zetty, Rock put the plan in motion and did as she told him. Africa was now holding an ID with her photo, but Kitty's information on it, with the help of some Superglue and razor blades.

On the train ride back to Brooklyn, Rock had Africa practice Kitty's signature to perfection. Before she entered the bank, they reviewed the plan once more. Rock then disappeared into a pizza shop across the street.

Africa walked inside and left that nervousness outside with Rock. She gathered her composure and walked over to the table where the withdrawal and deposit slips were kept. She filled out a withdrawal slip for $25,000 of Kitty's balance of $30,000. Zetty had advised them not to wipe out the account. That would raise eyebrows with the tellers. When she finished filling out the form, she patiently waited in line.

When it was her turn, she handed over the withdrawal request and her ID and smiled. The woman looked over the ID for a second then back up at Africa.

"Please hold for a minute, ma'am."

Africa damn near shit bricks, wondering if she should haul ass out of there before she was ushered out in handcuffs. She watched the teller scan over the information with another employee of the bank. They had forty-five minutes before Kitty was dismissed from school.

"Miss Kitty Smith?" A voice came from behind. Africa turned to find a slim white man dressed as the average corporate asshole type. Her heart began pounding like an African drumbeat.

"Yes," she replied, answering to the name.

"I'm James Rice, bank supervisor. Would you come with me, please? Right this way."

Africa sized him up, wondering if a well placed kick in the nuts would clear her path for the door. But then she thought better of it and followed him. He led her to an office away from the tellers, where he took a seat and had her do the same.

"Is there a problem, sir?" Her mind was reeling with fear at this point.

"No problem, Miss Smith. Bank policy requires that any withdrawals over five thousand dollars be handled by a supervisor."

Africa thought the cops were going to arrive at any moment. She wasn't sure if this was a bunch of crock. Mr. Rice began making small talk, asking her stupid questions. She thought for sure he was buying time, but under the extreme pressure, she remained calm and cordial. However, on the inside, she was burning with fire. The wait seemed to be forever, but when another corporate bullshitter walked into the room holding a small money sack in front of her, she knew she was getting away without incident.

"Sorry for the delay, Miss Smith. For future reference, please call ahead of time and we'll handle you promptly."

Africa wanted to grab the money sack and run the hell up out of there and never look back, but she did exactly as Zetty instructed. She took her time, counting all the money as if she had all the time in the world. She signed off on the paperwork, scooped up her ID, placed the money inside of her bag and casually strolled out of the bank.

Rock told her to walk past the pizza shop so he could watch to see if she was being followed. The smile on her face told him she had pulled it off. If he could run with his bad feet, he would have, but he paced himself with his new cane for balance.

That night, in the heat of pleasure, Rock said "I love you," to Africa. She wanted to believe it, but knew it wasn't true.

The next morning, she went with Rock to a car dealership, where he thought Africa was going to buy him a car. There was a huge sign next to the dealership that read: PALM READER. Africa had never had a reading before and wanted to try it out.

"Rock, let's go get our palms read."

"Hell no! Give me the money. I can tell you your future for free . . . I am your future!" He laughed.

"Come on and stop being a chump about it!"

Rock couldn't disrespect her in return because she had power over the money. Funny how that reversed their roles.

"I'll be waiting in the dealership for you. You go get your reading."

"Yeah, you keep waiting." She snickered softly and he didn't hear her.

The heavyset Indian woman sat behind a small table with the lights lowly dimmed. "Come, child, sit down. I'll read your palm, and if you agree with what I say, you pay me what you can afford. Fair enough?"

"Fair enough," Africa replied, placing her hands on the table.

The woman took her hands, closed her eyes and began tracing the line of Africa's palms. She continued this for about two minutes before she finally opened her eyes. The warm expression quickly turned into a mask of worry. Then, a single tear fell from her chubby cheek.

"You've deceived one person that truly loved you as a child behind the lust demon."

Africa acknowledged with tears swelling in her eyes. She had to be talking about her mother, Metta.

"The man that abused you is very concerned about your life. He believes he's the reason you are the way you are. He wants to help you, and in your last plea for help, he will be there for you."

Africa was trying to steady her shaking hands. The reader was on point.

"Proceed with caution like the laws of Karma. Beware of your knight in shining armor. There is a cloud of darkness above him."

Africa froze. "What's that supposed to mean?"

"I only read palms; I don't translate the readings. My messages can only be comprehended by those that they are meant for, because only you know what's real in your life."

Africa knew what that meant, but she didn't want to accept it. She wanted to chalk it up and file it under "C" for coincidence, but her internal warning system knew that this was more than just a coincidence.

"Take care of yourself, Queen of Africa. Your chariot awaits."

Africa thanked her and slid her a $100 bill. The woman watched as Africa walked off to meet Rock. She clutched the bill in her hand and placed it to her heart, for she knew she just handled a lost soul.

Chapter Nine

Rock had Africa full of pride once more. They were back together like they'd never been apart. Africa wanted to visit with her cousins, but Rock wasn't with that.

"If you're going over there, you can go alone. I don't have time for Zulu to run up on me. They don't fuck with you like that anyway. I don't know why you wanna go there."

"Yes, they do, and you know what, Rock? I'm learning that your bark is louder than your bite. You ain't 'bout shit, nigga! Come to think of it, you ain't even try to fight back when Zulu was pistol-whipping ya ass."

Rock still hadn't gained access to the money, so he played it cool, but wanted to smack her teeth out of her mouth.

"Why don't you call Zulu on the phone?" If he could get Africa to pay off the debt, it was possible Zulu would let up off of him.

"I don't think so. I'm telling you, he's not messing with us."

"I have a suggestion." Rock played with her intelligence. "Why don't we pay Zulu what we owe to him and get it poppin' again?"

"Zulu ain't fuckin' wit' us no more."

"Not me, but he'll fuck with you. You wit' it?"

"That's damn near all the money."

"I'm sure he'll settle for a lower payment. Call him." he handed her the phone.

She dialed the number slowly. Maybe it was a good idea to pay off the debt.

"Zulu, baby, this is Chocolate. I got some cash for you. When can I get up with you?"

"Chocolate, don't play with me."

"I'm not playing. I came into some cash."

"Don't we all know . . . You came into Kitty's cash. That's fucked up how you snubbed her out like that."

Damn! Africa gripped her fist to her mouth and wondered, *How the fuck did he know that?*

"They took you in, Chocolate girl. What the fuck? You creating a path to destruction for ya'self."

"Do Fire and Marcy know about this?"

"You know damn well they do. How did you think I found out about it?"

"Are they angry with me?"

"Angry ain't the word. They gon' stomp ya ass out. This was Fire's friend and her daughter that you shitted on."

"Damn! I guess I have to go all out now, huh?"

"Might as well. What do you have to lose? I know you think you love dat nigga, but it's one-sided."

"Zu, I'm not sure if I ever knew what love is. As for Rock, I love how he makes my pussy feel. If that's love, then I've been stung."

"Why you ain't tell me that shit? I coulda been offed that cat. Your ass ain't in love, you dick-whipped! There is a difference."

"Honestly, I'm all right with the way our relationship is. Why can't everybody else be?"

"Yo, he got you robbing family. Y'all got me for mines."

"That was different, Zu. It wasn't intentional. Shit just went wrong. That's why I try'na make it right with you."

"I know how you can make it right with me . . ." He explained what he wanted her to do.

Africa was partly in accord with him, but only on one condition.

◆ ◆ ◆

Africa was trying preparing herself mentally and physically to let Rock go forever. But after she expended her entire arsenal of farewells, Rock hit her ass with the unexpected—he cried. He actually broke down in front of her, gaming her of course, and told her she was the only woman he truly cared for. He told her he'd understand if she didn't want anything to do with him, and she'd be right because he didn't deserve a woman like her, who would do anything for her man. His emotional outburst cracked the outer defensive shell she'd forged for herself. He'd done it again with his way with words. She was his putty to mold over again.

Chapter Ten

The dynamic duo crime wave continued. They put their hardhats on and went to work. Yet every crime they pulled was based around Africa. She was the foundation of all of Rock's good fortune since she hooked up with him.

They teamed up with a Dominican guy named Yogi, who made a living by paying off American women to marry Dominicans in exchange for citizenship. Using fake IDs, Africa had married over ten men, coming off with $7000 per marriage. They were low-balled, but still coming out in the plus with what they were making. They were in a plush position. She had paid off Zulu and even passed off $25,000 to make amends with Kitty. This hustle was paying off dearly. It was Rock that wanted to fuck it up by robbing one of Africa's husbands, Hassan.

"It ain't gon' make a difference if we rob him. Let the mothafucka go back where he came from," he tried to convince her.

"I'm not in on this. I got paid my money, and I don't want to fuck this up. If you rob him, you do that shit solo."

Shortly after, Rock broke into Hassan's home, tied him up and robbed him, clumsily dropping a fake ID with his picture on it. He came off with $30,000 in a cash box.

Africa didn't have anything to do with the robbery. In fact, Yogi was giving her extra cash for finding other women—mostly prostitutes she knew from Midnight. She got six hundred dollars for each woman that would agree to marry for citizenship funds as well. That should have been enough to satisfy Rock's hefty appetite for the bottomless pit of money that Africa kept feeding.

Yogi learned of the robbery when Hassan showed him the ID left behind. Yogi put out a hit on Rock's and Africa's lives. He was taking care of them financially, and didn't understand why they would betray them like that. Luckily for Africa, one of the young prostitutes named Tee-Tee, who she'd had a threesome with before, put her on to the hit.

"Africa, don't come around no more. Yogi got a hit on your life."

Africa knew it had to be behind Rock's dumb shit. This time, she had nothing to do with it. "What for, Tee-Tee?"

"From stealin' from one of dem Dominican dudes you married."

"I ain't have anything to do with that shit. That was Rock's doing. You gotta tell Yogi that for me. I'ma lay low until shit simmers down."

"Stay outta dodge from dem bullets, girl. I'll let Yogi know, if he'll listen. I'll try to help you out."

"Thanks, Tee-Tee. I owe you."

"No, you don't. All the pleasure you've given me . . ."

"I'll holla, Tee-Tee. Peace!" Africa quickly disengaged in that conversation. Her past kept coming back to haunt her.

Chapter Eleven

Zulu had three sisters on his dad's side, all of them in their late teens—the twins, Tracey and Tilla, and Larae. He purchased a small house in Far Rockaway, Queens for them, giving them one rule: No niggas are allowed in the house! He had been responsible for them ever since their father was charged in a drug scandal that got him nine years.

Africa went to Zulu as last effort to help hide her out until the confusion was cleared with Yogi. She explained the entire situation to him, hoping he would offer his assistance. He was cautious because of his past dealings with her, giving her fair warning that if she did anything slick that Rock had put her up to, he would hurt her. Then he would make her watch as he carved Rock up with a straight razor, and after he did that, he would put her out of her misery.

Africa knew how serious Zulu was about his sisters, and she knew his threats were lethal. So, she guarded her three cousins with her life. Larae, Tracy and Tilla were pretty girls, and undoubtedly attracted the cream of the crop of drug dealers. They reminded her of the pretty girls that lived in her building when she lived with her mother in Sutter Gardens. The three beauties had all of the attention. But Africa was conditioned for this. When she got settled in with them, she tried to convince them to slow down with the drug dealers, but they wouldn't listen to her. Eventually, with Africa being a follower, she started hanging out with them in the parks while their friends were slinging crack.

One day they were in the park when a cherry red Mercedes Benz convertible pulled up. A thick, pitch-black nigga stepped out of it. Anyone could tell he'd done some time in jail; his face looked murderous. He walked up and made eye contact with Africa. The way they were looking at each other, Africa prayed this wasn't the hit man Yogi hired.

"Yo, who the fuck is you?" He asked.

"That's my cousin Chocolate, Shamell. She's cool," Larae responded promptly.

Shamell was the big man that supplied the girl's little boyfriends with packages. He usually came around to pick up money and drop off work. The girls were clueless that he was seriously envious of their brother. Zulu was getting more than he was. Shamell had plans of finding a way to get at him.

After the scare from the run-in with Shamell, Africa decided to find out a little more about him. If he was gangsta like they said he was, he had to have major power in the game. She didn't want to gamble with her life by getting into something she couldn't handle. She told Zulu about him, and he agreed with her getting on the inside to find out what Shamell was really about.

Africa had Larae's man, Bake, hook her up with Shamell for a job. She told them she'd sold drugs before and she was good at moving product. Shamell was hesitant, but wanted to use her for knowledge about Zulu. He gave her a simple interview for the job and let her know if she fucked him, he'd fuck her with a spiked bat. She immediately got the message. Everybody that she was coming into contact with was trying to put her under.

Taking the late shift to ease up off her cousins wasn't the smartest decision Africa could've made. The girls had their friends in and out of the crib, knowing Zulu's schedule.

Although she didn't go sneak with Rock, Africa did still call from time to time, dialing for pain. She told Rock that she was living at one of Zulu's cribs and hustling for a kid named Shamell. Rock knew Shamell from Elmira, so he knew what kind of grimy dude he was.

"Let's set that nigga Shamell up, Chocolate."

"Noooo! Rock, I can't do this with you anymore. I already have Yogi looking to kill me because of you."

"Why not?" Rock asked, surprised. When it came down to robberies, she was always with it.

"Not him, Rock."

"You putting that nigga before me? You fuckin' him or something?" He was acting jealous to win her over.

"No, I'm doing what's good for the both of us. If some shit jump off around those girls, Zulu gon' be on my ass. I don't want to fuck it up with him. You know what happened the last time. If not, check your toes!"

"Fuck you, Chocolate, a'ight. Those bitches don't have to be nowhere in the vicinity when we hit that nigga."

"No, Rock!"

"We won't do it around them, baby. We professionals with our shit."

"No, we're not! Our shit is sloppy. That's why we get caught up. There's other ways of getting money without walking down that road," Africa said, determined.

"Like what, Chocolate?"

"I'm sure if we put our heads together we'll come up with something."

"Fuck it! I won't involve you, that's all. I'll do this shit on my own."

Africa sat quietly, knowing it was a lost cause. They were going to be cut to pieces and thrown in an old trash bin somewhere in Brooklyn by Zulu's goons, Yogi's goons or Shamell's goons. In her heart, she knew that something would go wrong.

"How are you gonna do it, Rock?"

"You know Shamell's schedule, right?

"Yes."

"Well, I'll get the drop on him and hit him up."

"That won't work. He has too many people on the block to get him that way. Too much shit could go wrong with one man trying to rob a dealer in his territory. You know this!" The last thing she wanted to happen was for them to die behind making poor choices.

"I'll help, but let me plan this one," she huffed.

Chapter Twelve

Africa worked with Bake and his boys from ten o'clock at night until four o'clock in the morning. Then the three of them would chill back at the hotel, where they would wait for Shamell to pick up money. One night, Africa surprised them with pound of weed laced with PCP.

"Where'd you get all that weed from, Chocolate?" the little nigga named Nap asked her.

"Are you gonna play FBI and ask questions all night, or are we gonna get high up in this bitch?"

"Let's get high. Fuck what Nap talkin' 'bout," Bake chipped in.

"Well, let's get the smoke-out session goin'," Africa announced, pulling out a box of blunts from her bag to complement the weed. "We're gonna roll up all this weed and smoke out 'til y'all young boys pass the fuck out."

"You must be outta your mind if you think you can smoke mo' shit than us," Nap challenged.

"Don't talk about it, nigga, be about it. Start rolling." She tossed them the weed and a box of cigars. They kept rolling and smoking, repeating the process until the weed was damn near gone.

Africa was only inhaling the first blunt. Anything after that, she would blow the smoke out. In a matter of time, the young boys were fucked up and out of it—with the exception of Remix. He was higher than Snoop Dog on a concert night, but was paying close attention to Africa's moves.

"Yo, you still fuckin' wit' that bum-ass nigga? Where dat nigga at?" Remix pried, looking at her through smoke-filled, glazed eyes.

"He's probably somewhere putting dick in your mother, son," she messed with him.

"Fuck you. Why are you fucking with that old dude anyway? What's he like forty?"

"I'm starting to think you got a crush on him, you talkin' 'bout him more than I do. How you know him anyway?"

"Shamell been put us down on y'all. He did time with Rock. He know the nigga ain't shit. Hittin' them mothafuckin' punks off in Elmira. That nigga a bitch!" This wasn't the truth. He wanted to watch her squirm.

Africa was steamed. "You don't know shit, you piss-ass young boy."

"Don't get all defensive. I'm sayin', I got a brother that's more your age. He'd love to slide dick in you . . . I would, too, if you let me," he said, observing her fat ass with his sexual hormones coming alive.

"You wouldn't know what to do with this pussy, young boy. I think I'll stick with my old dude if you don't mind," she told him while walking toward the door.

"Where are you going?" He lifted partway from his seat.

"Just making sure the door is locked," she replied, but instead of locking it, she unlocked it.

When she turned around, Remix had his hard dick out in the open. "Come sit on this dick and make it go down, Chocolate. I heard you got that bomb shit and you ain't scared to fuck."

Africa looked around at Nap and Bake, who were snoring. "All right, young boy, I got you." Instead of wrapping her thick pussy lips around him, she dove in with her mouth action. She had Remix moaning and shit while she eased one finger in and out of his ass. He had to enjoy that shit more than she did because he didn't even stop her. She sucked him into heaven, the way Rock had taught her. She bobbed her head up and down his pole, force-fucking his dick in her hot mouth. As he erupted, a spray of semen went down her throat. Africa showed him she wasn't afraid to swallow. His eyes had rolled to the back of his head. That nigga was past heaven—he was at the judgment center, in front of God for his wrongdoings, pleading for mercy.

"I'm getting in the shower," she lied to him on her way to the bathroom, hoping that she eased his suspicions. She turned on the shower and made the call to Rock, who was in the area waiting on her call.

"It's about time. Damn, what, was you in there fucking the little niggas?" Rock exploded.

"Sort of. Now it's done. Let's go," she said and waited for him to come.

Remix was slouched down in a chair with his pants still at his ankles when he saw the door open. He shook off the weariness and realized this wasn't a fucking dream. Someone had come up in the room, and that someone had on a mask, holding a big ass gun. He tried to snap into action, reaching for the gun he had tucked in his waistline, but his reaction time was slowed from the weed.

Rock cleared the space between them and hopped over a chair to pepper spray him. Remix bent over, coughing and wiping his burning eyes before Rock brought down the butt of his gun to the back of his head.

Rock quickly hit Nap and Bake simultaneously. They were high and out of it. He had the gun to Nap's face and was tying Bake up. "Who's in the shower?" Rock asked Nap, disguising his voice.

"It's a chick. She ain't no threat. Take what you want and go," he responded.

"One word out of you and I'll kill those two," Rock told him. Nap didn't move after that. Rock secured some cuffs on Nap's wrists and walked into the bathroom. Africa was waiting for her cue.

"Where's the money, bitch?" Rock had her by the neck, putting on a performance for them.

"We all have money on us," Africa screamed as if she was full of fear. The gun was to her head for the benefit of those watching.

"Listen up, I ain't try'na be here all night, so we gotta do this the messy way. I'm going to ask the questions, and every time I'm lied to, somebody's getting shot." He put fear in them. He walked toward Bake and pressed his gun to his throat. "The worst death has to be getting shot in the throat, 'cause that shot will slowly drown you in your own blood. Where's the money?"

"In my pants pockets," Bake replied.

"In the box under the bed," Nap pointed.

"In my dick." Remix had a straight grill on his face. "Come get it, nigga!"

"Oh, this li'l nigga is the smart-ass." Rock cocked the gun and shot Remix in the shoulder.

In less than a minute, Rock fumbled for the door with the money in his bag and quickly left the scene.

"Fuck! I'm a hemophiliac. I could bleed to death," Remix alerted them.

Chapter Thirteen

Shamell showed up at the hotel room about fifteen minutes too late. Rock had made off with all the loot. Upon his arrival, Shamell found the front door open and his four workers with dishonorable expressions on their face.

"I'm not even gonna ask what the fuck is going on up in here," Shamell grilled, taking the key that was thrown to the floor to see if it freed the confines of the handcuffs.

"Remix is shot. We need to get him to the hospital." Africa wanted to help him before he bled to death. But mostly importantly she wanted to flee.

"I don't give a fuck about that. How many niggas came up in here?" Shamell pulled out a gun and laid it across his lap. The room went silent. "Don't everybody speak at once, mothafuckas. I might get antsy and shoot somebody." His memo was duly noted and well received.

Bake spoke up. "It was one nigga that came in and robbed us."

"What? One nigga did four of you in?"

"He was packin', man, and the only nigga with a gun had his pants to the floor." Nap pointed to Remix.

Shamell turned to face Remix. "What the fuck was you doin'? Jackin', bitch?"

"No, I was getting some head from Chocolate," he admitted.

"I told you mothafuckas not to fuck with the bitch like that! How did the mothafucka get in anyway?"

"I don't know. Maybe he had a key, maybe the door was left open for him." Remix was leading up to Africa.

"This shit smells funny. Y'all keepin' something from me?" Shamell raised his gun.

"Man, we were outta it. I'm still fucked up!" Bake yelled, talking about him and Nap.

101

"What?"

"We got high and fell asleep, but a nigga woke us up with a gun to our heads. He already had the drop on us."

"Oh, that's good then." Shamell smiled.

"What do you mean that's good?" Remix was distressed by Shamell's evil grin.

"I mean if two of you were 'sleep, the other two had to see the nigga."

"He had a mask on," Africa spit out before the suspicion rose any higher.

"All you bitches gon' either work this shit off or sell some ass to get me my money. Whichever you choose. I don't give a fuck as long as I get paid."

Everyone was listening to Shamell except Remix. He stared angrily at Africa, holding a towel to his shoulder. He was replaying the chain of events that transpired that evening. It was Chocolate who suggested that they get high; it was Chocolate that was fucking around with the front door. And was it by coincidence that she sucked him off because he hadn't fallen asleep like the other two? He put the pieces of the puzzle together. The finished picture was looking more like one person . . . Africa.

"Rock! It was that nigga Rock!" Remix held his shoulder and another towel that Africa had thrown to him to double-pad his wound.

At the mention of Rock's name, Africa's heart dropped to the floor and her mouth dried up.

"What the hell are you talking about?" Africa asked, trying to convince them differently.

"You know what I'm talking about, bitch. You sneaky-ass ho! It was your punk-ass man that robbed us, and you set it up," Remix proclaimed.

"Boy, you are buggin'."

Shamell had his fingers on his chin. "Are you sure?"

"Yes, I'm sure. You know how grimy that nigga is. You put me up on him. Think about it . . ." Remix insisted.

"Yeah, she was the only one that wasn't high like that," Bake agreed.

"It ain't my fault y'all niggas can't handle a little bit of weed."

"Oh yeah, then tell me this: Didn't you check the door to see if it was locked before you hit the shower?" Remix couldn't even feel the burning sensation from the gunshot. He had blocked it out.

"Yeah, so?"

"Then how the fuck did he get in two minutes later?"

"And that's why your dumb ass think it was me? Maybe he had a key or maybe you let him in. You were the only one woke when I went to take a shower." She switched the blame back on him.

"That's all you got, Remix?" Shamell had to let this scene play out. He'd suspected Africa all along, but wanted to see how far she would go on acting.

"Shamell, I ain't hallucinating. Trust me! That's their forte, robbin' niggas. It was that bitch-ass nigga Rock!"

"He might be right, 'cause the stick-up nigga somehow knew where we chilled. Don't nobody know about the room but us."

Africa watched helplessly as they all began to point the finger at her. She had no help; no one was there to side with her this time. She was scared, watching as Shamell burned a hole in her with his eyes. She could easily see where this was going, and it wasn't a nice place to visit.

"This is some bullshit! Y'all niggas so scared to take responsibility for fucking up, y'all wanna point the finger at me."

Remix paused as if a lightbulb had turned on in his head. He walked over and grabbed Africa's bag off the bed. He rummaged through it for few seconds before he found what he was looking for—her cell phone.

"I knew it, bitch! The last call on your cell phone was placed to Rock." That was mistake number one. Africa didn't know what to say to that. He searched more and found a knot of money in there. That was mistake number two.

"Why didn't he take this?" Remix asked, throwing her money on the bed.

By then, Africa was so terrified, all she could do was hunch her shoulders. "I don't know." She had no answers as Remix continued to dig her grave.

Shamell grabbed her phone and called Rock, who thought it was Africa following up with him.

"What up, Chocolate? You outta that bitch?"

"Nah, nigga," Shamell fumed. "We figured you and your bitch out. If you want to see her alive, nigga, bring that money back!"

"You sneaky bitch!" Remix kicked her in the face and finally fell out.

"Bake, you and Nap take Remix to the hospital. I'll handle this broad." Shamell helped Remix to his feet.

Before they left, Bake and Nap started beating Africa like a young boy getting initiated on introduction night to a gang—she got fucked up!

"I'm sorry, Shamell. I didn't want to do it . . . I swear." Africa started to cry. All her wrongdoings with Rock had finally come to an end.

"Bitch, I ain't try'na hear that. You've been tried and convicted. Now I'll let my gun judge you." Shamell opened the cylinder of his gun and emptied the bullets. He put one bullet back in the cylinder and spun it, preparing for a one-way game of Russian roulette. He aimed at Africa.

"I sure hope my gun likes you, Chocolate." He pulled the trigger.

Click! Africa saw the flash of gun muzzle shots before, and was relieved when the gun didn't go off. She started wondering if her death would affect any of her loved ones. With all the shit she'd done, probably not.

"You's a lucky bitch. My gun likes you. But you're still gonna get my money back. Do you think that nigga gon' come to your rescue?"

"I seriously doubt it, Shamell. If you spare me some time, I can get it back for you."

"Don't come back with my money and I will kill Zulu's pretty little sisters."

Africa couldn't let that happen. She'd rather face Shamell than face Zulu.

Africa went to Zulu and told him how she'd fucked up again. She warned him to take the girls to another location until the beef simmered down. It was to his benefit. He wanted Bake out of Larae's life, so he planned to help Africa get out of yet another jam.

"Why the fuck you keep listening to Rock? He's a con artist. You ready to die over him?"

Africa sat silently with tears plummeting down her face. "I don't know what to do, Zulu."

"Rid ya'self of that nigga once and for all!"

Chapter Fourteen

When Africa walked into Rock's apartment a day later, he gave her a friendly hug and let her go. He knew shit had gone haywire, but wasn't gonna come to her rescue. He took a long look at her face and apologized.

"I'm sorry, Chocolate. I see they fucked you up."

"They whipped my ass, baby, and they tried to shoot me. You didn't even come for me."

"They would've killed us both. Why would I?"

"Well, Shamell said if we don't bring that money back, we're both dead anyway."

Rock took her inside the bathroom and pulled out the Neosporin for her cuts. "You'll live."

"So, what we gonna do?" She wanted to give back the money and let Zulu handle it.

"We're gonna chill and spend this money like we normally do."

"No, I'm really asking you, what are you gonna do about them beatin' my ass and try'na kill me?"

"What do you want me to do?" Rock gritted his teeth.

"I want you to kill them niggas, Rock—all of them!"

Rock realized she was serious. "Calm down, girl. It ain't that serious. You'll get over this."

"It ain't that serious!" she shouted. "They tried to fuckin' kill me, and you ain't gon' do shit?"

Rock calmly answered, "No," went to his closet, opened his safe and took out the gun he used to complete the robbery.

"You want them dead, you kill 'em!"

"Why you can't do it?"

"They didn't do shit to me. They beat your ass, not mines."

"Time and time again, I won't let sleepin' dogs lie. I keep dealing with your ass, but this is seriously the end!"

106

"Chocolate, I'm on parole. If I get into any trouble, I'm done. You'll get a slap on the wrist if you commit the crime."

"Fuck you, Rock. Fuck you! You never cared about your parole officer before, and nigga, since when you know a murderer get a slap on the wrist? You know what? You're right. Let's forget that I asked you. Give me the gun. Real bitches do real things, not pussies like you!"

Rock laughed loudly. "You ain't never been a real bitch! You ain't nothin' but another bitch that I gamed! Stay the fuck outta my life!"

"It was never shit between us. This was all my imagination that you would change. Can you answer this for me? Why did you insist on robbing Hassan after I told you Yogi was too good to us to do that?"

"Because that Arabian mothafucka had money that he wasn't deserving of. He shoulda stayed his ass in Iraq, that's why."

"Oh, one more thing." Africa's cheeks began to shine from her salty tears. "Did you ever care for me, even if it was just a little bit?"

Rock lit a blunt and snapped open a beer can. "Are you fuckin' kidding me? Have you looked in the mirror lately? I told you what I was about when I met you . . . You were no different. It was nothing but game, baby, and you let me play you over and over again." He knew this time it was finally over between them.

Africa stepped back, crying hysterically. *I love myself and I don't care what others think of me. I am not unattractive. I am beautiful and worthy to be loved.*

Yogi and his men came up the steps as Africa faded back. All she had to do was get Rock to admit that he was the one who robbed Hassan, and Yogi would let her live. Tee-Tee had to seriously convince them that Africa didn't have any parts of the robbery, and he agreed to speak with Africa after Tee-Tee's plea.

"You cocksucking motherfucker!" Yogi screamed. "You steal from me, you die!"

"What are you talkin' about, Yogi? Chocolate set this all up. She was in on it!" Rock began to shake uncontrollably. "Don't do this, man. I have money right here." He showed him the bag full of money.

"This is not about money. It's about dishonor."

Rock knelt to the floor. "Please don't kill me, Yogi. Take this money, please."

"Hit this coward before I do it!" Yogi had grown irritated with Rock's begging.

One of the Arabian men pulled the trigger and blasted on Rock. His body shuddered violently. Yogi took out his gun and shot Rock one time in the center of his head.

Africa couldn't believe she'd done it, but she was able to fulfill Zulu's request by ridding herself of Rock, once and for all.

✦✦✦

Zulu took Africa back to Far Rockaway to handle the remainder of their business. She waited in the cut for his crew to hit up Shamell, who was due to come through as usual. Zulu and his goons were close by in case Nap and Bake peeped her. They learned that Remix died from excessive bleeding.

Africa listened for Shamell's car. When she heard the loud music coming from the end of the street and saw the shine from the rims, she knew it was him. She had him in clear view. With a signal, one of Zulu's goons, with his energy from killing before, ran down the block openly with a gun in tote to blast him. Africa saw Shamell's head explode and his face caving in.

Shamell's people came out shooting. Africa knew her life was ending. With the gun that Zulu gave her for protection, she took off running instead of trying to use it. She ran for dear life and ran smack dab into Bake.

"What the fuck are you doing 'round here? Do you got that money, bitch?"

"It wasn't your money to begin with. This is between Shamell and me. Stay the fuck outta it, little boy," she told Bake, preparing to get away. He grabbed her arm roughly. Africa snatched it loose.

"Don't fuckin' touch me again," she yelled, hoping the others weren't getting close.

"What, bitch?"

"That shit you and them niggas did to me the other night is forgiven and forgotten, but if you put your hands on me again, you'll regret it, trust me!" Africa knew if he came near, she would have to use the gun.

Bake back-handed her and knocked her to the concrete. She reached up and pulled the trigger on him twice. He made her do it, she justified to herself, just like Rock did.

Bake's eyes froze and blood dribbled from his mouth. There it was again, that little kid's face, those young, inexperienced eyes she'd seen the first day she met him. He looked so pitiful, so sorry and hopeless. Regardless of how tough he tried to portray, he was a baby. It was bad enough she contributed to two deaths, Remix's and Rock's, now here was a third one. Was this her fate? Is this what the palm reader meant?

Africa turned as a barrage of bullets ricocheted around her, whizzing past her head, deflecting off the parked cars. She saw Shamell's Benz parked in the middle of the street, his goons running toward her, shouting lewd words. She dove for cover. She didn't see Zulu or his boys anywhere.

"Show me your fucking hands!" An officer shouted to Africa.

The police quickly put cuffs on her and Shamell's goons, and hauled them off to jail. It was all over the news.

◆⁕◆⁕◆⁕

It was eight months after Africa had been hauled off to jail, but today the steel didn't secure her, for she was at the hospital delivering her baby girl. The baby had come as a surprise. Africa didn't know a baby was growing inside of her until her entrance exam to the joint revealed a positive pregnancy test.

It was only a temporary stay until she was well enough to go back to prison. She was allowed to bond with her child for three days. The rest of baby Africa's life would be spent with someone else. She named her Africa because she knew her daughter was Mother Earth the day she gave birth to her.

Africa had written Zulu to find out how he made out. When he wrote back, she was relieved. She told him about her pregnancy and asked if he could locate her mother and stepfather. He did, and Africa sent numerous letters to them. It took everything Africa had in her to ask them to care for the baby because somehow she knew her mother would say no. It was surely no use in asking Fire or Marcy. They were through with her. Dorsey came to baby Africa's rescue from foster care.

Sadly, Metta did break when Dorsey came to her about raising baby Africa. It was ultimatum time. She made Dorsey choose between her and the baby. He selected the baby. He owed it to Africa to see that her baby would have a bright future, seeing as he was the beginning of her mother's misfortune.

Africa learned that she was powerless over some issues, and trying to get others to forgive you is one of them. Still, she questioned if her mother forgave her. On a collect call to her mother's house, she learned her answer.

"Africa, make this the last time to call my house collect. Your ass need to rot in jail 'cause you ain't learn yet how to stop spitting up on people. God don't like ugly, and he sho' don't like pretty—that's why he made you!"

"Ma, I'm sorry. But you need to know I love myself and I don't care what others think of me. I am not unattractive. I am beautiful and worthy to be loved, but it starts with me! I can look at myself now. For years, I never wanted to walk past a mirror, fretting my image. Not anymore. I can look at myself because I am beautiful on the inside and out!" Tears filled Africa's eyes. She'd finally interpreted what the palm reader was saying to her.

💣💣💣

There's no logic to being young and in love. It's a first-time trip from the realms of reality into an emotional state of existence, where all senses are intensified. Everything looks more beautiful, tastes much better, sounds more musical, smells much sweeter and feels sexier. However, when the ruler of your emotional realm is your lover who turns out to be a low down dirty dog, you'll soon discover that things also hurt much worse when it comes crashing down around your sensitive heart, especially if you have low self-esteem.

Africa was given five years for possessing a deadly weapon. She had enough time to revisit what her life should be like. Her cellmate thought she was crazy when she stood in front of the mirror, talking to herself . . .

"I love myself and I don't care what others think of me. I am not unattractive. I am beautiful and worthy to be loved, but it starts with me."

111

URBAN BOOKS PRESENTS

WANNA BE

A novella by JOY

Acknowledgments & Dedication

I must acknowledge Carl Weber for even calling me up to be a part of this project. He looked beyond both past book sales and experience and focused on my literary talent alone. There are so very few publishers, if any at all, who truly believe enough in an author to do that. I thank God so much for using and allowing Mr. Weber to pick up the phone at a time in my life when I needed to be picked up, when I needed confirmation that my years of struggle and hard work in the book business had not been in vain. Thank you for that confirmation.

Nikki and Kashamba, I'm humbled to be in the same company with you.

I would also like to acknowledge Aunti in Toledo, Ohio. I was told that if I wrote one more thing without mentioning your name, I would be in big trouble.

This book is dedicated to all of the readers who continue to give my voice a chance to be heard. I apologize if the use of the word *nigga*, the cursing, the explicit sex and the violence I sometimes use in my work offends anybody. Please don't get mad at me. This is just how it really goes down in the hood.

JOY

Prologue

Harmony ran her hands down her body—first her chest, her flat, tight stomach, her curvy hips and then her juicy thighs. "I don't remember feeling like this," she said softly to herself. She fought the pressure for long enough, and now she was allowing her body to give in to the seductive call for the very first time.

Heaven knows there ain't shit like the first time. Everybody remembers their first time for sure. Harmony repeated herself, only this time there was no sound at all. *I don't remember feeling like this.* The words played in her head. Her pouty lips, painted with a dark rose lipgloss, struggled to say them, but no sound came out. It was as if she was numb. It didn't matter. Harmony was so far gone anyway. She was too wrapped up in the way she was feeling at the moment to realize that she was even holding a conversation with herself.

She leaned back on the bed onto her elbows. Her tongue rolled across her front teeth in slow motion. Hell, at this point, everything was in slow motion. Harmony's life was idle, yet the world continued going 'round and 'round . . . in slow motion. Who knew the first time would feel this way?

Harmony moaned and threw her head back. She closed her eyes and took in the stimulating feeling. Caught up, the sensation of it all was not only fucking with her mind, but her body too.

This was an unfamiliar ecstasy for Harmony, as her body had always been her temple. She had guarded it well up until now. But she learned that life had a way of giving up that good-ass foreplay that will get a muthafucka wet every time—the shit that will have a muthafucka's ass so wide open, not giving a fuck about a damn thing. Harmony was proof of that as she sat there

114

soaking wet, longing for that orgasm, that point of no return that whispers to everybody, but only a few actually answer the call.

An unfamiliar feeling it was, but Harmony wouldn't mind getting better acquainted. She could get used to this. As a matter of fact, this shit could become addictive.

Chapter 1
Dope Boy

Harmony and her family had only lived in New York City for a few years. They moved there because of her father, Glen's work. Neither her mother, Veronica, nor herself had ventured out and made any *real* friends, so whenever they did go out and do something, it was typically with one another. There were a few girls Harmony hung around with at school, but even though she referred to them as "her girls," they were more or less just her associates. Outside of school, it was just her and her moms.

Veronica really didn't want it any other way. She was on the path to being something that, as a child, she vowed she would never be when she grew up and had a child of her own—she was becoming just like her mother, very overprotective.

Veronica wasn't nearly as bad as she thought she was. As a matter of fact, Harmony didn't see her mother as overprotective at all. Besides, Harmony never gave her mother much reason to be overprotective. Around her mother, Harmony was as pure as uncut coke and could do no wrong.

That's exactly what Harmony wanted her to think; both her parents, for that matter. But at school, there was a whole other side to her. At school was where she allowed her alter ego to make cameo appearances. It was that side of her that wanted to fit in, be cool, hip, and up on shit, so to speak. It was the side of her that most kids hid from their parents, the side that swears, smokes or drinks.

But that side of Harmony stayed at school, except for the times when, every now and again, she might let the latest slang she had learned from her girls slip out

116

around her mother. Veronica just shook her head at the lingo the teenagers used these days. But no matter what crazy words came out of her daughter's mouth, she knew she had a good child that would succeed in life, and she dedicated as much of her time as she could to make sure of that.

Whenever Veronica wasn't volunteering as a nurse at the clinic, she enjoyed spending time with Harmony. She had been a full-time head nurse until after Harmony's birth. And before Harmony started pre-school, she was a full-time stay-at-home mom. Glen made an obscene amount of money, and with Veronica handling all of the household bills, she had access to the account, so she really didn't need her job as a nurse to maintain the lifestyle of shopping and splurging she was used to. She rarely spent a dime of her own money anyway, creating a nice stack of "play money" in her own personal savings. But with Harmony out of the house for those few hours of pre-school, Veronica thought she'd go stir crazy. She sat at home worrying about Harmony and what was going on with her at school. And when she wasn't worrying about Harmony, she was worrying about her husband.

She loved and trusted Glen with every ounce of her being, but with him being away from home so much, her insecurities got the best of her. She had even gone as far as hiring a private investigator to follow him. She spent a whopping twenty thousand—not including the flight and hotel fees she had to pay the private eye to travel across the country to follow Glen. She had probably spent a total of thirty thousand dollars to find out that her husband was doing exactly what he was supposed to be doing. But for her peace of mind, she felt that it was worth every penny. However, after nearly depleting her savings and not wanting to splurge in such a way again, she decided to do volunteer work at the clinic to occupy some of her time. Still, she always made sure that she had plenty of time for her Harmony.

Harmony walked down the strip of the mall with her mother, Veronica, who looked more like one of Harmony's girlfriends that she was out kickin' it with than she did her mother. Although Veronica didn't look much older than her seventeen-year-old daughter, no one had ever mistaken them for sisters or anything cliché like that. This was probably due to the fact that Harmony looked nothing like her mother at all. She was actually the spittin' image of her pops, Glen. Whenever anyone saw Harmony and Glen side by side, there was no denying that the two were kin. But seeing Glen side by side with Harmony, or even his wife for that matter, was very rare.

Harmony had always been closer to her mother than she was to her father. And it wasn't because her father wasn't a good one. It was because he was away from home more often than not. He was frequently out of town on work-related business or putting in long hours at work, but it was for the sole purpose of providing a better life for his wife and daughter. He had never wanted for anything, and he wanted to see to it that his wife and child didn't either.

It was a life that Harmony and Veronica had never taken for granted; therefore, there were no complaints on their end about his long stints away from home. After all, the money Glen pulled in as a forensic specialist, testifying in court all over the country, allowed Harmony and Veronica the means for their shopping sprees.

"This is smokin'. I'm talking on fire," Harmony said as she fumbled through articles of clothing on the rack in Macy's, one of her favorite stores. She had already

118

made room in her walk-in closet at home, which was the size of the average apartment bedroom, for the new items she planned on purchasing during this little shopping spree. It was the final summer before she was off to college, and she planned on, for once maybe, spreading her wings a little, so she definitely needed a new wardrobe to set things off right.

"Smokin'? On fire?" her mother repeated, always amazed at the new words her daughter picked up and added to her vocabulary. Veronica observed the sexy little number her daughter was gently molesting with her fingertips. It was a soft yellow chiffon sundress with crimson flowers printed all over it. It had spaghetti straps and was cut low in the front. It zipped on the side, certain to hug the owner's hips. Veronica couldn't fathom her baby daughter in that Dorothy Dandridge-lookin' piece. She would have looked twice her age, giving young men the wrong impression.

As far as she knew, boys were the last thing on Harmony's mind, and she wanted to keep it that way. But being realistic, Veronica knew that it was only a matter of time before some young man caught the attention of her daughter. It was evident, walking down the mall and observing all of the men's heads turning to admire Harmony, that she had indeed already caught the attention of men. White and black men alike did double-takes at her.

Harmony had always looked a few years older than she really was. It was the way she carried herself, the way she dressed, even the way she wore her hair—not to mention the fact that she'd been allowed to wear make-up since eighth grade.

Standing five feet and nine inches tall, Harmony had always been taller than the other girls in her class, and most of the boys too. She grew out of the junior clothing department and into the misses in seventh grade. That's why her apparel was always a little more grown-up looking than most girls her age. She never got into the little mini skirts or midriff tops with matching colored tennis shoes. Harmony was more of a slacks with a collared button-up shirt and two-inch loafers type of girl.

Harmony didn't run to the hair salon every week getting up-dos, pin curls, twists and stuff like the girls she hung around at school. Unless she needed her hair trimmed, she rarely went to the hair salon at all. And when she did need a trim, she went to this place right around the corner from her house called Saturday's. It sounded nothing like the gossiping hair salons the girls she associated with at school frequented.

She had learned to do her naturally curly hair herself. She mostly wore it in a simple, easy-to-do style, straight back in a tight, slick ponytail. She didn't have any hair in her face or bangs or anything to take away from her facial features, which were pretty average, but pretty nonetheless. Her tanned skin tone had faint brown freckles sprinkled about. They were the same brown as her eyes. She had tiny little dimples that only revealed themselves when she smiled a certain way, sort of a half smile.

She didn't really need to wear make-up. That was just something her mother allowed her to do because Harmony had started asking about it. Veronica remembered how, when her mother forbade her to wear make-up in middle school, she just went into the girls' bathroom once she got to school and piled tons of it on anyway. She always got a high knowing that she was defying her mother. So, she felt that it was better to just go ahead and let Harmony wear a little bit than to have her curious about it, sneaking to wear it. That would only lead to sneaking to do other things as well, which

Veronica knew about firsthand, because for Veronica, along with sneaking on make-up in the girls' bathroom came smoking cigarettes in the girls' bathroom too.

Well developed, Harmony got her first training bra in third grade, and was now a perfect 32 C. Her body was evenly filled out, curvy and thick with a medium frame. She had a long torso, and legs that would have been flawless if it weren't for the scar running down the right side of the left one. She got it when she fell out of a tree when she was nine years old. Her mother warned her that picking the scab off would lead to a permanent scar, and she was absolutely right. But not even the scar took away from Harmony's appeal.

It didn't take some hundred-dollar sexy sundress to make her appealing to the human eye. She would look good in a Fruit of the Loom fleece jogging suit.

"The movie starts in fifteen minutes, honey," Veronica said. "We better head out of here and over to the theater. We'll have to finish up our shopping later."

"Oh, come on, Mom," Harmony whined. "You know they're going to show previews for the first ten minutes anyway, so technically we have almost a half hour before the movie starts."

"Yeah, but I want to get some popcorn, and who wants to have to try and find a seat in that pitch-dark theater?" Veronica reasoned. "Besides, this is only the second weekend of the showing, so you know it's going to be crowded, maybe sold out. I want a good seat."

Harmony sighed. She looked at her mother and then at the dress. "You really don't want me buying this dress, do you?" Harmony said to her mother.

Veronica laughed, realizing that her daughter was on to her. "No, I don't," she said, taking the dress out of Harmony's hand and placing it back on the rack. "Now, let's go." Veronica grabbed Harmony by the hand as the two headed out of the store.

Just as they exited the store and entered into the hallway, Harmony almost ran smack into a guy who was walking toward them. She looked up and immediately stopped in her tracks. She was literally two inches from running into the guy.

The two just stood there eye to eye. Not one of them said a word. Those four seconds they stood their staring into each other's eyes felt like a lifetime. Finally, the guy broke the silence.

"The word is 'excuse me'," he said in a dry tone as he gave Harmony a cold stare.

Harmony could have sworn she felt a sudden chill. Must have been from his glare; either that or the cool breeze of his cologne. Whatever it was had Harmony frozen.

"The word is 'excuse me'," he repeated.

Harmony swallowed then spoke. "Oh, I'm sorry." She searched her vocabulary for the words "excuse me" but couldn't find them. She just continued to stand there, not budging, and neither did he.

Veronica looked the guy up and down, observing his gear. He was wearing a powder blue and white plaid button-up. The first four buttons were undone, revealing his white ribbed wife beater T-shirt. His midnight blue jeans were at least three sizes too big, according to the excess material bagged at his ankles over his powder blue suede Lugz. Dangling from his neck was a white gold necklace with a cross at the end of it.

His skin was creamy, the color of a melted chocolate and vanilla twist ice cream cone. He had piercing brown eyes that told a story of suspense with a cliffhanger for an ending. He was wearing white gold hoops in each ear, which Veronica never did understand—the boys wearing

122

earrings thing. It wasn't the earrings that caught her attention, though, as much as it was the tattoo on the side of his neck that read: MOB.

"Come on, Harmony, let's go," Veronica said, tugging at Harmony's hand.

Harmony didn't want to go. She couldn't go. She couldn't move. It was as if she had on cement shoes. She didn't know what it was about this dude standing before her that made her just want to stand there and be swallowed up by his strong aura. Perhaps it was his mystery, that mystery in his eyes that forced her to want to play detective and solve the case. But what in the hell did she think she could do with a guy like that?

Harmony wasn't no virgin, but at the same time, she wasn't that experienced either. She had had sex before, but only one time in ninth grade, back in Pickerington, Ohio, right before she moved to New York City. It was with Jeremy, some nerdy white boy she went to the Sadie Hawkins dance with at Pickerington High School. They were both virgins at the time, and neither of them knew what in the hell they were doing. They did it in the janitor's closet at the school during the dance. She didn't even like him, and he wasn't even a cute white boy on top of that. But once again, Harmony's alter ego that just wanted to fit in took over. Both of the girls she used to eat lunch with at school had already lost their virginity, so Harmony decided she was going to have that one thing in common with them too. She also just wanted to get her first time over with so that when she met someone that she really liked, she'd be ready. But as she looked at the fine specimen before her, she didn't know if she'd ever be ready for him. As good looking as he was, certainly he had had more pussy thrown at him than Sammy Sosa had fast balls.

"Do you know me or something?" the guy asked, now agitated by Harmony's failure to step the fuck out of his way. "Do I know you?" He looked her up and down, checking out her crisp white Tommy Hilfiger blouse with the khaki Tommy Hilfiger flare slacks. He had to hold back his chuckle when he looked down and noticed that she actually had pennies embedded in her penny loafers.

"I don't think so," Veronica said, snatching Harmony by the arm and pulling her out of his path.

"I go to East Meadow High. I don't know. Maybe you know me from there," Harmony said, knowing darn well that her school was the last place she'd ever see a guy like him. It was a public school, but one of them suburban public schools that might as well have been a private school. Even if someone used their auntie's address to go there, it would be obvious that they didn't belong.

"Nah," he replied, shaking his head.

Veronica managed to move on, with Harmony in hand. After taking a few steps past the guy, Harmony looked back over her shoulder. The guy was still standing there, but coincidentally, he was looking over his shoulder too. Harmony tried to keep from smiling, but a half smile formed, displaying her dimples. He nodded as if to say, "I got your number, ma," then turned back around and kept it moving.

"Harmony, are you crazy?" Veronica asked. "Don't you know some of these people will shoot you for just looking at them the wrong way, let alone damn near running into them and having a stand-off?"

"I didn't run into him, I *almost* ran into him, and I wasn't having a stand-off with him." Harmony chuckled. "Besides, he hardly looked like he wanted to kill me."

"Humph. You could have fooled me. Looked just like one of them thugs. And did you see all that expensive stuff he was wearing? He hardly looks like the nine-to-five office worker, so one can only wonder where he got the money to buy it all. I bet he's one of them—what do you all call them? A dope boy? Yeah, he's a dope boy if I ever saw one."

Harmony stopped walking, spread out her arms and looked down at her name brand clothing. She held out the brown signature Coach purse she was carrying. She fingered the five-carat diamond bracelet that once belonged to her great-grandmother on her father's side. Her father had given it to her for her sixteenth birthday, which had just passed. "I have on expensive stuff," she said sarcastically. "Oh, no! Guess that makes me a dope boy too."

***

"So, what's up for the summer, yo?" Harmony asked as she began to choke from the strong pull she had just taken from a blunt.

"Slow down, baby," Nay-Nay said to her. "I told you that wasn't no home grown. That shit right there is the chronic."

"Yeah," Kendra added. "You know Nay-Nay's pops don't fuck with that weak shit that La-La's pops be pushin'."

All the girls burst out laughing; all of them except for La-La.

"Fuck y'all hoes," La-La said, snatching the blunt from Harmony to take a pull herself.

The girls had to be careful, even when they were just playing around with La-La. Her bland, standoffish demeanor was hard to read. They never knew when she was being serious or when she was joking, and the last thing they wanted was to piss her off. She was the type who just snapped and beat a muthafucka down in a minute, not just bitches, but dudes too. Hell, she fought

125

like a dude. She was so tomboyish that people at school whispered that she was a dyke. They whispered behind her back, of course. The way she dressed didn't help convince them otherwise. Jeans, T-shirts and kicks were her steelo. She wore her hair straight back in twisted cornrows, and wouldn't even wear as much as lipgloss. The only thing feminine about her was her mousy little voice and her titties. The one time the other girls were talking about their first time having sex, La-La never said a word. They figured La-La hadn't had sex before—with a boy, that is.

"Oh, girl, relax," Nay-Nay said to La-La as she leaned up against the shed.

The girls stood behind the sports equipment shed of their high school, blazing on a blunt, which is what they did whenever either Nay-Nay or La-La could manage to pinch some off of her father's stash. Whenever they did, they always told Harmony that it cost them, and they would make her pay money to blaze. It wasn't like they really needed the money. They just did it because they could.

Harmony's parents dropped her allowance into her bank account every week. She hardly ever touched it because she hardly ever did anything. Hell, somebody ought to spend it. At least that's how Nay-Nay still felt. La-La eventually stopped taxing Harmony. It wasn't funny anymore after so long, and in addition to that, she started to kind of like Harmony a little bit. But Nay-Nay kept right on pocketing the little bit of change, again, not because she needed it, but because she could.

Nay-Nay's father worked in the data processing department of an insurance company where he had initially started off working in the mailroom. He had been there for years now and made good money, a good enough salary that would have afforded them the life of a middle class African American family. But selling weed by major weight (he didn't even fuck with anybody who wasn't talkin' a minimum of ten pounds per sale) allowed them to live the life of an upper class African American family.

Nay-Nay's father had come from nothing from the Marcus Garvey Projects in Brownsville, Brooklyn, NY. He felt like the more he had, the less his chances of ever finding himself and his family back at the projects. But ironically enough, Marcus Garvey Projects would always be home in Nay-Nay's heart. That's where she went to kick it whenever she felt like she couldn't stomach the plastic world she was living in now. A girl she used to hang with in grade school, Fire, still lived there with her cousin. They were known to throw the dopest sets. Whenever Nay-Nay needed a dose of home, that's where she went to get it.

There was nothing that Nay-Nay wanted that she didn't get, right down to the black Ford Mustang her father presented her with two years ago for her sixteenth birthday. She had a standing appointment with her beautician twice a week and had a new burgundy weave, which she sometimes wore in an up-do with pin curls, sewn in on each visit. Most of the time she wore it straight, though, which was more becoming of her round, pudgy face. Her hair would be parted down the middle and fall to the sides, covering her puffy cheeks to slim her face. The hair color also seemed to compliment her peanut butter skin tone. She was a little chubbier than the other three girls, but as long as she wore clothes that fit her right, she didn't really look fat.

Although La-La's dad sold a little weed here and there, his main product, besides houses, was crack. On paper, La-La's dad was a real estate agent. Folks who wanted more house than they could prove income for came to him. He had a reputation as a shark in the real estate business and was known for making unethical transactions under the table in order to close on a deal. Ironically, the same people who bought new homes from him were the same ones he sold bricks to.

Harmony and Kendra were the only ones who had parents living a legitimate lifestyle. Kendra only lived with her mother. Her parents had never been married. Her mother told her that her father died in a car accident, but her gut feelings told her that her mother hadn't the foggiest idea of who her dad even was.

When Kendra was nine years old, her mother married her stepfather, who was deceased now. He was a police officer, about fifteen years her mother's senior. After the wedding and the honeymoon, it took him less than two months to start his very own honeymoon with Kendra. Initially, it was just him playing games with her that included fondling. Then oral sex became a part of the game. By the time Kendra was ten and her stepfather was convinced she wouldn't tell anyone what he was doing to her, he started having intercourse with her.

Despite what her stepfather thought, Kendra did tell someone after about a year of being molested by him. She told her neighbor, a sixteen-year-old girl who sometimes baby-sat her. Surprisingly, instead of being shocked and advising Kendra to tell her mom or the police, she taught Kendra just how powerful pussy was, even if it was young, ripe and had no business being picked.

Kenda didn't know that her stepfather had also been having sex with the neighbor girl. He would give her money and material things to keep quiet. She had been fucking since the sixth grade anyway, so she didn't even look at it as the man next door molesting her. She looked at it as a come-up, since she had fucked plenty of boys and got nothing in return except for a case of the crabs or an STD here and there. Not only did the neighbor convince Kendra that telling her mother would only make her mother angry and that the police probably wouldn't believe her, she schooled her on how to make him pay for the pussy he had been stealing from her. She even taught her a few tricks on how to make the old man cum quick in order to get the whole thing over with. So up until the day her stepfather dropped dead from cardiac arrest brought on by some terminal illness he had been living with, leaving a pension and a $500,000 insurance policy behind, Kendra lived this life in her own home, right underneath her own mother's nose.

Kendra used to wonder if her mother really knew what was going on and just did nothing about it. After all, Stepdaddy made pretty good money. Her mother knew that he was dying and that once he was gone, they would be set financially. But Kendra just let it go and moved on. Stepdaddy was gone, and it was just her and her mother living off of his money, which Kendra felt she had definitely earned.

Kendra's mother took some of the money and started her own interior designing business that turned out to be very successful. La-La's dad turned most of his clients on to her to decorate their new homes. Word was that La-La's dad and Kendra's mom were fucking. His finder's fee was a dick suck and hittin' it from the back.

"But anyway, I gotta go to fuckin' summer school this summer," Nay-Nay said, answering Harmony's initial question. "That bitch, Mrs. Glenwood, gave me an F on my science project."

"Girl, you put a seed in water and waited for it to burst open." Kendra giggled as she ran her fingers through her short layers of hair. It used to be down her back, but she fucked this girl named Cricket's boyfriend, who went to one of the inner-city public high schools. Cricket and her crew got a hold of Kendra and not only beat her ass, but cut all of her hair off. "We did that kind of mess in elementary school."

"Hell, does it matter what grade you do it in? It's still science," Nay-Nay said, shrugging her shoulders as she reached for the blunt and took a pull.

"Girl, you a trip," Harmony said. "And that's exactly why you're going to be in summer school while the rest of us are going to be playing in the sun."

"Pleeease," Nay-Nay said as she exhaled and handed the blunt to La-La, who took a pull and handed it to Kendra. "Although you could definitely use a little sun, your momma gonna have your ass on lock down this summer just like last summer."

"Yeah, we didn't see your ass out not once over the summer last year," Kendra added. "Not that we see you out now."

"Veronica don't even be having me on lock down," Harmony disagreed. "She lets me do whatever I want to do." Harmony snapped her neck and rolled her eyes, something she had practiced in the mirror.

"Yeah, right," Kendra jumped in. "If your momma knew you was sittin' here puffin' on the magic dragon with a couple of *dope boys'* daughters, she would have a heart attack."

"Harmony's momma would have a heart attack if she knew she was sittin' here with a couple of dope boys' daughters period," Nay-Nay added. "That's why she don't never do anything with us outside of school. She knows if her momma see us and how we do it, she gon' know what her baby girl is up to. You think you slick, but we been done figured out how you get down."

"That's not true." Harmony tried to lie, but she knew it was very much true. If she dared bring the girls around her mom, Veronica would take one look at them and figure her daughter was cut from the same cloth, giving her more than enough reason to be overprotective. Besides that, to Harmony, the girls were merely associates. Almost imaginary friends that her alter ego liked to play with. Nay-Nay, Kendra and La-La were cool to hang out with at school, but outside of school, she couldn't see it happening.

Unlike Harmony, the girls could care less about high school academics, while Harmony had already been accepted to Duke. While the girls were at the crib chit-chatting, gossiping on the phone, meeting up to get their drink and smoke on, Harmony was hittin' her books. Both her parents had graduated from college, and it was pretty much expected that she would do the same. But that wasn't the reason she wanted to go to college. She was truly dedicated to learning all that she could in life, and actually enjoyed her school studies.

She had kept a solid 4.0 grade point average throughout her entire four years of high school. Her father had always told her education first, friends and fun later. He told her that it was okay to have a few people to associate with at school, but once the final bell rang, cut 'em off. He said that friends were needy, and it took time and effort to be someone's true friend—time and effort that could be spent on more purposeful things. Plus, she'd have plenty of time for friends in her adulthood.

Although her father wasn't always around physically, mentally he was always there with wise words he had given Harmony. Just about the only time his words weren't in her head was when it was full of smoke from blazin'. But it was during those times when she didn't think of herself as the girl with a doctor for a father and a nurse for a mother. She was just one of the girls, period. The last thing she wanted to think about while smoking weed was her parents and what they would think of her if they saw her. She wouldn't be able to handle their disappointment.

Harmony knew how her parents would react to her smoking marijuana, but in all honesty, Harmony didn't see the harm in just a few puffs here and there, especially after the girls convinced her that it was just an herb, naturally grown in man's land. Besides that, the very first time the girls convinced her to smoke one day at recess, she went back into class and aced her government studies exam without even using her study notes. Kendra had even gotten a B+, and she was a C-student all day long. So from that point on, Harmony was convinced that weed was more harmless and helpful than it was hurtful.

"Y'all know y'all my girls," Harmony continued, trying too hard to make her words sound convincing.

"Whatever," Kendra said, handing the last of the blunt to Harmony.

Harmony took a pull, hoping the topic of conversation would die out.

"You better get going, Harmony," Nay-Nay said in a sarcastic tone. "Your little school bus might leave you. Kendra and La-La are cool 'cause they riding with me in my Mustang. They ain't ashamed."

"Don't even go there, Nay-Nay," Harmony said, shaking her head. "You know it's not even like that. You know I'm down with y'all." She wished the girls could look around and see the bigger picture, the picture her father had drawn for her about life, but there was no trying to explain it to them. Besides, there were only two more months of school left. Who cared what they thought at this point? It was senior year and Harmony would be on to bigger and better things. They would probably still be sitting around smoking blunts this same time next year, while she would be away at college.

"You better get going, Harmony," La-La said in a sincere tone, almost as if she was on her side.

"Yeah, I guess I better," Harmony said as she dropped the doobie and crushed it with her foot. "I'll check y'all out tomorrow." She picked up her books that were on the ground at her feet and headed for her bus. Just as she was halfway through the school yard, she could see her bus starting to pull off, so she picked up her pace. At least she thought she was picking up her pace, but that blunt was starting to hit her. She didn't even realize it was fucking with her motor skills and ability to react. "Wait!" she yelled, but the bus driver couldn't hear her over the roar of the motor and the ruckus from the kids on the bus, so anxious to be leaving the school that they weren't hardly looking back to see Harmony being left behind.

"Wait! Wait!" Harmony yelled at her bus driver to no avail.

By the time Harmony reached the front of the school where the buses lined up, her bus had pulled off and all of the others were now in a caravan down the school drive.

"Damn it to hell," Harmony said as she stomped her foot. She looked to the rear parking lot and saw the girls loading up in Nay-Nay's car. She wasn't about to bum a ride with them with the way their conversation had just ended. She thought about calling her mother to come pick her up but remembered that today she was volunteering at the clinic. She lived about four miles from the school, which was an hour of walking that she wasn't about to subject herself to.

Harmony dropped her books, bent down in a squat and started digging in her purse for the twenty-dollar bill she had. "Where is it?" she said under her breath. "I know I had money." Just then she remembered she had paid for her senior scrapbook during homeroom with the twenty dollars. There were only a few weeks of school left, and she had been spending money left and right on senior dues and stuff. She closed her eyes and sighed. She stayed there for a minute then she opened her eyes, scooped up her books into her arms and stood up. Parked in front of her was a soft yellow 1988 clean Cadillac with dark tinted windows. It was old, but it was clean. The tires were even glossed with Meguiar's Hot Shine. The car was dazzling and eye-catching, but as the front passenger side window rolled down, Harmony soon realized that the car wasn't nearly as eye-catching as the driver was.

There he sat in the driver's seat, staring at Harmony as if she had something that belonged to him and he wanted it back . . . now. As Harmony stared back at him, she couldn't resist speaking the first words he had ever spoken to her.

"Do you know me or something?" Harmony said instinctively, smacking him across the face with his own words. "Do I know you?"

In a sexy manner, he softly bit down on his bottom lip, put his head down and tried his best not to crack a smile. Harmony felt as though she had just checkmated his ass. She smiled a half smile, the same half smile she had given him the day she and her mother had seen him in the mall.

"A'ight, I'ma give you that one," he said in surrender.

"Oh, you didn't give me anything," Harmony said, snapping her neck. "I took mine." She laughed, but he just sat there staring at her. *Hmm, not much of a sense of humor*, she thought.

He sat there trippin' off of the fly mouth that was on this chick. He didn't expect such a fresh mouth on such a wholesome looking girl. "So, you ridin' or what?" he asked as if he knew her like that.

"Excuse me?" Harmony said, twisting up her face.

"Oh, so you do know how to say excuse me," he said, teasing her.

"Look, what do you want?" Harmony said, deciding right then and there that if he wanted to come off hard and crabby, two could play that game.

"I think the question is what do you want?" was his comeback. "But you really ain't even gotta answer that, 'cause never mind your wants. I know what you *need* right about now, and I can give it to you."

Harmony grew hot inside as her face blushed red. So far she had been able to hold her own in exchanging words with him. It was something she learned from Nay-Nay, who would shoot down the boys at school in a minute when they were trying to holler at her. But now Harmony was speechless. She thought for a few seconds then replied, leaning into the passenger window, "And just what is it that you think I need that you can give me?"

He licked his lips, leaned over toward Harmony and said, "A ride," then he positioned himself straight up in his seat again.

Feeling slightly salty that he didn't hit her with some comment with a sexual innuendo behind it like she was expecting him to, Harmony leaned back and said, "You don't know my name. I don't know yours either, so why would you think you could just come up here and I'd jump in the car with you?"

"Look, it's cool," he said, gunning his engine, preparing to pull off. "I just saw you chasing the bus and shit like you was Jackie Kersey Joyner, so I said to myself," he paused for a second then changed to a condescending, preppy tone, "that looks like Harmony being left by her bus. Maybe I should offer her a ride."

Harmony was shocked. "You do know my name."

"Yes I do, Alicia Keys."

Harmony giggled and eased up. She was delighted that he had done some investigating, not realizing that he had simply heard her mother call her by her name in the mall. "I still don't know yours, though."

"You still haven't asked."

"So, tell me, what's your name?"

"Nikko."

"Just Nikko?"

"Vosk. Nikko Vosk."

"Well, I don't know, Nikko Vosk," Harmony said, rolling her eyes in a flirtatious manner. "Still not sure if I should take a ride from someone I still really don't know." Harmony decided to play a game of tease. She was bound and determined to chip away at his ice shield. "What would my mother say to me taking a ride with someone I hardly know? What would your mother say about you picking up girls you hardly know?"

"She wouldn't say anything. She's dead."

"Oh, I'm so sorry," Harmony said regretfully. "I'm sorry. I didn't know."

"It's cool. How could you know?" Nikko said, looking dead into her eyes as if expecting an answer. Harmony just stood there looking crazy. "So, do you want a ride or not?"

Harmony still didn't answer. Although it was just a ride home, she knew what a ride home from a boy could lead to. "Which way are you going?" she asked, stalling, planning to say that she was going in the opposite direction of whichever way he said he was going so that she could humbly decline the ride.

Nikko looked her up and down with those pretty brown eyes of his and answered, "I'm going your way, ma."

Oooh, he lookin' good and he talkin' right. The words to Destiny Child's song ran through her head as, without further hesitation, Harmony quickly said, "You can drop me off at the library." The library was the first place that came to her mind. She didn't want some guy pulling up to her doorstep and knowing where she lived. The library was only a couple of blocks from her house, so she knew she could handle walking home from there.

"The library, huh?" he said, twisting his lips and shaking his head, definitely onto Harmony's move. He knew he wasn't exactly the type of guy that a girl could take home to Momma, especially a girl like Harmony. She might have had a fly mouth like she was all that, but Nikko could see right through her. In the mall she was like a deer caught in headlights. Now all of a sudden she was this totally different, outspoken girl. He knew right then and there that she was a wanna be. But he was willing to play along just as long as she was. "That's cool. Get in."

Get in, Harmony thought. *What happened to a guy opening up the door for a girl?* She shrugged her shoulders, figuring that chivalry must just happen in movies as she opened the door for herself and climbed into the passenger seat. She put her books on the floor, set her purse next to her, and slammed the door closed.

"Damn, girl!" Nikko said. "That ain't how you treat no Caddy. You got to be gentle." He mumbled under his breath, "Slamming doors and shit."

"Well, if you had gotten out of the car and opened the door for me like a *gentleman,* then I wouldn't have had to close the door behind myself in the first place."

"Shit, I ain't no gentleman," he said, so sincere. "I'm a thug." He put the car in gear and drove off.

By this time, Nay-Nay and the girls had pulled around from the rear parking lot and saw Harmony get in the car with Nikko.

"Can you believe that shit?" Kendra said. "That bitch act like she too good to roll with us, but she jumpin' in that nigga's car."

"And you do know who *that nigga* is, right?" Nay-Nay said. "That's Nikko. Wanna be gangsta. He's my dad's friend, old man Pursey's son, or at least the one he calls his son."

"That's Pursey's son?" Kendra asked as her mouth dropped open. Kendra had heard of Pursey. He was like a legend in the hustle game. She knew that Pursey used to be the star of New York, and he had a son in training to perhaps some day grow to take over his reigns.

"Hell yeah, it is. I can't believe that she can be so quick to jump in the car with a dope boy and ride around town, but she don't wanna roll with her girls." Nay-Nay shook her head in dismay.

"Fuck her," Kendra said as she glared at the Cadillac reaching the end of the school drive to stop at the light.

"What in the hell could he possibly see in her lame ass?" Nay-Nay complained.

"What do you care if he trying to get with Harmony or not, if he's just some wanna be gangsta?" La-La asked.

"He is," Nay-Nay said. "He don't never say shit to nobody. Always flossin' clean cut and shit. If he wasn't Pursey's boy, half of them niggaz in the hood been done broke him down by now.

"That don't sound like no wanna be gangsta to me," La-La said. "Sound like he just a smooth cat who don't fuck with nobody is all."

"Whatever," Nay-Nay said.

La-La looked over at Nay-Nay, who was mean-mugged up. She snickered at the fact that Nay-Nay couldn't really care less about Harmony choosing not to hang out with them. She was really pissed that Nikko would be into someone like Harmony, not her. La-La also laughed at just how much Nay-Nay reminded her of her cousin, Brianna, who lived in Richmond, Virginia.

"Come on, y'all, let's go," La-La said from the back seat, brushing the situation off. "We all know how Harmony is, so it ain't nothin' new. Besides, she wouldn't know what to do with that boy if he came with instructions. It ain't nothin'. Let's ride already."

"Yeah, come on, Nay-Nay, let's ride," Kendra said. "Just look at it this way: One wanna be deserves the other." Both Kendra and Nay-Nay laughed as they watched Nikko and Harmony turn left out of the school drive and ride off together.

"So, Nikko, what school do you go to?" Harmony asked in an attempt to make casual conversation, while at the same time hoping not to sound corny.

"I'm finished with school," Nikko replied.

"Oh yeah?"

"Yeah. I graduated at the top of my class."

"And you didn't go on to college?"

"Had scholarship offers," Nikko said nonchalantly as he drove. "But college couldn't teach me what I needed to know in order to do what I do."

"And what do you do?"

Nikko laughed disrespectfully then looked over at Harmony. It was his first time really noticing her freckles. He liked them. He smiled, but only briefly. "I make money."

The next question Harmony probably should have asked was how he made his money. But girls didn't ask questions like that when they already knew the answer.

Not knowing enabled them to play stupid, to really believe that the dude they were diggin' was into construction or real estate. The last thing Harmony wanted Nikko to do was to confirm her mother's suspicions about him, so she just nodded her head and said, "Oh."

"So, what do you do besides go to school?" Nikko asked, deciding to play questions right along with Harmony.

"That's pretty much it."

"You don't hang with no crew, party or nothing like that? Let me guess, you're really a square. One of them valley girls."

"No, I'm not," Harmony said defensively. "I have a couple of homegirls I hang out with at school. We get high and shit sometimes. You know how the sistahs do it."

"The sistahs, huh? Where are you from originally? I know you ain't from around here."

"Ohio. So what?" Harmony said, snapping her neck.

"Nothing. Damn, calm down." Nikko thought for a moment then asked, "So you and the *sistahs* be gettin' high and shit at school, huh? Then I take it y'all plan on getting a *higher* education."

"Ha-ha," Harmony said, rolling her eyes. "I have you know I have a solid 4.0 GPA."

"Oh, then you're just the little book worm too, huh?"

Harmony smiled. She couldn't hide her love for education. "Man, I know it sounds crazy, but I really do love school." Harmony's eyes lit up. "That doesn't make me a square, though. It just makes me someone who wants to do something with myself. I mean, I don't even know what I want to be when I grow up, but I'm going to college and just learn everything that there is out there for me to learn." She smiled as she looked out of the window that was still rolled down.

Nikko took note of the way Harmony expressed a genuine love for education. He grinned at first, but then he suddenly saw that same look of determination and sincerity in her that his father had once seen in him. Just thinking about it put a knot in Nikko's throat, quickly erasing the smile from his face.

"A book worm who fries her brain with drugs?" Nikko shook his head and laughed.

"I don't do drugs or nothing like that. I just smoke a little weed here and there," Harmony said in her defense.

"What the hell do you think weed is? It's a drug too. And you said you plan on going to college?" Nikko began to laugh again. Harmony became agitated by his patronizing attitude and the way he seemed to be getting off on making her feel stupid.

Before she could even catch the words, they spilled out of her mouth. "You're an asshole."

He shrugged his shoulders as if he didn't care. "Been called worse."

"Look, you can just let me out right here. I don't know what it was that attracted me to you in the first place. Just stop this goddamn car and let me out now""

Nikko smiled. He had gotten under this girl's skin and he liked it. But even more, he liked hearing her say that she was attracted to him. He knew he was up one. Nonetheless, he wasn't no pussy, and never wanted a woman to think that he was sniffin' after hers, so he stopped the car right there in the middle of the two-lane road, put it in park, leaned over across Harmony and opened the door for her.

"There," he said, "I opened the door for you . . . like a gentleman."

Harmony couldn't believe he had called her bluff and actually stopped the car to let her get out. She looked up at Nikko to try to read the expression on his face. She wanted to see if this fool was for real about putting her out of the car in the middle of the street. He was looking at her like "Bitch, what are you waiting for? Get the fuck out."

"Asshole," she mumbled as she proceeded to pick up her books from the floor. By now the drivers stuck behind them were starting to blow their horns. Harmony managed to grab all of her books and get out of the car. She was fixing her mouth to say one last thing to Nikko as she slammed the car door, but he quickly pulled off, leaving her standing there in the middle of the street. She could see the passenger side window rolling up as he drove away.

Harmony hurried out of the middle of the street to the side where there was gravel and grass instead of a sidewalk. She was in complete disbelief as she walked the rest of the way home. She couldn't believe that the first boy she had given the time of day to since forever had put her out of his car. It must have been a sign from God that she was supposed to stick to her game plan of not dealing with boyfriends until she was where she needed to be in life. Maybe he was bad news, a poison that she should be glad to be rid of.

When Harmony walked around the corner to her street, she immediately noticed the yellow Cadillac parked in front of her house. Once she was about six feet from the car, the driver's side window started to roll down. It stopped midway before a hand emerged, holding her purse out of the window. She knew that he must have gone into her purse and found her address on her ID.

This boy just doesn't stop, Harmony thought as she approached the car. Although infuriated by the fact that he put her out of his car in the middle of the street, at the same time she was flattered that he had taken the initiative to return her purse. She took her purse from Nikko's hand and said, "Thanks," rolling her eyes and stomping off, heading toward her porch.

"Why you seem mad?" he asked.

"Why do I seem mad?" Harmony flung around. "Dude, you just put me out of your car in the middle of the street."

Nikko laughed at the little white girl cheerleader voice she didn't realize she was now using in anger instead of the hip *sistah* voice she had been using before.

"Like I said, why are you mad at me?" Nikko got out of his car and began approaching Harmony with a smirk on his face. This only pissed off Harmony even more. "You told me to stop the car and let you out. You see, I'm young, but I'm old schooled. I was always taught that a man is supposed to give a lady what she wants and to do what a lady wants done. Not to ask questions, but to just do it. Well, that's the kind of man I am." By now, Nikko was completely in Harmony's face. She could feel his breath hitting her lips as he spoke. "I only did what you wanted. If I'm wrong for that, I'm sorry. I thought most girls liked a man to do what they want. But I can see that you're not like most girls." He looked her up and down. "Are you?"

Harmony was caught up in Nikko's web of game, like a fly too tired to continue fighting its way out of a spider's web.

Oh God, please let him kiss me. Please let him stick his tongue down my throat right this very minute, Harmony thought as Nikko's closeness made her body tingle.

"Sure you're not. I can just look at you and tell that you're not like most girls," Nikko continued.

Harmony's bra strap had managed to slide down her

143

shoulder from under her short-sleeved blouse. With his index finger, Nikko slowly placed it back up on her shoulder. He turned around and headed back to his car.

"Wait! Don't go. Do you wanna come inside for a drink or something? Where can I find you? How can I get a hold of you again?" Those were all of the things Harmony wanted to call out to him. Something about his chemistry had her wanting to do a science project about his ass. If chemistry had anything to do with him, then she wanted to take the class every semester. She wanted him to be the instructor of the class, teaching her everything. Teaching her how to kiss him like he liked to be kissed, how to suck, how to fuck and how to cuddle just the way he liked it. Instead, she just watched him get in his car and drive away.

Harmony let out a deep sigh then turned around to go inside her house. She unzipped her purse to get her house keys, and sitting right there in her purse was a piece of paper with Nikko's name and phone number on it.

If getting put out of Nikko's car was a sign from God that he was poison, then the devil must have been working overtime that day to intervene in God's work. But Harmony would find out soon enough who was working with her . . . God or Satan.

Chapter 2
New York's Rising Star

Genius or not, when it came to school, Nikko was jaded. He had made straight A's all throughout high school and even had scholarship offers to universities across the country. But one of the things that kept him from pursuing a higher education was the fact that his thirst for knowledge wasn't something that was natural or embedded in him, it was something that was beat into him.

His pops had been a college bound student back when he was in high school. His biggest dream was to get a degree one day, but when Nikko's mother got pregnant with him the summer before their senior year of high school, they knew that both of them couldn't continue going to school if they were going to raise a baby. Both Nikko's father and his mother had aspirations of becoming the first in their families to graduate college and make something of themselves. Nikko's father wanted to become an entrepreneur, running one of the most successful businesses in the world, while his mother wanted to do something in the legal field. But one of them would have to put their dreams on hold and go out and get a job in order to be able to provide. Being the man, the one who had been labeled by society as the provider, Nikko's father stepped up to his responsibility. He dropped out of high school to get a job. It was decided that his mother would continue her education, land a high paying job, and then help put his father through school. In his father's mind, becoming a teenage parent wouldn't ruin his dream, only defer it.

Nikko's mother, with the help of her auntie who baby-sat for her, was able to finish high school while his father worked two jobs. Eventually she went on to college, where she would start a relationship with a lawyer who was the professor for her legal research and writing course. One minute she was this lawyer's student, and the next minute she was the lawyer's intern. By the time Nikko turned four years old, his mother left him and his father to be with her new lover. Soon after she graduated college, she moved to the West Coast with the professor, where they started their own legal practice. Nikko would never see his mother again. She worked as the professor's paralegal and for a minute there, she sent Nikko letters and called him on the phone, promising to send for him. But once she got pregnant and started a new family, she forgot all about Nikko and his father.

The bitterness of his father was soon transferred to Nikko. Not only had his mother started another family, but she had done so through artificial insemination. She and the professor couldn't have children of their own since they were both women. He couldn't believe that his mother went through such extremes to have a child with another bitch when she already had one child that needed to be loved. Since Nikko's mother was nowhere around for his father to take out his anger on, he took it all out on Nikko, at the same time attempting to redeem his dream through Nikko.

Nikko's father felt as though he had given up his dreams for nothing. But he saw Nikko as an extension to what could have been, a second chance for himself, so he pushed Nikko extremely hard when it came to education. Nikko's life revolved around schoolwork. No extracurricular activities were allowed, and he was given a lick with his father's belt for every point his missed on a test. If he only scored ninety-five out of a hundred points, then he could expect five licks of leather when he got home. Once he was too old for licks, it was blows to the chest.

Nikko feared the times his father would sit him down to study. His father would drill him like a dentist does a tooth with a cavity, and it was just as painful because every incorrect answer meant a slap across the face and some derogatory name like "idiot" or "stupid nigger." Sometimes, to this day, Nikko's father's voice woke him up out of his sleep at night. "I'm not going to have no stupid nigger for a son," he would say to Nikko. "Stupid nigger."

Nikko didn't realize just how offensive the word "nigger" was until he was in fourth grade. His teacher showed them a movie on the Civil Rights movement that included footage of some interviews from several citizens in Mississippi. From that day forward, whenever his father called him a nigger, it hurt far worse than any lick, blow or slap he had ever given him. Nikko hated the N-word, and he hated it all the same, even if it was a black person saying it. He heard black folks calling one another that name like it was a badge of honor. "Nigger," "nigga" or "niggaz" all meant the same thing to Nikko and hurt the same as well.

While all of the other kids in Nikko's neighborhood were running around gang bangin', hustlin', getting high or drinking, Nikko was in the house with his face buried in a book. He always felt as though he was missing something, but promised himself that just as soon as the opportunity presented itself, he would find out exactly what it was that he was missing. And that is exactly what he did.

Nikko did eventually graduate high school at the top of his class, but ironically, his father wasn't there to see it. He had been killed a month before Nikko's graduation ceremony at the steel plant where he worked, when a piece of operating equipment malfunctioned. Nikko was only two weeks shy of his eighteenth birthday the day his father was killed. He received a lump sum from social security as well as a settlement from his father's employer. By the time the checks were cut, Nikko had already turned eighteen, so the money was released to him instead of a guardian. His father surely would have wanted him to use it towards higher education, but how Nikko saw it, he had enough book smarts. What he lacked were street smarts. Now on his own, experiencing freedom from his father's wrath, it took Nikko no time at all to find out what he had been missing on the streets.

He started running with a couple of knuckleheads from around the way. They had ambitions to be a rider once they got put on by an old G named Pursey. They promised Nikko that if he stuck around long enough with them, they could get him put on too. Every cat in the hood dreamed of being like Pursey. He had it all—money, cash, respect and bitches. What he didn't have was a left leg. He lost it when he was younger in a motorcycle accident, and got put on permanent disability. Death would have been better than living on a fixed income for the rest of his life, so he started hustling. At first cats used to try to get over on him. For some reason, fools thought that just because he only had one leg meant he couldn't catch their asses. Maybe he couldn't physically catch them, but he definitely reached out to muthafuckas.

From the moment Pursey met Nikko, he was impressed by the young blood's intellect and the fact that he was quiet, smooth and always listening. He wasn't like the other loudmouths running around thinking that they already had the game figured out. He couldn't believe how smart the boy was. Pursey was getting old and had made enough money in the game to live two

148

more lives if reincarnated. He knew that once he bowed out gracefully, cats would be at war trying to reach his status. But out of all the young cats under him, he felt that Nikko was the one with the most potential, so he took it upon himself to start schooling Nikko. The first thing he told Nikko was to stop running with those two knucklehead friends of his. Nikko did so, and three weeks later, they were both killed by some fiend they had sold wax to, passing it off for crack. They were memorialized with the names Mop and Glow in the hood.

Pursey took Nikko under his wing and treated him like the son he never had. He even introduced Nikko as his son, and Nikko was more proud to acknowledge Pursey than he had been his own biological father. Unlike what others might have tried to do with young Nikko, like manipulate him for the money he got from his father's death, Pursey instead taught Nikko how to invest his money—not on Wall Street, though, but on their own streets. After a year of shadowing Pursey and following his advice, Nikko had managed to double his money on the streets.

Nikko worked hard and paid attention to everything, almost never sleeping and never blinking both eyes at the same time, afraid that he would miss something. But he never tired. His dreams of someday retiring as a millionaire from the streets is what kept him on the grind. He vowed that he would never end up like his father, a man who died striving for what the white man, his forefathers, had told him was the American dream. And he damn sure wouldn't let a broad fuck up his shit either. So yeah, Nikko dreamed of someday getting married and having a family, but in his mind, he would get married to the streets, and his family would be the loyal soldiers he accumulated.

It had been a year since Pursey retired from the game. Once Pursey's newborn, Nikko was now having to birth his own soldiers. As of now, this kid named Boogie was his newborn. He needed a little toilet training, but Nikko knew that he could mold Boogie the same way Pursey had molded him.

Enjoying the weather, Nikko and Boogie stood leaning against Nikko's Caddy. All of the honeys that passed by were checking for them. Although Nikko was low-key, everybody knew who he was because of his relationship with Pursey. Hoping that one day Nikko would grow up to be just like the man who claimed him as his son, gold diggers were on him like white girls on high school athletes. They figured they'd get in good with Nikko now, in hopes that in the future he'd be worth every dime of their time.

Nikko paid no mind to all the ladies walking by, begging for his attention. He had seen pretty girls come and go. He had even boned several of them, but unlike some of the other hustlers who had a broad on each side of town in addition to their wifey or so-called main squeeze, Nikko flew solo. There had been a few broads that he enjoyed fucking a lot, he may have even liked one or two of them, but as far as being in that unconditional love bullshit, it wasn't happening.

"What up, young blood?" Nikko heard a voice behind him. When he turned around, pulled up next to his car was the cleanest Caddy that had ever rolled through the neighborhood. It made Nikko's Caddy look like a hooptie. It was silver with black tinted windows. The driver's side window was up, but the back passenger window was down. Nikko squinted, his eyes focusing in on the passenger in the back seat.

"Don't tell me you done forgot what your old man looks like. It ain't been that long," the voice from the back seat said.

"Pursey?" Nikko said, walking in closer.

"Who else would it be? You only got one old man," Pursey said as he leaned his head out the window.

Nikko gave Pursey a hug through the window. He hadn't seen Pursey in a few months. It seemed as though once Pursey moved out of the neighborhood, Nikko saw less and less of him. And the more work Nikko put in, the less he managed to make it up Pursey's way to see him.

"How's business?" Pursey asked.

"Couldn't be better." Nikko smiled. "But then again, what did you expect? I learned from the best."

"So, I take it in a few more years you'll be moving up out of here too."

Nikko looked around. "Nah, there's no place like home."

"I hear you, but there comes a time when a man gets too big for his home and must uproot in order to recognize his true potential."

"Oh yeah, and have you recognized your true potential?" Nikko asked.

"I'm looking at it." Pursey then looked over at Boogie. "One person can't do it all. Why do you think God used Jesus?"

"I ain't hardly no Jesus." Nikko snickered.

"Maybe not literally. But in certain situations, we have to take on superior roles. Take a doctor, for instance, who performs emergency open-heart surgery on a man and saves his life. No, he's not God, not in the spiritual sense, but to that man whose life he just saved, he's God-like. Take a man on death row and his attorney, who through appeal, gets the governor to stay his

151

execution. No, that attorney is not God, but in that situation at that time, he's God-like to that man who just got saved."

"I don't get it," Nikko said. "I mean, I understand what you're saying, but I don't understand what that has to do with you and me and this here lifestyle we live."

"You'll see, young blood. Oh, you'll see." Pursey nodded his head with a smile on his face. "Well, I was just riding through. You know, checking out things."

"You mean checking on me," Nikko said.

"That too. But I see that you're doing all right." Pursey looked over at Boogie, who was waiting for Nikko over at his car. "Is he one of yours?"

"Yeah, that's my man, Boogie. He's young, but he's hungry."

"I see. Well, you know what to do with him. Keep him fed, but not full." Pursey stuck his hand out of the window to shake Nikko's.

"All right then, Pops."

"All right then, young blood. Stay cool." Pursey rolled the window up as the driver drove off.

Nikko walked back over to Boogie.

"Who was that in that phat-ass Caddy?" Boogie asked. "See, that right there, that's what I'm talking about. I'm trying to be like that right there. That's why I'm down with you. A few more years on your team, and that's all me, son. That's all me."

Nikko was quiet. He heard Boogie's words, but at the same time was thinking about what Pursey had just preached to him.

"Did you hear me, man?" Boogie asked. "Who was that?"

Nikko looked down. He smiled then he looked up at Boogie and replied, "That, my friend, to me, was God."

Chapter 3
Lay Back, Kick It and Enjoy the Ride

For the past couple of days, Harmony had hardly been able to focus in class. She was too busy fantasizing about Nikko. The feeling she got just thinking about him put a smile on her face. The thought of Nikko gave her a high that no blunt ever had. She didn't even feel this high when she got skipped from fourth grade to fifth grade.

She sat in her government studies class dazed. She wasn't thinking about Nikko holding her, kissing or touching her as she had dreamed the night before. This time, she was thinking about whether he was thinking about her as well. Not even her teacher calling her name twice to answer a question snapped her out of her daze. It was Kendra's elbow that got her attention. Harmony looked over at La-La, who nodded her head towards their teacher.

"Are you okay, Ms. Hiles?" her teacher asked, unaccustomed to calling on Harmony and her not being able to answer.

"Yes, I'm fine," Harmony replied.

"Then please answer the question."

"Excuse me?"

"Answer the question I just asked you."

Harmony felt as though she was on the game show *Jeopardy* during the final round and that stupid music was playing while she struggled to come up with the correct answer. Seeing that Harmony had no clue what the teacher had asked her, Kendra decided to intervene.

"Stop playing," Kendra said. "Everybody knows who takes over the presidency of the country if both the President and Vice President were to expire."

The teacher gave Kendra a stern look.

"The Speaker of the House," Harmony said, saving herself.

The teacher's eyes darted to Kendra then to Harmony. She rolled her eyes and walked away. Just then the lunch bell rang and the students started gathering their belongings.

"I dismiss this class, not that bell," their teacher said. Everyone settled and turned their attention back to her. "Homework is the review questions from chapter twenty and the definitions. I'd suggest you study all past reviews and definitions because you never know which ones are going to be on your final exams. Class dismissed."

Once again, the students gathered their belongings to exit the class.

"Thanks, girl," Harmony said to Kendra.

"That's what friends are for, right?" Kendra said with hidden sarcasm as they headed out of the class together. "What's got your mind all twisted anyway? You been acting funny these past couple days."

Harmony took a deep breath then smiled. "Girl, I met someone."

"What? For real?" Kendra acted surprised.

"Yeah, this guy."

"And since when do you have time for a guy?"

"I don't have time. That's one of the reasons I haven't called him. He doesn't have my number, but he gave me his."

"Some dude has got you thinking about him, daydreaming and shit in class, over school work, and you haven't called him? Well, if he's got you fiendin' like this now where you can't even answer a lousy question in class, then you can kiss your final exams goodbye."

Harmony put her head down. She knew Kendra was right. No matter how hard she tried, she just couldn't stop thinking about Nikko and the what-if-she-called-him, what-if-she-didn't-call-him thing.

"What? What's wrong? He got one eye or something? Why you trippin' off just calling the guy?"

"Scared."

"Of what?"

"The dick," Nay-Nay jumped in from behind. Both Harmony and Kendra turned around and laughed.

"You crazy," Harmony said.

"You crazy 'cause I know exactly who you talking about, and if I still had a cherry, you best believe I wouldn't hesitate to put it on his sundae."

"Just nasty," Kendra said to Nay-Nay.

"No, but for real," Nay-Nay continued, "everybody knows Nikko's got the hots for you."

Harmony stopped in her tracks and looked at Nay-Nay with shock. Maybe Nay-Nay could read her mind or something. How else in the world did she know that it was Nikko who had her head in the clouds?

"Don't look at me all funny. You can keep a lot of things secret, but not true love," Nay-Nay said.

"True love? I wouldn't go that far," Harmony said, downplaying the situation. "Besides, how do you know about Nikko?"

"Now, you know ain't nothing a secret in the hood, and that's where I'm from," Nay-Nay said proudly. "You know I still got eyes and ears there, and you and Nikko are the talk on every block."

"For real?" Harmony asked, not able to hide her excitement.

"For real," Nay-Nay assured her. "And girl, the sistahs be checking for his fine yellow ass, so if I were you, I'd be calling him all day every day."

Harmony still had doubt and hesitation on her face.

"He's really feeling you, girl," Nay-Nay added.

"I know I would be callin' him, girl," Kendra

pressured. After a few seconds of watching Harmony be indecisive, Nay-Nay pulled out her cell phone and held it out to Harmony.

Harmony looked down at the phone. "What am I supposed to say?" she asked.

Nay-Nay sighed. "Just go with the flow. Look, we'll be right here. You know I know how to shoot game, so I'll tell you what to say if you freeze up or something."

Harmony thought about it for a moment before taking the phone out of Nay-Nay's hand. "Okay," she agreed.

The girls stood outside of the lunchroom in the hallway where kids hung out during the lunch period. Nay-Nay and Kendra watched anxiously as Harmony took the number out of her purse and dialed. After two rings, Harmony heard Nikko's voice.

"Talk to me," he said in Harmony's ear.

"Uh, hello. May I speak to Nikko?"

"Yes, you may," he said with a pause.

Harmony just sat there for a moment. "Hello," she finally said.

"Yes."

"May I speak to Nikko?"

"Yes, you may."

"Then can you put him on the phone, please?" Harmony laughed, knowing it was Nikko being Nikko.

"This is Nikko," he gave in.

"Hey, it's Harmony."

"I know."

"So, what's up?"

"The sky."

"Do you ever just conversate without always saying something slick? Can't you just talk to me?"

There was a brief moment of silence. "So, what's up, lady?"

It was something about the way he said "lady" that made Harmony feel like a woman.

"You," she said with confidence. "That's why I'm calling."

"I see."

Nay-Nay waved her hands at Harmony, telling her to keep the conversation moving. "So, what are you doing?" Harmony asked off the top of her head.

"Just sittin' here chillin' for the time being. 'Bout to make a move in a minute here."

"'Bout to make a move, huh?" Harmony repeated.

Nay-Nay jumped in and fed Harmony a line to regurgitate to Nikko.

"I wouldn't mind you making a move," Harmony said, repeating part of the line Nay-Nay had whispered. Nay-Nay nudged her to finish the sentence, which Harmony did. "On me."

A little thrown off at Harmony's frankness, Nikko paused. "Is that so?" he asked.

"Yeah," she replied. "That's very much so."

"So what you 'bout to get into?" Nikko asked, moving the conversation along.

"Nothing. Just at school. It's lunchtime."

"So, what's up with you after school?"

"What am I doing after school?" Harmony repeated then looked at the girls frantically.

"Is something wrong with your phone? Can you hear me now? Why do you keep repeating everything I say?"

"No, I can hear you fine," Harmony replied.

"Tell him to come scoop you up after school," Nay-Nay whispered.

"Girl, I can't," Harmony whispered back. "My mom."

"Tell her you're staying at school late with your study group or something. I don't know. We'll worry about that later."

"Hello," Nikko said.

"Uh, yeah, after school is fine," Harmony said.

"Fine for what?"

"For if you want to come scoop me up or something."

"Do you want me to come *scoop you up*?" Nikko asked, mocking Harmony's phrase.

Harmony paused. "Yeah, I'm definitely sure."

"Then I'll see you in a couple of hours."

A huge grin covered Harmony's face as she replied, "Okay then, bye." There was no response from Nikko. To her surprise, he had already hung up the phone without even saying bye. She handed Nay-Nay her cell phone.

"Well?" Kendra and Nay-Nay both said in anticipation.

"Well," Harmony lingered, "he's coming to scoop me up after school today."

The girls started screaming. Nearby students looked at them as if they were crazy.

"You go, girl," Nay-Nay said to Harmony, giving her a high five.

Just then Harmony's smile turned to a frown.

"What's wrong?" Kendra asked.

"What am I going to tell my mom about where I'm going after school?" Harmony asked. "I never do anything after school."

"That's all the more reason why she shouldn't suspect that you're up to something," Nay-Nay said.

"Or that's all the more reason why she will suspect that I'm up to something."

"Seems as though your double life is a double-edged sword." Nay-Nay sighed.

"Girl, we'll think of something," Kendra interjected. "Right now let's go grab something to eat because I'm starved." She grabbed Harmony by the arm and pulled her toward the cafeteria.

"I'll meet y'all in there. I have to go to the bathroom first," Nay-Nay said as she turned around and headed towards the girl's bathroom, running smack into La-La.

"What's going on?" La-La asked. "I heard y'all screaming all the way down the hall."

"Girl," Nay-Nay said in a devious whisper. "We just talked Harmony into hooking up with Nikko. She wanna be down so much and act like she's one of us, well, Nikko ain't nothing like that little white boy back in Ohio she fucked with. You know what they say; Once you go black, you never go back." Nay-Nay began to laugh.

"Y'all are crazy," La-La said. "I told y'all that girl wouldn't know what to do with that boy if she had instructions. She ain't never been around no real brotha. The brothas at this school all remind me of Carlton from *The Fresh Prince of Bel Air.*"

"No, she's crazy for thinking she could play with the big dawgs at her own convenience, when and where she wants to, like we some fuckin' guinea pigs, making us look stupid." Nay-Nay became more serious. "Well, now the big dawgs are about to play her. At the end of the game, she's the one who's going to be looking stupid. Mark my word."

***

Harmony watched the second hand go around the clock the last two times before the final school bell of the day rang. She was both nervous and excited at the same time. She didn't know if she was more nervous about hooking up with Nikko or getting caught in a lie by her mother. Harmony had told Veronica that she was staying after school because they were offering tutoring and study groups for the final exams.

"It's your last year of high school," Veronica questioned, "and now you want to take advantage of an after school program?"

Harmony could sense that Veronica was skeptical. "Exactly," Harmony said, thinking quick on her feet. "Any other year if I messed up, I had the next year to make up for it. But I'm a senior now. There is no next year, and you know how important going to Duke is to me."

With fingers crossed, Harmony waited on her mother's response. After a few seconds of silence and a deep sigh, Veronica eventually gave in. Although a little nervous at first, Harmony knew her mom would come through. After all, she had never given Veronica any reason to doubt her. But it was still in the back of her mind how bad she would be busted if her mother just happened to come up to the school and see that she wasn't there.

Once Harmony walked out of the school doors and saw that yellow Caddy, she forgot all about her mother.

When she approached Nikko's car, she waited at the passenger door for a second before she realized that he wasn't about to get out of the car and come around to open the door for her. She hopped in and the two of them drove to his apartment. The closer they got to his place, the more foreign everything started to look to Harmony. She had never been in the parts of the boroughs he was touring her through. Nikko watched her face as they drove through his hood. He could tell that she was way beyond her comfort zone.

Once they arrived at his place, he double-parked next to his neighbor's car. Everything looked so dirty to Harmony, but inside Nikko's apartment, it wasn't as bad as she had presumed it would be.

"Not bad," Harmony said, eyeballing his red velvet-like couch with matching chaise. In between them was a black wooden table with two doors. Harmony couldn't tell if they were faux cabinets or ones that really opened.

"Thank you," Nikko said. "Have a seat." He walked

over to the couch and sat down. Harmony sat down as well, but over on the chaise. Nikko began to chuckle.

"What?" Harmony asked, still looking around, checking out his pad.

"I won't bite," he said, patting the spot next to him.

"Oh." Harmony got up to sit by him on the couch.

"So tell me, what's the real?"

"Come again?" she asked.

"What do you want from me?" he replied.

"What do I want from you? Shouldn't the question be what do you want from me?"

"You called me."

"You gave me your phone number," she reminded him.

"But you chose to use it. Why?"

"Because," Harmony said, sounding like a six-year-old.

"Because you were curious." Nikko answered for her.

Harmony was, in fact, very curious, and perhaps curiosity was getting the best of her. She had to admit it to herself, but no way was she going to confess it to Nikko, not verbally anyway, so she said nothing, hoping her silence said it all.

"I'm curious too, Harmony. I'm curious about you."

"What about me?"

"I don't know, everything. So why don't you tell me about yourself?"

"Not much to tell. I'm originally from Ohio. Moved to New York City my freshman year of high school. My dad's a doctor. My mom's a nurse."

"Stick out your tongue," Nikko said as if he were a doctor and wanted to examine Harmony.

"What?"

"Stick out your tongue."

"Why?"

"I want to see if there's still any silver on your tongue from that spoon you were born with in your mouth."

"Cute." Harmony giggled.

"Yeah, well, you're pretty cute too."

Harmony blushed and looked down. Nikko placed his index finger on her chin, lifted her head and looked deep in her eyes. "Don't ever let what anyone has to say about you make you put your head down, whether it's good or bad."

Harmony nodded her head to Nikko's words, which seemed so sincere. There was just something about the way he said it that made her certain that he meant it. Not only that, but his words hit home for Harmony. She was quick to allow what others said or thought about her to make her second guess herself. It was as if Nikko was in her head or something.

As Nikko sat there, still looking into Harmony's eyes, she wanted to grab him by the face and plant one on him. Instead, she just sat there twiddling her thumbs. All of a sudden, there was a loud boom, and Harmony ducked and covered her head. Nikko busted out laughing.

"What are you doing? That was just a car backfiring. Relax," Nikko said, still laughing.

This agitated Harmony. She wasn't comfortable being out of her element, and she knew he could see that. She was embarrassed, frustrated and making a complete fool of herself.

"Look, I'm ready to go," she said, jumping up. She didn't know why she had let Nay-Nay and Kendra talk her into this mess.

"Okay, okay, I'm sorry," Nikko said, pulling Harmony back down next to him on the couch. "I didn't mean to laugh at you. Sit down and just try to relax."

"I can't relax. I'm nervous. Being here makes me

nervous. You make me nervous." Harmony's eyes began to water. She couldn't believe she was in breakdown mode on her first date with Nikko, if it was even considered a date. As far as she could tell, she was just making a fool out of herself. "This is embarrassing." Harmony wiped a tear that fell from her eye. She just wanted to go home, back to where she was comfortable and could be her real self.

Nikko put his hand on Harmony's. "You don't have to be nervous around me. Just loosen up and relax like you just chillin' with your homegirls and shit." Nikko paused. "I know something that will make you relax. It works for me every time the world is going 'round and 'round and I seem to be standing still."

"What?" Harmony asked, wiping her tears away. "What is it?"

Just then, Nikko opened the cabinet doors on his living room table, pulled out a plate and set it on his lap. On the plate was a pile of white powder, a piece of paper and a rolled dollar bill.

"What's that?" Harmony asked, pretty much already knowing the answer.

"It's like weed, only not," Nikko said as he picked up the piece of paper and started to scrape some of the white powder into lines.

Once he had made three lines, Harmony watched him pick up the dollar bill and place it in his right nostril, holding his left nostril shut with his index finger. He proceeded to snort one of the three lines he had formed, then leaned back against the couch and sighed. "See, all relaxed now. Try it."

"Nah," Harmony said, shaking her head.

"You said you smoke weed, right?"

"Yeah, but—"

"This ain't no different. 'Spite popular opinion, a drug

is a drug. Doing this ain't no worse than smoking weed." Nikko snorted the second of the three lines. Snortin' lines wasn't something that Nikko did on the regular. He just always put a stash for himself to the side before it got cooked up.

Harmony watched him as he leaned back and closed his eyes. After a few seconds, he picked up a remote from the table and turned on the CD player. Sade was singing, "It's never quite like the first time." Nikko then leaned back and started tapping his foot to the beat of the music. Then he started humming. When he opened his eyes, Harmony's were locked on his.

"Remember when you asked me which way I was going?"

"Mm-hmm," Harmony answered.

"I said I was going where you were going. You remember that?"

"Yes."

Nikko sat up and leaned into Harmony. "Now I want you to go where I'm going." Nikko licked his lips and said, "Come with me." He pecked Harmony on the lips. "Come with me." He kissed her again. She moved in to kiss him back deeply, but he pulled away, leaving her there mesmerized, wanting him. "Come with me," he whispered one last time before he handed her the rolled dollar bill.

Slowly, Harmony took the dollar bill from Nikko and leaned her head in over the plate. She hesitated, asking herself, *What in the hell am I doing?* Then she thought, *Can't be worse than a blunt. Like Nikko said, a drug is a drug. Mouth, nose, what's the difference where it enters the body? The point is that it enters it.* Over her own thoughts, Harmony heard Nikko's words playing in her head as well.

Come with me.

She looked up into his eyes. He looked okay. She was sure it wasn't his first time doing coke, and it hadn't seemed to have affected him any. He wasn't out on the corner like some fiend. He had a nice ride, crib, clothes and jewelry. *Come with me.* She wanted to go.

The next thing Harmony knew, she leaned over Nikko's lap and was assuming the position. She placed the rolled dollar bill in her right nostril as she held down her left nostril with her index finger, just as she had seen Nikko do. Nikko softly cupped the back of her head, pushing it closer to the plate as he massaged her head with his fingers. Harmony snorted the last line on the plate.

She began choking and snorting, holding her hand over her nose.

"It burns," she said.

"Just lean back," Nikko said, grabbing her shoulders and pulling her toward his chest. "Just hold your head back. It'll be okay. You'll start to feel it in a minute."

At first, Harmony felt nothing but a stinging up her nostrils. She twitched her nose. Then a couple minutes later, drainage began seeping down her throat.

"Yuck," she said, attempting to sit up, but Nikko pulled her back against him.

"Just relax and let it flow."

In increments, like codeine in an IV, the powder turned to liquid and flowed down the back of Harmony's throat, eventually giving her a feeling that marijuana never had. Before Nikko knew it, Harmony had taken the liberty to scrape up another line and snort it.

"Who's this?" she asked, realizing that the piece of paper she had used to form a line of coke was a picture of a couple.

Nikko looked down. "That's my mom and dad."

Harmony stared at the picture. "Your dad is white?"

"Yeah," Nikko said.

The photo of Nikko's black mother and white father explained his creamy skin tone.

"They looked like a happy couple. Your dad must really miss her."

"He's dead too," Nikko said nonchalantly.

Harmony dropped the photo back onto the plate. She couldn't imagine how it must feel for Nikko to have lost both his mother and father.

"He raised me after my mom died," Nikko added. "He was a son-of-a-bitch. You remind me of him."

"Oh, so I'm a son-of-a-bitch?" Harmony said.

"No, I don't mean it like that. I mean how you are with school and all. How your face lights up when you talk about education, going to college and all."

"Your dad went to college?"

"No. He wanted to, but never got the chance. But he was going to see that I made up for that by any means necessary, even if it meant beating the shit out of me." Nikko didn't realize that he was letting his guard down with Harmony. He had never discussed his parents with anyone before.

There was silence for a moment. Harmony looked up at Nikko, who was leaned back with his eyes closed. She took the plate from his lap and placed it on the table. Her hands fumbling with his jeans made him open his eyes. He looked down at her.

"You're going to have to teach me," she said, looking up at him. She had never given head before, so she didn't know how, but for some reason, she wasn't embarrassed that Nikko would have to be the one to teach her.

Harmony pulled Nikko's dick out and put about two inches in her mouth, bobbing her head up and down. "Is that right?" she asked.

"That's just fine," Nikko said, so she continued

slobbing up the two inches. Eventually, he pushed her head down to take in about two more inches. He began to moan. Harmony looked up at him as she continued, making sure she wasn't hurting him, scraping her teeth up against him or anything.

It seemed as though all of a sudden Harmony was going ninety miles per hour. Nikko couldn't tell that she hadn't done it before by the way she was going at it.

"Slow down. Don't move up and down so much, just suck on it."

"Like this?" Harmony asked as she held a good five inches in her mouth and basically slapped her tongue around on it.

"Hold it like this." Nikko took her hand and placed it around the part of his penis that wasn't in her mouth. "Squeeze it and move your hand up and down." He began to moan as Harmony followed his instructions to the tee.

The more he moaned, the faster Harmony went. Suddenly, he stopped her.

"What? What's wrong," she asked. "What did I do?"

"I think you started something you're not going to be able to finish." Nikko started to zip his pants.

Harmony put her hands on his to stop him. "I can finish. I've done *it* before, but only once, so you still might have to teach me . . . how you like it."

"Hold on." Nikko got the plate and cut two more lines. He snorted one then gave the plate to Harmony to snort the other. He laid Harmony down on the couch. She just lay there, swallowing the drainage, feeling good.

Nikko unbuttoned her pink Old Navy blouse and rubbed her breasts through her white bra. He placed himself on top of her and gently began kissing her neck, pulling her breasts out of her bra and sucking on them.

Not even in Harmony's late night fantasies had she imagined a feeling that good. Nikko was right. She lay there enjoying the feeling as he slipped her slacks off of her. Her eyes did open wide once she felt his hand go down her panties.

"Wait a minute," Harmony said quickly. She had only had sex once, and that was over three years ago. Jeremy was a boy, a white boy, and Nikko was a man, a black man, and if the myth was true, he was a black man who was probably going to burst her wide open.

"Just relax," Nikko assured her. "I got this, ma."

Harmony lay back and tried to relax, but she was fidgety. She began breathing heavily as Nikko's fingers found their way to her clit.

"Oh," she moaned as she jerked her body.

"I'm just gonna touch you here," Nikko whispered as he began rubbing his finger up and down her clit.

"Ohh," she softly moaned. "Ohh."

Each time Nikko slid his finger down her clit, he went closer and closer to her opening. Once Harmony realized that the tip of his finger was inside of her, she grabbed his hand.

"Please go slow."

"I will."

Nikko decided that now was the time to stuff her mouth with his tongue because this would be the part where she would lose it. After a few seconds of kissing her passionately, he pushed his finger halfway inside of her. She jerked and tried to pull away, but he kept her tight to him and continued doing what he was doing. He knew that it would only be a matter of seconds before it hurt so good. With each stroke of his finger going deeper inside of her, Harmony gave in, rocking her hips to his rhythm. Once her body was limp with ecstasy, Nikko pulled his hand out of her panties and laid his body flat on hers. He wasn't inside of her, not yet.

Harmony helped Nikko remove his pants. He took off

his shirt then he slid her panties off of her. He placed three of his fingers in his mouth, soaked them with saliva then rubbed her pussy to make her wet. Going down wasn't something Nikko did and wasn't about to start doing. But fortunately, Harmony was sticky wet, as if she might have already cum just from grinding.

Nikko couldn't help diving into Harmony's pool as he placed himself inside of her. He had wanted to start off slow, but from the moment the tip of his dick made contact with her pussy, it was over.

"Ohhh," Harmony yelled in a tone that sounded of both pain and ecstasy.

"Damn," Nikko said as he thrust in and out of Harmony like he was a male dog who had just run up on a bitch and started humping her.

Harmony grabbed hold of Nikko's ass cheeks. She found herself fucking him back, moving just as quickly as him, but struggling to keep up. Finally she decided to just lay back, kick it and enjoy the ride. It wasn't two minutes after that before Nikko's body tightened up and he let out a loud moan. He thrust himself deep inside of her then he just held the position. That's when Harmony decided to get hers off, crooning herself on Nikko's dick.

"Fuck that dick, baby," Nikko moaned as the last of his nut filled the condom he had gotten from the cabinet and placed on himself before running up in Harmony.

A rush came over Harmony's body. It felt like she was being drowned by a tidal wave. Her eyes opened wide and her mouth opened as the orgasm left her limp.

Nikko kissed her lips then rested his body on top of hers, where he lay for the next half-hour. It was then that the sound of Harmony whispering his name woke him out of his sleep.

"Nikko, Nikko," she said. "Get up. I gotta go."

"Huh, what?" Nikko said, yawning.

"Get up."

Nikko looked down at Harmony like "who the fuck is this and what the fuck did we just do?" until enough time set in for him to recall the scene. "You all right?" he asked as she got up and started dressing.

"Yeah, I'm fine," Harmony lied. She really felt like crap. She didn't know what was going on, she just didn't feel like herself. She looked around for her panties. Nikko saw them and picked them up and handed them to her along with her pants.

"I gotta go to the bathroom," he said. "I'll be right back."

Harmony got dressed then sat on the couch and waited for Nikko. "I need to get home," she said as soon as he came out of the bathroom.

"You wanna go to the bathroom and clean up?" he asked her.

"No, I'll do that at home."

Nikko grabbed his keys and they headed out of the apartment to his car. He was walking about three paces ahead of Harmony, and she waited to see if he was going to open the car door for her. To her dismay, he walked right on around the car, past the passenger door, and got in.

She stopped in her tracks, shook her head and smiled. *At least he's keepin' it real,* she thought to as she got into the car.

Nikko started the engine. "You hungry?" he asked without waiting for a response. "Let's go get something to eat."

Nikko took Harmony to some little Mom and Pop soul food joint not too far from where he lived. Harmony felt funny at first, as if everyone was staring at them, as if everybody could smell the sex on them, see sex on them, and knew they had been fucking. But after a while,

Harmony didn't care anymore. She and Nikko just sat at the table eating and talking until the sun started to go down. Not once did Harmony feel nervous or have to think about what she had to say to Nikko. She was just being herself, and corny or not, Nikko seemed to enjoy her company.

When Nikko dropped Harmony off at the library like she instructed, she knew that would probably be the last time they hooked up. Although she had had a wonderful time with him, she had seen enough movies and had read enough books about the girl who dates the boy from the wrong side of the tracks to know that nothing but drama could possible become of their relationship. On top of that, the main thing that had attracted her to him was his mystery and her own curiosity. Now she no longer had to fantasize about what it would feel like to be with Nikko. She knew firsthand, and it was memory enough to last her a lifetime.

Although her memory of Nikko's touch might have been enough to last her a lifetime, Harmony would soon come face to face with a thirst that memory alone wouldn't be able to quench.

Chapter 4
Back to the Hood of Things

It only took Harmony a couple of days to call Nikko and hook up with him again. Although he'd never admit it to anyone, or even himself for that matter, he was hoping that she would call. He even found himself checking his cell phone to make sure that it was on or that he hadn't missed her call.

Nikko had never let his guard down with a woman as much as he had with Harmony, and even though it seemed like a little bit, for him it was a lot. After the way his mother did his father, it had been difficult for Nikko to let a woman in. He just found it too hard to trust them. If you can't trust your own mother, then what other woman can you trust? That's why Nikko killed her off in his heart. She wasn't really dead in the physical. She was still breathing and living somewhere with her new family. But as far as Nikko was concerned, she was dead. In addition to that, lying and just telling people that she was dead made a long story short.

Speaking of truth and lies, Harmony found herself making up all kinds of lies to tell her mother in order to spend time with Nikko. Veronica tried not to seem too suspicious at first about Harmony wanting to spend more and more time out of the house. She knew that Harmony wasn't a baby anymore. She was growing into a fine young woman and she'd be heading off to college soon. She knew it was only a matter of time before Harmony would want to leave the nest.

She didn't want to be like her mother and make Harmony feel as though she had to sneak around to do things. At the same time, she didn't want to give her the green light to just go buck wild either, so she allowed Harmony some space and decided to let her fly. It didn't

172

take long, though, for her mother's intuition to start nagging at her, telling her that perhaps Harmony was straying too far from the nest and flying in the wrong direction.

Harmony was flying all right. She was flying high, higher than she ever imagined. Every time she met up with Nikko, she was always glad to see him. Being with him gave her a high, but not as good a high as the coke he kept on the plate in his living room table made her feel. Harmony didn't even realize that her brain associated Nikko with getting high. The sex got better and better each time, the conversation was good, but the high was great.

Every time Nikko left her alone in the living room or went to the bathroom or something, she made her way to the plate of coke, in so much of a hurry sometimes that she snorted it right off the pile.

The girls hardly noticed the change in Harmony because now it was to the point where she barely even hung out with them at school anymore. She was too busy up under Nikko. She had even missed a couple of homework assignments, claiming to have left them at home. For once, something was definitely more important to Harmony than school, and it was starting to become evident through her grades.

"A C-minus?" Kendra said as she looked over Harmony's shoulder at the test paper she was holding in her hand. Just then the bell rang and the teacher dismissed the class.

Harmony had never seen a C-minus on any paper that had her name on it. Although she was a little shaken by it, she didn't worry much. It was only a practice test, and on top of that, there were only three more weeks of school. She had been a straight A student as long as she could remember. A C-minus on one lousy test wasn't going to keep her from going to college, so she brushed it off.

"Girl, it ain't nothing," she said to Kendra as she gathered her things and headed out of the classroom.

At lunch, Harmony wasn't saying much, like she was just dazed. That's pretty much how the rest of her day went until the final bell of the day rang.

"Oh yeah," Kendra said to Nay-Nay as the two of them stood at their lockers next to Harmony's. "Can you believe Harmony got a C-minus on her test in government class today?"

"Why are you making such a milestone occasion out of it?" Harmony snapped, slamming her locker closed. "You of all people have seen a C-minus enough times not to get so excited about it. If I wanted Nay-Nay to know my grades, I would tell her."

"Oooh, she told yo' ass," Nay-Nay said as both she and Kendra closed their lockers.

"Damn, my bad," Kendra said, rolling her eyes. "You don't mind tellin' everybody what your grades are when you running around with A papers."

"And I don't see you quick to tell anybody about my A papers either," Harmony came back.

"Squash it already," Nay-Nay said. Harmony walked off, and Nay-Nay and Kendra followed behind. "Oh yeah, Kendra, guess what? My girl Fire, from my old neighborhood, called me. It's on. They having a set at her place."

"I don't know if I'm trying to hit up another one of Fire's sets," Kendra said. "The last time I went to one of them damn sets, I swear on everything there was more than just weed in that blunt. I don't care what nobody says. I was fucked up, headache the next morning and all."

"They don't even get down like that. I mean yeah,

they be doing other thangs besides weed, but they don't be trying to trick a muthafucka or nothing by slipping them no coke or no shit like that. You just ain't used to the fo' real fo' real chronic that yo' ass ain't gon' get nowhere else but in the PJs."

"Umm, I'll let you know if I'ma roll or not," Kendra said.

"Well, La-La said she's going," Nay-Nay added.

"Yeah, I bet she is. Bitch walked away with almost five hundred in winnings from playing cards the last time."

Harmony was walking a couple steps ahead of Nay-Nay and Kendra. Nay-Nay looked over at Kendra and winked before she said, "Hey, Harmony, you wanna go?" Kendra giggled under her breath.

"No, I promised Nikko I would hang out with him."

"You been spending hella time with his ass," Nay-Nay said.

"Yeah, well," Harmony said without elaborating. "Look, I gotta go. Nikko's probably out there waiting for me. He's supposed to be picking me up after school today."

"You don't even want to blaze one with us first?" Kendra asked.

"Yeah, you ain't blazed one with us in a minute. You always running off with Nikko."

"Sorry, girls, maybe another time," Harmony said as she eagerly made her way down the hall and through the exit.

As Harmony walked away, La-La came up behind Nay-Nay and Kendra and started walking with them. "Where's Harmony running off to like she done stole something?"

"Where else?" Kendra said, smacking her lips. "To be with Nikko."

175

"Yeah," Nay-Nay said with a mischievous grin on her face. "Who knew that she would fall head over heels and start slippin' up?" She winked at Kendra.

"Yeah, that nigga got her ass sprung," Kendra added.

"I don't know," Nay-Nay said. "He might have her a little more than sprung. I mean, come on, a C-minus on a test."

"Who, Harmony?" La-La was surprised.

"Yep," Kendra answered.

The girls exited the school, where they saw Harmony hopping into Nikko's car.

"He's fine and all, but we talking about a chick who don't even get A-minuses, let alone a C-minus," La-La said. "I don't know, but if you ask me, her ass is sprung on something other than just some dick."

***

When Harmony got in Nikko's car, she leaned over and hugged him. He just sat there with his hands on the steering wheel and let her. He wasn't a touchy-feely kind of person.

"So, let's head to your house," Harmony said.

It seemed like whenever Nikko picked up Harmony, the first thing she wanted to do was to go back to his place. A couple of times he had convinced her to go get something to eat with him, catch a movie or go shopping or something. These were big steps for Nikko to take. Even those chicks he called himself liking a lot at some point never got to go shopping. But with Harmony it was different. She came from money, so he knew she wasn't after his. He didn't mind taking her to the mall and hooking her up with a nice pair of earrings or something. Hell, she pretty much already had everything she wanted, and it wouldn't be hard for her to get her parents to give her anything she didn't already have. But with the girls from the hood he had kicked it with before, he always felt suspicious of their greedy asses. They might have gotten a meal or two and a movie out of him, but the mall was off limits. Although one or two of the girls might have genuinely cared for Nikko in the end, in the beginning they had simply been on the paper chase. But Nikko wasn't plum dumb. He knew after only a couple of weeks that Harmony might not have been on a paper chase, but she was definitely on a chase for something.

"I gotta meet this cat up at the bowling alley to take care of some business," Nikko said. "I thought we'd bowl a couple games while we were there."

"Nah," Harmony said. "I'll wait for you in the car, though, while you do whatever you have to do. I'd rather just go back to your place."

"I'm starting to think you don't want to be seen with me."

"Oh God, not you too." Harmony sighed. "I've heard the same thing from my girls a thousand times. Do you mean I have to start hearing it from you as well?"

"Well, shit, I always gotta beg to take you somewhere. Most girls would jump at the opportunity."

"Well, like you said in the beginning, I ain't like most girls." Harmony looked over at Nikko and winked. She loved it whenever she could make him eat his own words.

Nikko made his pit stop at the bowling alley then they went back to his crib. Harmony brushed by Nikko into his apartment before he could even get the key out of the lock. Almost unconsciously, she walked over to the living room table and opened up the cabinets to pull the plate out, the plate that had been there for her use every other time she had come to his apartment. But this time, there was no plate. Harmony felt around inside the cabinet just to make sure. There was nothing but condoms in there. She closed the cabinet and sat back on the couch. She thought for a minute then got up.

"Where you going?" Nikko asked.

"Uh, I gotta go to the bathroom," Harmony said.

Nikko watched her sniff her way to the bathroom like a canine working with 5-0 on a drug bust. Once she got there, she immediately started looking in Nikko's medicine cabinet. She looked in the cabinet under his sink. She found nothing.

"Damn it," she whispered, burying her face in her hands with a sigh. Then all of a sudden she started laughing. "What am I doing?" she asked herself. "This is crazy. I'm cool. Harmony, you're cool." She straightened herself up and exited the bathroom to join Nikko, who was in the kitchen.

"What are you doing?" Harmony asked.

"Making spaghetti."

"You can make spaghetti?"

Nikko looked up at Harmony, who was fidgeting. "Yeah, there's a lot of things I can do."

Harmony just stood there as if something was on her mind but she just didn't know how to say it.

"You okay?" Nikko asked as he stirred the boiling noodles.

"Yeah, I'm cool," Harmony said. She paused for a few seconds then spoke up. "Hey, you moved the stuff."

"What stuff?" Nikko asked, playing dumb.

"You know, the stuff." She nodded her head toward the living room.

"I don't know what you're talking about." He continued to play dumb, all the while praying that his suspicions wouldn't be confirmed.

"You know, the stuff, the powder. Where is it? I need to relax. I had a crazy day at school today." Nikko remained silent. "So, where's the stuff?"

Nikko stopped stirring the noodles and looked over at Harmony.

"You can't even say it." He shook his head. "You can't even fix your mouth to say it, to call it what it is."

"What?" Harmony asked, not knowing where Nikko was going with this.

Nikko looked up and started laughing. "Bitches," he said. "All alike. Y'all all might be out for something different, but nevertheless, y'all always out for something. And just to think I—" Nikko paused and put his head down. "Oh, I almost caught myself slippin' and shit." He continued laughing.

"Baby, I don't know what you're talking about." Harmony walked over and put her hand on his face. He closed his eyes, put his hand on top of hers and kindly moved it off of his cheek.

Nikko left the kitchen and went into his bedroom. He came back with the plate. Harmony busted a nut at the sight of the coke. Her energy level skyrocketed at just the thought of it.

"You mean this stuff?"

"You knew what I was talking about," Harmony said excitedly, almost dancing a jig. "I don't know why you play with me so much."

"It's called coke, cocaine, coca." Watching her reaction to the plate, Nikko shook his head. "Why do you come here, Harmony? Why you fuck with me? I mean for real, why do you really fuck with me?"

Harmony remained silent.

"Huh!" Nikko shouted, startling her.

"Because," she said, frightened by his sudden anger. "Because I like being with you, Nikko," she said honestly. She did like being with him, but she liked what he could give her more.

"I'm glad to hear that because for a minute there, I was starting to think otherwise." Just then, Nikko walked the plate over to the sink. Harmony watched, rubbing her arms as if she was cold. "You chilly?" Nikko taunted as he held the plate over the sink.

"No, no, I'm fine," she said nervously, praying to God that boy didn't do what she thought he was about to do. But this was one prayer God wasn't about to answer. Nikko turned on the water and allowed the flow to start washing the coke down the drain.

Nikko watched Harmony as she pretended not care. Once she could no longer hold it in any longer, she yelled, "No! Stop it! Don't do that!" She ran over and tried to retrieve the plate from Nikko, but he fought her off with his other hand as the water continued to wash the coke down the drain.

"What the fuck are you doing?" Harmony cried as she continued trying to out-wrestle Nikko. He managed to hold her off with one arm while he washed the last of the coke down the drain. Harmony felt like getting a tool set and taking the fucking sink apart to see if she could retrieve just a line. She was pissed.

"Why did you do that? Huh? Why did you do that? What are you, some kind of stupid nig—"

Before Harmony could even get the entire N-word out of her mouth, she found herself laid out on the kitchen floor. She looked up in shock at Nikko. He had the same look of shock on his face. He had hit her. He was shocked that he had done it, but he wasn't sorry for doing it. He wished he hadn't just hit a woman, but he wasn't sorry. Every time his father called him that word, he wanted to do the same thing to him, but couldn't. Seeing Harmony fix her lips to say it just triggered something inside of him.

"Is that all I am to you?" He got down in her face and yelled. "Is that all I am to you?" He got up and grabbed the plate that had once had the coke on it. "Is this all I am to you, a fix?"

"Fuck you!" Harmony yelled as she managed to pick herself up off the kitchen floor. She held the right side of her face, the side that had Nikko's hand print on it. It hurt, but not as much as watching him flush that coke down the drain.

"It's gone," Nikko said, waving the plate in her face. "It's all gone, so now you don't have to come 'round here no more pretending to be something that you're not, pretending you enjoy kickin' it with me and shit. You think just 'cause you from the 'burbs, got money and go to a good school and all, that you all that? I don't give a fuck where you from. Yo' ass ain't no better than them girls from the hood. Matter o' fact, your kind is worse. At least they keep it real."

Harmony had no response to Nikko's words. She wanted to say something, but what could she? So she just made her way over to the door, unlocked it, turned the doorknob and opened the door. Before walking out, she turned and said to Nikko, "I wasn't pretending. I really did like being with you, Nikko."

Her words sounded sincere. They really did, but Nikko wasn't about to be no sucka. "Fuck you!" he shouted as he threw the plate towards Harmony. Not at her—he wasn't trying to hit her.

The plate hit the wall about three feet away from her and shattered. She quickly exited Nikko's apartment, closing the door behind her. When she told Nikko that she really did like being with him, at that very second, Harmony was nothing but sincere, but no sooner than she closed the door behind her, the thought of that coke down the drain took over her mind again and then fear took over. It was at that moment when Harmony realized that something that had been readily accessible to her no longer was. She had waited all day long for that get high feeling. Still, in her mind, it wasn't something that she needed, it was just something that she wanted. And right now, she wanted it bad and didn't have the foggiest idea where she could get it. As she exited Nikko's apartment building, the answer to her dilemma hit her out of nowhere, the same way Nikko had hit her.

***

Nay-Nay couldn't believe her ears when she answered her cell phone and heard Harmony on the other end asking if she could hang out with them at the set they were talking about earlier at school. The pay phone Harmony had called from wasn't too far out of the way from where they were headed, so Nay-Nay, Kendra and La-La picked Harmony up on their way.

"Look, we got to do something with you," Nay-Nay said to Harmony as they got out of the car to head to Fire's apartment. "They gon' clown me fo' sho' if I show up with you looking like that."

Nay-Nay proceeded to unbutton the top three buttons on Harmony's blouse and the bottom three buttons, leaving only two buttoned. She tied a knot at the bottom of her blouse, exposing her belly button. She pulled Harmony's belt off so that the lacy trim of her panties would show, and made her take her hair out of a ponytail and wear it down, a little wild.

"Yeah, that looks better," Nay-Nay said, proud of the transformation she had just performed on Harmony. She looked down. "And for Pete's sake, can you please take those damn pennies out of your shoes?"

Kendra and La-La laughed.

"Girl, you gon' be all right," La-La said as they headed off.

Ordinarily, Harmony would have hyperventilated in such an atmosphere. That little-ass apartment was stacked, and you could hardly see through the smoke. But Harmony's mind was focused on one thing, and not shit else that was going on around her mattered.

Nay-Nay introduced Harmony to her peoples, and Harmony tried to be cool, laughing harder than anyone else did at jokes and conversing with everybody who walked by her. The others might have thought that she was being overly friendly, but she was just trying to find out who had what she was looking for and how she could go about getting it.

After standing around feeling a little awkward, Harmony found a place on the couch where she then took the liberty of introducing herself to some guy named Talib. He then introduced her to his uncles, Foots and Stoney, who in the past enjoyed sniffing coke, but had now escalated to cooking it.

It wasn't long before Harmony witnessed Foots and Stoney whispering. Foots pulled something out of his pocket then the two of them eased their way back to one of the bedrooms. Nay-Nay was off to the side with a blunt in her hand and a forty-ounce in the other, playing catch-up with her people from the hood. La-La was regulating the card table while Kendra acted as her cheerleader. No one even notice Harmony slip away to the bedroom to find Foots and Stoney. She had no idea what they had, but she knew it wasn't weed, because no one else seemed to mind blazing out in the open. Harmony remembered Nay-Nay saying something to Kendra about coke earlier at school. If it was her lucky night, then her instincts wouldn't lead her astray.

When Harmony walked in on Foots and Stoney, they were sitting on the bed preparing their spread. When they looked up and saw her, though, they began to scramble, putting their shit out of sight. For all they knew, Harmony was 5-0. She was friendly and all, but she definitely stood out from everybody else at the set, in more ways than one. After Harmony convinced them otherwise, they let her in on their little pipe dream.

Harmony wasn't with it at first, but once she realized that was as good as it was going to get for her, she convinced herself that coke was coke, cooked or not. Even though Foots and Stoney were sucking it in from a pipe, she just told herself that it wasn't any different than how the powder transformed into a liquid and flowed down her throat. All that mattered to Harmony was that she got that feeling, that feeling that Nikko had flushed down the drain.

Harmony sat down on the bed next to Foots and watched the two of them take a hit before taking her very first hit of the pipe. Harmony didn't know what hit her. She got a feeling like no other. "I don't remember feeling like this," she said softly to herself. It was a high that no blunt or line of coke could compare to.

Foots and Stoney couldn't help but laugh at the way that shit had her trippin'. They each thought back to their first time. Ain't shit like the first time.

Harmony took another hit and repeated herself, only this time there was no sound at all. *I don't remember feeling like this.* The words played in her head. Her pouty lips, painted with a dark rose lip-gloss, struggled to say them, but no sound came out. It was as if she was numb. It didn't matter. Harmony was so far gone anyway. She was too wrapped up in the way she was feeling at the moment to realize that she was even holding a conversation with herself.

She leaned back on the bed onto her elbows. Her tongue rolled across her front teeth in slow motion. Hell, at this point, everything was in slow motion. Harmony's life was idle, yet the world continued going 'round and 'round . . . in slow motion. Who knew the first time would feel this way?

Harmony moaned and threw her head back. She closed her eyes and took in the stimulating feeling. Caught up, the sensation of it all was not only fucking with her mind, but her body too.

This was an unfamiliar ecstasy for Harmony, as her body had always been her temple. She had guarded it well up until now. But she learned that life has a way of giving up that good-ass foreplay that will get a muthafucka wet every time—the shit that will have a muthafucka's ass so wide open, not giving a fuck about a damn thing. Harmony was proof of that as she sat there soaking wet, longing for that orgasm, that point of no return that whispers to everybody, but only a few actually answer the call.

An unfamiliar feeling it was, but Harmony wouldn't mind getting better acquainted. She could get used to this. As a matter of fact, this shit could become addictive.

She was glad that Nikko had flushed the contents of that plate down the drain. It didn't have shit on the way this was making her feel. What Harmony didn't realize was that Nikko might have flushed that coke down the drain, but she was now flushing her life down the drain.

Chapter 5
Can't Fly With No Wings

Harmony struggled to finish up her last weeks of school. Something that it seemed like just yesterday she loved so much was now the biggest burden ever. But she did manage to pass her exams and graduate. Her father surprised her and was in town to watch her walk across the stage and get her diploma.

As Harmony crossed the stage, she looked out and saw her parents in the audience. She wanted to break down and cry. If only they knew the other side to their little girl. For the past couple of weeks, Harmony had managed to smoke more crack than a little bit. She told herself that she would only do it until it was time to go off to college. She had no idea that crack was runnin' thangs, not her.

Harmony turned her attention back to her graduation and took her diploma from the principal's hand. As she did so, the principal looked at her strangely. He signaled to her by touching his own nose that something was wrong with hers. Harmony put her hand under her nose and caught the blood that had begun to ooze out. She had to walk off the stage and straight to the bathroom to clean herself up. She wasn't even sure she had gotten all of the blood off. She was too ashamed to look at herself in the mirror to see.

After the graduation ceremony, Harmony and her parents went out to dinner. She only picked at her food. She hadn't really had an appetite lately, and leave it to Veronica to take notice.

"Honey, you barely took one bite of your food," Veronica said. "And look at you, how skinny you are getting. I just told you the other day that your pants looked like they were going to fall right off of you."

"Please, Mom," Harmony whined. "Like I told you already, I've been so stressed out with final exams and the fact that I'm going to be leaving home to go off to college. I mean, why do you think I've been trying to free myself from you more and more? You're all I know, Mom. I have to get used to being on my own, being with other people besides you."

"Fine, and I understand that, Harmony. That's why I've been giving you your space. You're all I know, too, and it's hard for me. I can't seem to get two minutes alone with you these days. You just don't seem the same. You don't even look the same. It's like you're—"

"Leave the girl alone," Glen interjected with a mouth full of food. He continued to chew then swallowed before saying, "She looks just fine." He winked at Harmony and she smiled at the fact that her father had her back.

Her father wasn't able to stay in town, but he did give her $1,000 to go shopping for a graduation gift. Needless to say, Harmony spent most of it on getting high.

She was like a whole different person, but she hid it well. She started spending a little more time with Veronica, but it was usually only to go shopping. The sad thing was, whatever Veronica bought her, she would take back to the store, get the cash for it, and go get high with the money.

Harmony thought about Nikko on occasion. He thought about her too. How was she doing? But his main thoughts were on money. His name was starting to get out there and before long, him and Boogie would be the go-to men in the hood. Although he had started to let down his guard a little with Harmony, he reminded himself of the tat on his neck—MOB, money over bitches—and vowed to never slip up like that again. What was he thinking, almost fallin' for some chick? Hadn't he learned anything from his father?

The question for Harmony was hadn't she learned anything from hers? She had watched her father work very hard for years, even sacrificing time with his family. He did all of this to make sure that his family had everything they needed and wanted. But at the end of the day, it still wasn't enough for Harmony.

How can I do this to my father, to my mother? Harmony wondered as she lay in her bed, tired and burnt out from getting high the night before at one of Fire's sets, which she now went to without Nay-Nay. She was even still wearing the same clothes from the night before. She looked down at herself. The dirt from the New York streets settled on her clothes, in her skin, her hair. *On second thought, how can I do this to myself?*

This was the first time in a long time Harmony had thought about anything other than getting her high on. She hadn't thought twice about what she was doing to her parents. The way she was living her life would destroy them and could perhaps destroy what she had grown up to know as a perfect family unit. Harmony had never taken anything for granted. She had always acknowledged, respected, and appreciated the life her parents had provided for her. In return, she had worked so hard to make them proud of her. She couldn't go out like that. She just couldn't. She refused to let her life thus far be in vain.

Harmony jumped up out of bed and went into the bathroom to start the shower. At that very moment, not only had she decided that she was going to clean up her body, she was going to clean up her act altogether. Today was going to be a new day, the long overdue new beginning. It was time to let drugs go, cold turkey. She wouldn't even as much as smoke a blunt. It was mind over matter, Harmony thought. She didn't need some rehab center or some counselor telling her that she didn't need to do drugs. Hell, she already knew that. Harmony told herself that it couldn't be as hard as people made it out to be. She didn't need it. She could live her life without it the same as she had done before. Harmony had come too far in life to fuck up now. College had always been a dream of hers and she couldn't just let her dream die. She wasn't going to throw her life away in the name of an urge.

Harmony was determined to make herself feel brand new. She had cracked open a new Victoria's Secret shower gel and lotion set that her mother had purchased for her. She had originally planned on taking it back to the store to get the money because she had spent her last dime the night before. She took a long, hot shower in hopes of washing the past few weeks down the drain. She grabbed her bottles of Pantene and washed and conditioned her hair as well. It had been a few days since she had done that. She had barely felt like brushing it, let alone washing it.

Stepping out of the shower and drying off, Harmony wrapped a towel around her body and proceeded to work the tangles out of her hair. She stood at the bathroom mirror, watching the comb stroke her long strands of hair. From the roots, the comb seemed to straighten Harmony's hair, but once it reached the ends, her hair would bounce back into its curly form. With each stroke, it seemed as though she could hear the sound of the comb running through her hair. For a minute, it seemed so loud that it was going to make her eardrums burst. Harmony's hand began to tremble as she continued combing her hair, listening to the aggravating sound.

Suddenly Harmony stopped, threw the comb down, and closed her eyes. "I know what it is," Harmony said to herself, figuring out why it seemed as though the comb was making such a loud noise. "It's too damn quiet in here. Yeah, that's what it is."

Harmony exited the bathroom and entered her bedroom. She fumbled through her CDs and put in Whitney Houston. She turned up the volume then snapped her fingers as she headed back into the bathroom, hoping Whitney's five octaves would be louder than the call of a crack rock.

After blow drying and putting her hair into a ponytail, Harmony went over to her drawer and picked out a matching white bra and panty set. She hummed along with Whitney as she slipped them onto her body, purposely trying to keep herself distracted by the music. She went over to her closet and grabbed a cute little white blouse with three-quarter length sleeves and a pair of tan drawstring slacks to put on. She put on a comfortable pair of loafers then walked over to her jewelry box to find some matching accessories.

When she opened it, with Whitney still blowing tunes, reality slapped Harmony across the face. There were only a few pieces to choose from. Before there had been enough jewelry in the box to start her own boutique—before crack cocaine, anyway.

Harmony realized that she had pawned, sold, or traded on the streets all of the pieces of jewelry that were worth anything. She hadn't sold or bartered pussy, which is something she had been told crackheads did, so still she didn't consider herself that bad off. She was selling and bartering her jewelry, though; all except for the diamond bracelet that was like a family heirloom. After draining the bank account that her allowance went into, Harmony had no other choice but to sell her belongings. There was only $101 dollars left in her custodial account. The only reason Harmony hadn't smoked that up was because once her account fell under

$100 the custodian, who was her mother, would be made aware of the balance and she would need to sign for any withdrawals. The last thing Harmony wanted to do was involve Veronica, and she didn't have the street smarts to figure out another way to get the money.

In a sense, the heirloom bracelet represented to Harmony that she wasn't a crackhead like the ones she saw hangin' out on the main streets in the hood. They had earned their titles. Crackheads didn't give a fuck about sentimental shit, but Harmony saw herself as different from them. The bracelet was one of the most special, sentimental and expensive gifts ever given to her. She felt as though no high in the world was worth trading it for.

The bracelet sat in the jewelry box where Harmony had taken it off and placed it. She didn't even wear it anymore, not wanting to tempt herself out there on the streets in search of a hit. She didn't want to tempt some other person out on a mission to cop some drugs who might decide to knock her over the head and take it from her. The last thing she wanted was for somebody else to be out there gettin' high off the proceeds from her shit. Hell, if that was the case, she might as well smoke the bracelet her damn self.

The phone rang, startling Harmony. She slammed the jewelry box shut without finding any decent accessories, and walked over to her bed. She sat down as she picked up the phone.

"Hello," Harmony said.

"Harmony, darling," the voice on the other end said. "I finally caught you. Do you know how long and how hard I've been trying to reach you?"

"Daddy," Harmony said. "I swear I was just thinking about you. I swear I was."

"Okay, dear. I believe you," her father said with a chuckle. "You okay? Where's Mom?"

"Probably at the clinic," Harmony replied. "Yeah, I'm fine. I miss you, Daddy."

"I miss you too, darling."

Harmony closed her eyes tight and squeezed her lips together. Hearing her father's voice wasn't enough. She needed him there.

"So when are you coming home, Dad?" Harmony asked, wiping the tear that had fallen from her eye.

"I'm really not sure. I was going to try to fly home this weekend, but it doesn't look like I'm going to be able to pull that off."

Harmony could hear someone in the background talking to her father.

"Look, Harmony. I'm needed, so I have to go, but I'll call you again soon. Okay, dear?"

"Okay," Harmony said in a trembling tone, trying not to burst out crying.

You're right. You are needed. I need you, Daddy. Please come home. Just sit with me. Just stay with me. You have no idea what I'm going through. Please, Daddy, come home.

"I love you, little Harmony," her father said.

"I love you too, Daddy." Harmony hung up the phone and buried her head in her hands. She took a couple of deep breaths then wiped away her tears. Hearing her father's voice gave Harmony a burst of strength she didn't know she had. She had always made her parents proud. Yeah, she acted different at school than she did when she was around them, but never had she done anything like she was doing now. The first few times she smoked with the girls, she never even really inhaled. She was just trying to fit in. They seemed so cool that she just wanted to be like them. She knew she wasn't anything like them, but it didn't hurt pretending to be. Once she came home, she was just Harmony. For now on, that's all she wanted to be, just Harmony. She didn't care if she never had a friend or if a boy ever liked her again. She just wanted to do what she had always dreamed of doing, going to college.

Harmony reached into her nightstand drawer and pulled out some of the college brochures from Duke University. She flipped through them, comprehending nothing. It was just an attempt to keep busy. A failed attempt. Harmony pushed the brochures aside and lay down. She grabbed her favorite teddy bear and started stroking it. Harmony soon found herself making silly goo-goo remarks to the teddy bear as if it were a real baby or something. Once she realized how stupid she sounded, she threw the bear back down then walked over to her bedroom window. Harmony lifted the blinds and opened the window. The birds were trying to upstage Whitney. Harmony smiled at the innocent competition.

The sun was blazing. It was a nice, clear summer day. Perhaps it was too clear for Harmony. Through the tall, beautiful trees, blue sky, and green grass, Harmony could only see one thing—smoke pearling up over the city. The funnel of happiness. She envisioned herself hitting the pipe, blowing the smoke over the city so that everyone could experience the high. The feeling of the high was too good to keep to herself. The bird's serenade ceased and she could hear them no more. All she could hear were the streets calling.

Snapping back into reality, Harmony slammed the window shut and closed the blinds. She went back over to her bed and sat down. For a little while, she tried sleeping, but only tossed and turned. She got up out of bed and began pacing back and forth, forth and back until she started to wear a path. Then all of a sudden she felt like she had to throw up. She started gagging, but nothing came up. Beads of sweat started to form on her body. She felt as though she was walking through fire.

Just a minute ago I was fine, Harmony thought. *This shit is in my head. This shit is* all *in my head,* she told herself repeatedly.

"Shit, it's hot," Harmony said as she quickly, almost angrily removed her blouse. When that didn't seem to cool her off, she removed her pants as well. She now stood pacing with nothing on but a bra, panties and a pair of loafers. Still sweating profusely, Harmony walked into her bathroom and began running cold water, splashing it on her face. She filled her hands with water and slapped it on her neck. Water dripped down to her chest, soaking her bra.

Harmony walked over to the toilet and sat down on the lid, rocking back and forth, breathing heavily. She needed to get high. But she couldn't fly with no wings. She hadn't a dime to her name. For the very first time, Harmony contemplated doing the unthinkable to get money. She considered selling herself, but then she remembered that it was that time of the month.

Fuck! she thought. *I'd have to find a dude grimy enough to want to fight the bloody battle. I'll be dead by the time I luck up on one of those kind of triflin'-ass men, otherwise I'd probably have to do some ol' freaky shit like sucking dick, balls, licking ass or another bitch's pussy or some shit. Fuck that!*

Just as quickly as the thought of selling herself for a hit came into Harmony's head, it was gone. She continued rocking back and forth. One minute Harmony would be telling herself that she was fine, that she could do this. She could fight the urge. She told herself that everything was going to be okay. She just had to get through this day and then the days would get better. But

194

the next minute, Harmony would be telling herself that one more hit wouldn't hurt. She could stop after that one more hit. Just one last hit. The inner voices bickering back and forth at one another were starting to drive Harmony insane. She put her hands over her ears, pulled her feet up onto the toilet seat and sat there, rocking back and forth. Even if the part of Harmony that wanted to answer the call of the streets prevailed, she would still find herself with a bad case of the shorts. Even if she wanted to smoke, with no money or means to cop, she couldn't . . . or could she?

***

"Hey, pretty lady," the owner of the pawn shop said to Harmony in a heavy accent. He was Arabic or some nationality that Harmony didn't too much care to concern herself with. "You back to get your fancy CD player?"

Harmony shot him a fake smile that left her face just as quickly as it had come. "No. No, I, uh, got something else for you," Harmony said with hesitation.

"Let's see what you got. I'm sure it will be pretty like you."

Harmony took a deep breath then reached down in her purse. The pawn shop owner greedily waited for her to place the item on the counter.

"Oh, nice," he said, picking up the diamond bracelet that had once belonged to her great-grandmother. He held it up and observed it carefully. "Diamonds, huh? Not Cubic Zirconia? Let me take to back of store and examine. I be right back. Don't go nowhere, pretty lady." He quickly dashed to the back of the store, admiring the bracelet the entire way.

Hell no, I ain't goin' nowhere, Harmony thought. *Not as long as you got my shit anyway. Stupid towel head.*

As Harmony stood at the counter waiting impatiently, she looked around the shop.

I wonder how many hits the owner got off of that, Harmony thought as she looked at a pearly, midnight blue electric guitar. Her eyes moved on to a fairly new mountain bike. *Oh, I know they got plenty of hits off of that.* It seemed as though everything amounted up to hits on the crack pipe. Nothing had a monetary value anymore.

"Not fake," the pawn shop owner said, coming from the back. "How much money you try to borrow?"

"How much can you give me for it?" Harmony asked in an anxious tone.

"To borrow, three hundred, but I give you good deal if you sell to me," he said, smiling.

"Only three hundred? Do you know how much that thing is worth?" Harmony asked, disappointed. *How much if I sell to you?* she wanted to ask, but she didn't want to be tempted by the answer. Having every intention of coming back for the bracelet, Harmony said, "Three fifty. I need to borrow three fifty."

The owner eyeballed the bracelet a little longer. "I give you $325.00. That's best I can do."

"Okay," Harmony said, nodding her head.

Harmony couldn't wait to get that money in her hand. She needed that high. With every inch of her soul, Harmony had intended on giving up crack. Perhaps now she would realize that she couldn't do it alone.

After handling her business at the pawn shop and going to cop some rocks, Harmony found a spot in the back of the building where she had gone to buy the rocks. At first, nobody wanted to fuck with her, thinking that she might be 5-0 as out of place as she was, but after copping a couple of times with Fire, dealers knew she was cool. Now she didn't need Fire or anybody else to cop for her or to smoke with.

Harmony damn near burned her fingers off lighting up her shit. She had learned how to smoke crack without a pipe by placing some Brillo pad into a valve. She was nervous, trembling in anticipation of getting high. After that first hit, which felt like she'd been awaiting forever, she closed her eyes and let her head fall back. She exhaled then opened her eyes. When Harmony raised her hand to her mouth in order to take that next hit, she looked at her vacant wrist and realized that she had given up something that meant a great deal to her and her family. But just as soon as that high kicked in, she really didn't feel so bad, seeing that the outcome led to such a feel-good high.

Harmony had to give up the bracelet. It was the wings that would give her flight. At that moment, she knew she was no longer becoming a crackhead. She had, in fact, already become one.

Chapter 6
The Streets Raised Me

After selling the bracelet in the pawn shop, Harmony went back home, where she found Veronica asleep on the couch. Harmony knew she had been waiting up for her. In her mother's hand were some balled-up tissues. It was obvious that Veronica had been crying from the smudged eyeliner around her eyes. The gig was up and Harmony knew it.

Tiptoeing past Veronica to her bedroom, Harmony quickly packed up some of her things and left. She never went back home after that. It had been nearly three months now. Something just wouldn't let her go home, not while she was doing what she was doing. She didn't want her parents to see her like that. She didn't want anyone who knew her to see her like that.

She had managed to distance herself from Nay-Nay, Kendra and La-La those last couple weeks of school. It was summer break, so she didn't worry about alienating herself from them. As high a pedestal as she had placed herself on, there was no way she could let them see her now anyway.

She had heard from Fire that Nay-Nay ended up moving back to her old hood with some dude who sold dope. Supposedly she was going to be throwing La-La and Kendra a going away party. They were going to be heading to Atlanta, where they would be room mates at Clark.

Everyone that Harmony pictured herself doing better than after high school was going to end up doing better than her at the rate she was going. Although all Nay-Nay might have been doing was laying up under some man, it was still far better than what Harmony was doing.

Nay-Nay had heard the rumor through Fire, who heard from Talib, who heard from his uncles that Harmony was smokin'. Nay-Nay refused to believe it. She didn't want to believe it. She would hate to think that egging Harmony on to try to be something she wasn't led to something as drastic as addiction.

La-La said she suspected that something wasn't kosher a long time ago with Harmony when her grades started slipping. When Veronica and Glen went on a hunt to find information on Harmony, the school staff led them to the girls. The girls informed Harmony's parents of the rumors about her, but they, too, refused to believe it. Veronica had her suspicions but preferred the comfort of denial—until she took inventory of Harmony's room and found things missing. They especially knew something was wrong when they found the pawn ticket for the bracelet.

Nikko hadn't heard from Harmony either, but he had long gotten over the feelings for her that had started to take root. He and Boogie and the other couple of soldiers he had recently put on in his army were making more money than a little bit. Pursey even had a sit down with him, telling him that he felt it was time to put him on to the major connects. With that would come more money, and with more money would definitely come problems. It wouldn't be long before a couple of cats would be overcome with envy and he'd have to watch his back, but he trusted Boogie out of everybody to always have his back. He still had to work on the MOB aspect of the game with his other couple of soldiers, though. They loved them some women. That was something Nikko would definitely have to break them on.

Nikko parked his car a few blocks from the spot where one of his soldiers was supposed to be working. He got out of the car and started walking. As he passed this alley, he saw this dude about to get his dick sucked by some white girl. Nikko took a double take and realized that it was one of the young cats that he was letting make a few dollars by doing corner work. But how in the hell did he expect to make any money if he was taking head for crack instead of money?

"I told his little ass," Nikko said to himself as he clenched his teeth and balled his fist. He immediately went to holler at ol' dude.

By the time Nikko had reached the soldier, the white girl was down on her knees, doing what she did. She was bobbing her head and jerking ol' dude's dick. He grabbed the back of her head and began milking the cow, pushing her head up and down on his dick. Her curly blond ponytail swung back and forth as her head moved.

Dude's head leaned against the wall and he was moaning. Nikko didn't care that he was about to fuck up dude's nut.

"Man, what the fuck you doing?" Nikko said, scaring the shit out of both him and the fiend. The girl quickly stood up, not even turning to look at Nikko. She turned her back to both men as she brushed off the knees of her tan slacks and straightened the collar to her dingy white blouse.

"Oh, my bad, boss," the soldier said to Nikko.

"You damn right your bad. What I tell y'all about this shit? Money over bitches, always. Y'all ain't gon' be satisfied until y'all's dicks fall off. Let a pocket full of money make your ass want to bust a nut, you hear me?"

"Yes, boss. Yes," he said as he put his dick back in his pants and hurried away.

"Hey, wait a minute!" the girl turned around and yelled when she heard him running off. "I started, so you got to give me something." Her words meant nothing to the dude, who was well on his way down the alley as she stood there pissed off.

Just then, Nikko took a closer look at the white girl. He focused in and realized just who she was. It was at that same time that the girl looked up at him for the first time and realized who the man was who had just fucked up her next high. Nikko was speechless. He was disgusted, and she could detect his thoughts about her all over his face. He rolled his eyes and walked away.

"Wait a minute, Nikko," she called to him, but he just kept walking. "Can you just wait a minute, please? You owe me that much."

Nikko stopped in his tracks and turned around to face her. He still couldn't believe that it was Harmony standing in front of him. He stared at her, remembering how one time he had tried to count the little brown freckles on her face. He wished he had been able to take an accurate count because he would have counted them again just to make sure that this really was her before him.

"I know you're probably trippin' right now," Harmony said to him. "Can't believe your eyes? Well, whenever I look in a mirror, I can't believe mine either." She started to break down but managed to hold herself together. "I haven't been home in days, weeks." She became confused. "Months, I think. I don't know anymore. I lost track. I can't go home. My mom and dad . . ." Harmony began to cry. "Can't let them see me like this."

Nikko swallowed and maintained his composure. "So, why are you telling me all this? What do you want from me?"

"Nothing. It's just that I don't have any money or anyplace to go. I haven't eaten in a while."

"Oh, so I guess you was suckin' my boy's dick in exchange for a sandwich?"

Nikko sucked his teeth, shook his head at Harmony then turned away and started walking.

"Please, Nikko, help me, please." Just as he was about to turn the corner, she yelled, "You did this to me! This is your fault. You did this to me."

Nikko stopped in his tracks. Harmony's words cut him like a knife. He turned around and looked at her.

"I did this?" he said, taking a few steps toward her. "I did this to you?"

"That's right, I said it!" Harmony yelled at him. "You did this to me. Yeah, I might have smoked a little weed when you met me, but I didn't know what the fuck coke was. I had no idea what you were turning me on to or what affect it would have on me."

"A couple lines of coke here and there ain't no comparison to smoking crack," Nikko said. "Besides, I didn't put no gun to your head. You did it the same reason why you do everything else; 'cause you wanna fit in, 'cause you wanna be cool. The bottom line is you just a wanna be, period. But the biggest reason of them all is that you wanna be black." Nikko took a breath and continued. "Yeah, a white man might have raised me from a black boy, but the streets raised me into a black man. You think running around with black people, fucking black men and so-called talking black is going to make you black? Look at you. This was just a game to you, but this right here," Nikko said, pointing to his skin, "ain't no game. We can't pretend to be black in the streets and then be white when it comes to dealing with society. There ain't no on and off switch. This life ain't no game, yet you took it for one, and look who got played. You played yourself, Harmony, so don't you dare stand there and say I did this to you."

Harmony just stood there crying. Nikko hated to see her like this, but he refused to take the blame like she wanted him to do so that she wouldn't have to take any blame herself. But Nikko would be damned if he got labeled as the black guy who turned the white girl out on drugs.

"This is what you wanted to be a part of, Harmony. Welcome to the hood," Nikko said as he threw his hands up and walked away, this time clearing the corner. He headed back to his car, trying to convince himself that he was right in every word he said to Harmony. For some reason, though, he still felt a sudden sense of guilt.

As he got into his car, he saw Harmony coming around the corner toward him. He hurried to start the car. He tried to pull off, but there were cars lined up next to him at a traffic light.

"Nikko," Harmony called as she came running toward his car. "Nikko!"

She ran up to the passenger side. His windows were so darkly tinted that she could barely see into his car, but he could see her. "Nikko, please help me. Just help me, please. I'm sorry, Nikko. It's not your fault. It's mine. It's all my fault. I take the blame. Just don't leave me here. I don't want to do this anymore. Please help me, Nikko, please!"

Nikko turned his head. He couldn't even look at her pleading with him anymore. Just then, the light changed and the cars next to him began to pull off, leaving an opening for him, which he took.

As he drove off, Harmony watched in tears, still calling out his name. But he continued to drive, leaving her there alone.

Once Nikko got to the corner to make a right turn, Harmony noticed that his car stopped. She began walking slowly. Once she got to the car, she hesitated, but then slowly approached the passenger door and put her hand on the handle.

Nikko got out of the car and said, "Get away from the car."

Harmony couldn't believe what he had just said. It was the same feeling and the same look on her face as the day he stopped his car in the middle of the street to make her get out.

"You heard me. Get away from the car," he repeated.

Nikko began walking around the car toward Harmony. She slowly backed away from the door. He stopped, and they stared at one another momentarily.

"Let me get that for you," Nikko said. He turned and opened the passenger door.

Harmony broke down into tears, her body shaking. Nikko looked up to the sky, praying to God that she got into the car before he changed his mind. She did, and Nikko closed the door behind her then went around to the driver's side and got in the car.

"Thank you," Harmony said. "Thank you so much."

Nikko looked over at her. Through the pain, humiliation, and embarrassment, she was able to crack a half smile at him. Her dimples were showing. She was looking at Nikko as if he had just saved her life. She wasn't looking at him as though he was God, but at the moment, at the weakest point in her life, he was the next best thing or, according to Pursey, God-like.

"I ain't even gon' lie," Nikko said to her. "I'm trippin' right now. I can't believe this is you. It seems like just yesterday you were sitting over there in that passenger's seat talking about going to college. I hate to tell you this, but you're a long way from college right now, baby girl."

Harmony put her head down.

Nikko placed his index finger on her chin and lifted her head. "Don't ever let what anyone has to say about you make you put your head down, whether it's good or bad. It's a sign of weakness, defeat. You haven't even started the battle yet."

Harmony sniffed, then held her head up.

"Look, I want to try to help you," Nikko said, "but before we go any further, you have to let me know what you want, Harmony."

Harmony wiped her tears and looked up at Nikko. "I just wanna be that same girl you ran into at the mall that day, minus that slick talkin' and weed smokin'. I just wanna be that same college bound girl who sat in your car months ago. I don't wanna be cool. I don't wanna be hip. I don't wanna be something that I'm not anymore. I just wanna be—" Harmony paused, thought for a moment then said, "I just *want to be* me."

URBAN BOOKS PRESENTS

JOY is the *Essence* magazine bestselling author of *Dollar Bill* and *If I Ruled the World*. You can visit this author at www.JoylynnJossel.com.

Nikki Turner

Once A Hoodrat...
Always A Hoodrat

Getting Beat for the Head

"Push, baby girl, PUUUSH!"

Unique flexed her thigh muscles as hard as she could, forcing the pedals of the leg press machine to the floor.

"There you go, girl! Push that shit!" Kitty continued to urge her.

That's what Unique liked about Kitty, her stamina and what seemed like her inability to quit or let anyone around her be a quitter either. Although Kitty was just a few years older than Unique, the hard life she had lived mentally, emotionally and physically had added many more years onto her body and mind. Unique gathered wisdom from her and worked out with her. She also shared a cell with her, and more often than not, shared a bunk as well.

Kitty had been down fifteen years on a murder charge for setting up and killing a major player in Atlanta for her man, Big Time. Kitty told Unique that she never even knew why Big Time wanted the man dead. All she knew was that when Big Time asked her to do something, regardless of the task or the consequences, she obeyed his instructions to the letter. This wasn't her first bit, and she had been exposed to the street life since she was thirteen years old, so Kitty had seen it all and done it all twice, on the streets and in jail. Knowing the rules of the game and how to play the cards made her well connected in the penal system. That was the very reason why Unique had chosen her to woman up with for the two and a half years she had been down.

Unique did her thirty presses then got off the bench to give a turn to some nappy-headed female who was standing next to the machine.

"Come on, Kitty," Unique said. "This place is getting too crowded for my tastes."

The nappy-headed female caught her by the arm and said, "Don't you know me, girl?"

Unique took a good look at her. "Well, if it ain't Nosy Rosie"

"Yup. I just got in yesterday. Heard you was down here for a fifteen-year bit. What a shame. Baby Jon is sho' enjoying that money."

Unique sucked her teeth. She had been sent to Danbury Women's Federal Institution for a crime she did not commit. Baby Jon, a local dude she used to fuck with, had actually perpetrated the crimes and left her to hold the bag. Still, Unique was guilty of many things: grand larceny, prostitution, accessory to robbery, extortion, manipulation, conspiracy to mastermind a robbery, robbery of a dead man, operating an illegal gambling house, fraud . . . and most of all, she was guilty of being a grimy hood rat. Guns and drugs were never her M.O., but that's what she got charged with, so now she had to press the bunk and do the time.

"Welcome to Danbury, Rosie. We'll have to catch up later," Unique said with a fake smile.

"Okay, but, hey, you know Took got out, right?"

Unique nodded and lied, "He writes me sometimes to tell me how he's doing and all." She took Kitty's hand and led her out of the weight room.

When they got back in the cell they shared, Kitty said, "You ain't never got no letter from Took, girl. You've hardly ever mentioned him. But I know him by rep. A few of the Richmond chicks said that Took took whatever he wanted."

Unique sat down on her bunk and said, "Yup. Took was my man for five years, and those were the best years of my life. He gave me everything I needed, wanted and desired. Clothes. I had the flyest clothes from the best stores, too. And I drove a brand new car every year. Then he went down, and I was left having to fend for myself."

Kitty leaned against the wall, crossed her arms and said, "He didn't leave you any scratch? You was broke?"

Unique nodded her head. She didn't like to think of the ninety grand she had blown like she was running a marathon. Being Took's wifey-boo, him treating her like royalty, getting everything she wanted, plenty of the finest fashions, money, sex, and attention from one man, had enabled her to retire all the other trick-ass dudes. Never did she work a job or save a dime, because she was sure that Took would retire from his game a multi-millionaire and they would raise their kids in a huge mansion with a tall fence. It was too bad that a snitch had other plans for him. The state of Virginia gave him an early retirement plan to a state facility with a tall razor-wired fence surrounding the brick condominium where he would live for the next few years along with a six-digit state number, 972345.

The "man" might have hauled off Took, but they left his money behind for Unique to continue to floss. Ninety thousand dollars sounds like it would last forever. Unique thought that it would too, even though she was spending it like it was Monopoly money. It took no time at all for her to run through the cash. She splurged on name brand clothing, cars, designer purses, luggage, jewelry, and fine dining, until her well ran dry. When Took's money was all gone, so was Unique, leaving him to rot in jail without a single visit from her nor a Dear John letter. She left him and started her career down the path to becoming a legendary hood rat.

"Well, I understand if you don't want to talk about your previous life. We here now, and the past don't make no difference no how," Kitty said. "I'm going to the canteen. Want something?"

Unique was about to say no, but just like when she was on the streets, she had to get something at every opportunity. She smiled at Kitty and said, "Bring me something sweet. I'm hungry."

"I got something sweet for you," Kitty said with a leer. Unique held the fake smile on her face so Kitty wouldn't see her disgust.

"Later for that. Bring me some cookies, a Twinkie, and some plain M&Ms. Hold on, I'm going to do a list."

Kitty left and Unique was finally alone to think. Her conniving mind hadn't changed a bit since her old days in the hood. Scheming was something that came natural to her. All her life, besides the five years she was with Took, Unique had been molded into the worst kind of woman. She wished there was some way she could get Took to forget about what she did to him, how she had hunted down every man with a dollar to his name and taken him for all she could.

Unique would do anything she could to get what she wanted. She wasn't working for squat. If it was true that hard work built character, then she was one no-character-having bitch. Why should she, as pretty as she was? She believed that men would always take care of her just to be able to say they had a trophy like her up on their shelf. And if they didn't, then she would just take what she wanted by any means necessary. Men with long and deep pockets were her preference, but when that kind wasn't at her disposal, she certainly didn't discriminate. She was down for any scheme, even if it meant robbing the dead or stealing money out of a sucker's pocket as she rode his dick and her girl Strolla roamed the house, helping herself to whatever they needed out of his refrigerator or cupboard. If that wasn't enough, Unique would take the towels, wash cloths and soap out of the bathroom when she was supposed to be washing up after the sex she had been paid for. No matter what Unique had to do, at the end of the day when all the dust settled, Unique was going to be on top. That was her creed. But her devious ways had cost her Took and even, in the end, Strolla.

Strolla had been her best friend for many years, the only person who ever seriously had her back. Being down for the cause was one thing, but it was almost like the blind leading the blind when it came to Strolla and Unique. Strolla was just as low-lifed as Unique. Inseparable, they had been two peas in a pod or two beans in a bucket and basically said "fuck it!" Strolla would have done anything for Unique. However, Unique only did whatever it took to make sure Unique was okay, and if Strolla happened to be around, then she could reap the benefits of Unique's scams.

Unique wondered what Strolla was up to and decided to find Rosie and do a little interrogation. She found her still in the weight room.

"Hey, Rosie," Unique said with her charm turned on high. "Catch me up on everyone in Richmond. You know they can't tell everything in a letter."

Unique sat down on the machine next to Rosie and started working out. As Unique had hoped, the first name out of Rosie's mouth was Strolla's.

"Girl, Strolla and Train be living high on the hog. They got practically a mansion and the cutest little girl. But I guess you know that. You two sure was close . . . though I heard she was plenty mad about you not letting her know that Train was looking at her. Why you do some evil shit like that?"

"I just thought Train wasn't good enough for her," Unique said, trying to defend herself. The truth was that

Unique didn't want to lose her friend. Strolla was useful to Unique, and if she was with Train, he would put an end to their criminal partnership.

"Well, I guess you were wrong about that. He might even get out of the game, go legit. He sure has made plenty money." Rosie paused then said, "I was sorry to hear about your momma, Unique."

Unique rolled her eyes. She generally didn't let anyone know what she was thinking, but it was hard to hide the fact that she didn't care her momma had died in a crack house, her body left to rot outside in the alley. Unique's mother had been a straight dope-fiend and was unable to take care of both Unique and her drug habit. She had to make a choice and with her dependency, the narcotics took priority. From the time Unique was three years old, she was forced to use her cute, childish face and mannerisms to get neighbors and family friends to give her food. So the fact that her mother was dead meant no more to her than if some total stranger had died. Maybe it meant even less.

Having a mother like hers had done something to Unique. She never learned how to care about anyone else. Everyone she met was just a meal ticket of some kind. And no one ever got anything back from her. Just about the time she got sent to the penitentiary, most people had come to see she was nothing but poison. For the first time, she felt like the game had finally played her, leaving her with nothing. She had no support on the outside. She received no letters, and she had no numbers to call. Nothing! Everyone cut her off, even Strolla. Sure, she had done some shiesty stuff to Strolla at times, but she never thought her best friend would leave her dead and stinking when she needed her most. It was just something that Unique never really quite understood. Yeah, it was wrong that Train, now Strolla's fiancé, had been wanting to get with Strolla for years but never got a chance to get at her due to Unique's lies. There was also the huge ghetto heist that Unique had pulled. She walked away with more than fifty grand and didn't let Strolla in on it, though Strolla unknowingly aided and abetted the entire thing. Unique laughed, remembering how slick she had been, but somehow Strolla found out about that.

Unique turned to Rosie and said, "I'm glad Strolla is happy now. She writes me and tells me how great her life is. That means a lot to me."

In fact, Strolla had only written Unique once and the letter said: *You are not a team player, Unique. You think I'm your mascot, but I have washed my hands of you. Everyone who comes near you gets infected by your poison. Don't expect not a got damn thing from me, girl. We are through.*

At first Unique was hurt, but her vengeful side assured her that one day she'd get Strolla back and everybody else who had crossed her. *That bitch, Strolla, and that motherfucking Baby Jon can't ever leave me for dead unless they sew my mouth together,* she thought, *but as long as I got these lips, jaws and tongue, a bitch can't never be doing bad or broke. Believe that!* Unique could've taught the art of giving good head as a profession. Man or woman, once she performed her high-tech oral gymnastics on them, they were putty in her hands, and Unique knew this. Although it's been said that money is indeed the root of all evil, in Unique's eyes, it was sex. She knew that her sex was the key to get her what she needed from anyone, male or female. Because of her tongue skills, her time on the compound had been nothing but gravy.

Kitty walked in the door, looking for Unique.

"Over here, baby," Unique said.

"Lookin' good, baby girl, real good," Kitty leered, palming Unique's ass as she stood up from the workout machine. Unique grabbed her towel and wiped the dripping sweat from her face and neck. She started to say something smart to Kitty about that feel she just stole, trying to let another bulldagger know on the sly that Unique belonged to her, but she let it go. Unique wasn't trying to take it to the streets with Kitty anyway. Kitty always bragged on her gangsta bitch days. Unique believed her because Kitty had the war marks to prove it—the long cut on her face, her earlobe torn, multiple stab wounds all over her body and a bullet still in her shoulder. So, Unique reminded herself, *I'm a lover not a fighter.*

Unique never really liked the bucktooth, bad skin having, cock-eyed bitch, but as long as Kitty kept Unique with all the weed, money and simple amenities not available to the average inmate, Unique would tolerate her rubbing and touching on her whenever and wherever she wanted to.

"See ya later, Rosie," she said as she and Kitty left the weight room.

Back in the cell they shared, Unique stood in front of the full-length mirror in the corner of the room and smiled, admiring her shapely frame. *Damn, I look good.* She always had a banging body, but on the streets she never worked out, so the excess baby fat here and there held her back from really shining. But now, hands down, Unique was a straight-up bad bitch, head to toe. She wasn't too chiseled the way some chicks get, losing their femininity. She simply toned herself up a bit. Her calf muscles and thick thighs gave her bow legs, a stallion-like stance, while her ghetto booty poked perfectly from her shorts, curved enough to put Ki Toy, the big booty video chick in Outkast's video, to shame.

Unique lived up to her name. She was unique in many ways, from the unique mole on the left side of her top lip, which, if you stared at it long enough, looked heart-shaped, to her unique scams that usually raked in whatever funds she needed or desired. But her award-winning, unique blow jobs really set her apart from the field.

Even if her mama hadn't given her the name, she probably would have had it changed to Unique herself. As far as she was concerned, she was one of a kind. Her skin was flawless except for the mole, which she claimed was a beauty mark. She stood 5 feet 4 inches, and her body was a perfect ten all day. She was a C-cup with firm breasts and a big badooka butt with a small waist, light-colored skin, long, flowing sandy brown hair and slanted hazel eyes. No matter what Unique wore, she made it look like a million dollars, right down to her fed-issued khaki suit. She was definitely easy on the eyes, but she had little to no book sense whatsoever. She had dropped out of high school in the tenth grade. The only reason she even went to school that long was because she liked showing off whenever she had boosted a new outfit. After she met Took, he was so mesmerized by her beauty that he automatically fell into position as her man/slot machine and began to take care of her. Took put her in only the best designer gear, but showing off was the last thing on her mind at that point. She'd rather stay home and show off for Took, and that's exactly what she did until he was hauled off to prison.

As Unique admired her new and improved physique in the mirror, Kitty came up behind her and started kissing on her neck and groping her left breast. Unique knew that the time was 69. She didn't mind because just the day before, Kitty had gotten a huge money slip. Big Time kept her locker running over with money slips and everything else she needed. She knew that if anybody, man or woman, had a dime in their piggybank, pocket, safe or inmate account, she could get it. Although nothing about Kitty turned her on, she reasoned with herself that nothing about a whole bunch of niggas she had fucked turned her on either. But money was money, and it was all green.

She lay across the bunk, spread her legs and allowed Kitty to lick between her thighs. Unique popped that coochie like a Luke dancer. Although Kitty couldn't get Unique to where she had to go even if she had a road map, fake but very convincing moans of ecstasy dripped from Unique's lips. Unique stroked Kitty's ego just like she had done many times with men.

"Ummm, ulllll, ummm, ummm," Unique whined, topping off her performance as she went on to fake an orgasm that a porn star would envy. She did it quickly because if Kitty was down there too long, she would feel that she wasn't pleasing Unique.

Unique wished she could just lie there all day. She hated going down on Kitty, whose pussy always smelled like something had died down there. But Unique held her breath and accepted that it was a part of the pimp game. It was her time to fulfill Kitty's needs if she wanted to continue having full access to all of Kitty's prison possessions.

When Kitty pulled off her white Fruit of the Loom grandma bloomers, Unique began to caress Kitty's breasts with one hand, fingering her fish market with the other. Before she got deep into it, she heard a voice call out, "Bryant, Bryant!"

Unique jumped up and peeped her head out of the cell to see who was calling her name.

"Legal mail," one of the inmates informed her.

"I got legal mail. I don't know what the fuck for," Unique said to Kitty as she slipped on her shower shoes and her sweats.

She went to the podium in the day room to sign for the correspondence. It was from a lawyer, but not the same one who had sold her out during the original trial. He was a court appointed lawyer who did nothing to help Unique prove her innocence. Unique was facing seventy-five years. Her options were to take the fifteen-year plea bargain or grow old in prison. Well, there was a third option, but she had never told on anyone in her life, and she didn't intend on staring then. Unique pleaded guilty and took the fifteen years.

She didn't recognize the lawyer's name on the legal mail. "What the fuck these motherfuckers want? Don't tell me it's a judgment or an old bill or something," Unique mumbled as she tore open the envelope. She sat in the commons area to read the letter, trying to take her time in hopes that Kitty would be out of the mood when she got back to the cell.

Re: Case Number: 17870000625353555-US
The United States Government v. Unique Bryant
Dear Unique Bryant:
I have been retained to conduct an appeal of your case. After researching your case records, I was able to get the United States Court of Appeals to grant you a new trial based on questionable conduct by your previous counsel. Your appeal bond has been set at twenty-five thousand dollars, which will need to be secured in cash or property. If you are able to raise bail, please keep me informed of your whereabouts so we can come up with our strategy for your new trial. Otherwise, I will visit you in due time to discuss your case further.
Sincerely,

R.W. Emerson, Esquire

"Hmmm," Unique said to herself. "R.W. Emerson? I hope it's not just some phony-ass public pretender trying to get a paycheck or something."

After reading the letter again, Unique was happier than she had been in a long time. She had another chance at freedom. Hopefully she would get a fair chance to be exonerated for the crimes that she didn't commit. Her emotions were running wild. She felt as though she had been given a get out of jail free card. However, it didn't take long for her spirits to get dampened. When she thought about all the ballers, gamblers, hustlers and stick-up kids that she had known, she knew that not one of them was thinking about her. Her bond might as well have been a million dollars, because she wasn't going nowhere. There was no way she was going to pass go, and she wasn't going to collect two hundred dollars.

Damn, I can't let this shit get me down, Unique thought as she put the letter back inside the envelope. *I ain't never let nobody hold me up from what I got to do, and I ain't gonna start now. Where there's a will, there's always a motherfuckin' way! And especially where I'm concerned!*

On her way back to the cell, Unique thought that maybe she could get Kitty to convince Big Time to put up bail. Maybe things would work out better for her if Kitty was still in the mood.

"Hey, Kitty, my sweet Kitty Kat," Unique sang as she walked over to Kitty, who was now lying down.

"What, baby?" Kitty replied with a smile on her face as she ran her fingers through Unique's bone-straight hair.

"You know I love you, right?" she asked, looking directly into Kitty's eyes.

"I know," Kitty said. Unique leaned in and put her tongue in Kitty's mouth, trying to get her back in the mood.

"You know . . . I'd do anything . . . in my power . . . to please you . . . too, right?" Unique whispered hot and heavy into Kitty's ear while licking it between words.

"And I'd do anything for you too, baby," Kitty said, sliding her hand between Unique's thighs and putting her fingers in Unique's canal. Kitty then pulled out and put them in her mouth like she was sucking on a chicken bone and it was finger licking good.

Unique closed her eyes. For a second there she wanted to throw up, but she quickly snapped back into "fuck the shit out of Kitty" mode. By no means could she mess this up. She desperately needed something from Kitty, and if she had to suck this nasty bitch's fishy pussy dry to get it, so be it.

Unique opened her eyes, licked her lips and smiled. "I need a huge, huge favor from you," she said.

"As good as you treat me, anything, baby. Just name it." Kitty's hormones were on fire.

Unique knew her magic was working. Inhaling all that toxic pussy would finally pay off. "Look," she started, "I just got a letter from my lawyer, and they just granted me an appeal bond. I need you to get that nigga, Big Time, to put up the twenty-five thousand dollar bail to get me out."

Kitty looked like she was going to shit a brick. That wasn't what she was expecting to come out of Unique's mouth. "For real," Kitty said nonchalantly, with slight disbelief. "Let me see the letter."

"It's an appeal bond," Kitty said after reading the letter. "But a nigga gotta pay the whole twenty-five to get you out. It's not a bondsman in the country that will get you out for ten percent on an appeal bond."

"I know," Unique said with a straight face while playing with Kitty's cat. "But what's twenty-five to Big Time as a favor to you? You traded in your freedom for his. That ain't shit to a nigga balling out of control like him. So, all you gotta do is ask him and it's done, right?"

"You know what? You right, it ain't nothing but a phone call."

Kitty's words were like music to Unique's ears, and it gave her the motivation that she needed. To show her gratitude, Unique began working on Kitty's cat like never before. She started with her finger then finally used her tongue, giving it all she had to give. The things she did with her tongue even had Unique amazed, but when it came to a bitch's freedom, Unique was willing to work her tongue like a Komodo dragon. When she saw that Kitty's eyes were rolling in the back of her head, she knew that the deal was sealed.

Strolla, Baby Jon, watch out. All hell is about to break loose. A bitch is about to hit the bricks, and I'm going for you! Unique mused. She didn't even notice Kitty's odor; she was so caught up in the idea of soon becoming a free woman.

Once Kitty came, still lying on the bunk trying to get herself together, Unique asked, "So, you gonna make the call to Big Time before the phones cut off?"

Kitty paused in between breaths for a moment and replied, "Uhhh . . . Nope."

"What you mean, nope?" Unique asked, trying to keep calm and not get an attitude. "Why?" Everything was weighing on Kitty. She had no other resources.

"Because I can't let you go after what you just gave me. That was *the* best head I ever had in my life. I can't let you go out into that world without me with you. Besides, I know Big Time is going to want you. You his type. I be damned if I'ma lose my pussy and my dick at the same time."

"I'm not gonna fuck no damn Big Time," Unique said, not believing the bullshit spewing from Kitty's mouth.

"You got it twisted. It ain't about you wanting Big Time. See, Big Time gets whatever he wants," Kitty replied with a stern face. "You couldn't turn him down. Plus that nigga got so much motherfuckin' money to back up his wants. That nigga got a Bentley and fucking millions, and he loves red bitches just like you."

"I ain't interested in him," Unique said bluntly, trying to keep the discussion focused on her getting out and not the ongoing, forever and a day spiel that Kitty usually got into. Somehow Kitty always managed to brag in-depth about how long Big Time's money was. "I just want him to post my daggone bail on the strength of you."

"If I was to do it, what are you going to tell him?" Kitty asked curiously. "That you were fucking me, so he can't have you? You gon' have to tell that nigga something, because he ain't gonna have no type of understanding as to why he can't have you. Like I said, Big Time gets what Big Time wants."

"I mean . . ." Unique tried to come up with something to say, but the words couldn't come out quick enough.

"Naw, that shit ain't going down like that." Kitty shook her head as the thoughts marinated. "That nigga don't know that I'm in here bumping coochies or licking them, for that matter."

"You know there ain't no way I would tell him that," Unique tried to convince Kitty.

"I know, because I ain't going to put you in a position to. That's final. I want you to myself, and you ain't going nowhere but right here with me," Kitty said with authority. "And don't ask me no motherfuckin' mo'. That shit is off limits. I'll get you out when I get out."

Bitch, you get out in thirty-one fuckin' mo' years, and that's with good behavior, Unique thought, looking at Kitty like she was crazy. *By then I'll be out and would have forgotten all about your triflin', can't-make-a-pussy-cum-but-call-yourself-a-motherfuckin'-bulldagger   ass.* Unique was fuming, but she never let anybody see her true emotions, especially when she was boiling with anger.

"Okay, I understand. I would probably feel the same way," Unique said before getting out of the bunk, climbing over Kitty and placing her pussy in her face. *Bitch, smell it now, because this is the last time you ever will in this lifetime,* she thought with a slight snicker as she moved over to her bunk. *Ain't no nigga on God's green earth ever beat me for my head. And I damn sure ain't gonna let a bitch beat me for my shit. This bitch gon' get it, too.*

Back on the Block

If this is a dream, please don't wake me up. Damn, it seems like bitches is always coming out of the woodwork when I least expect them to. I knew sooner or later this bitch right here would come to her senses. This bitch needs me like a fiend needs a pipe. I'm this bitch's drug. Always have been, always will be. This bitch can't make it without me.

Once she came out of the Richmond airport, Unique hopped into Strolla's candy apple red Lexus and the scent of the leather permeated her nose. She smelled everything. The little things that she never cared about all of a sudden mattered to her. Unique could not believe that her best friend/sidekick since the sandbox, but her enemy for the past two and half years, had come through for her. Two years ago, Unique had finally written Strolla off, after spending six months expecting a letter from Strolla, talking shit about how they were supposed to be better than that, and begging for an explanation as to how Unique could have shitted on her like she did. That letter did not, nor did any other letter, ever come, except for the very first one where Strolla had washed her hands of Unique.

Unique thought she knew Strolla like the back of her hand, but to her surprise, Strolla had flipped the script on her. Then Strolla threw Unique for a loop when the lawyer showed up with Strolla's money order for twenty-five thousand, her signature on the dotted line and a plane ticket home. This had to be a dream, but it wasn't. It was Strolla, live in the flesh behind the wheel of her Lexus.

The ride was silent for the first few minutes, until Unique dramatically burst into tears. "Thank you so much for coming to get me. You came through for me, girl, in a major way."

"It ain"t nothin'." Strolla threw her hand up. "Don't be gettin' all emotional on me."

"Yes, it is. Especially knowing that I might not have done the same thing for you three years ago."

"Yeah, you right, you left me fucked up, but I'm over it," Strolla said nonchalantly.

"Girl, my mind wasn't right."

"It's cool. I'm a'ight," she said as she maneuvered the steering wheel to whip her Lexus into a right turn. Unique noticed the ice on Strolla's wrist and had to do a double take at the rock on her left ring finger.

"Damn, Train looking out for you real decent. How many times he done married you since I've been gone?"

Strolla smiled at Unique, just like old times. However, they both knew it wasn't old times, and Unique had a bunch of explaining, apologizing and ass kissing to do. Even that, though, didn't seem so awful for Unique, after having to smell Kitty's fish dinner for the past couple of years.

"So, you and Train been together for how long?"

"Since you got locked up."

"Damn, look like he treating you good." Before the words had rolled off of her tongue good, she noticed a little baby picture hanging from the mirror. "Who is this?" she asked, surprised even though she had heard from Rosie that Strolla had a little girl.

"That's Treniece." Strolla smiled. "That's my daughter. Well, me and Train's daughter."

"For real? Oh my God, Strolla. I'm so happy for you. I really am," Unique said with deep sincerity. "How old is she? She is so cute."

225

"She's only thirteen months now, but growing every day. She's what makes my life complete. So, you hungry?" Strolla changed the subject.

"Yes, starving."

Unique and Strolla ate lunch at Applebees and chit-chatted about everybody and everything. Unique noticed how Strolla had changed. She was more guarded toward Unique with her responses.

"My, my, my, we've gotten to be real cagey out the mouth. You acting like we don't go back like Easy Bake ovens," Unique said, enjoying her first sample of free world food in two and a half years.

Strolla exhaled a bewitching laugh. "Girl, sorry, you know how it is when you have a man with sooo much damn paper and everybody want him." She casually added, "After you crossed me, I don't fuck with no girls at all. I'm just used to being kinda standoffish, so please forgive me." Then Strolla began to lighten up like old times.

"So, I'll let you stay with me for a couple of days until you get on your feet. If I still know you, it ain't gonna take but a few days."

"What Train gonna say about that? You know he can't stand me."

"That's why I said a few days." She chuckled. "He's out of the country now, setting some things up, and won't be back for a few days."

"Damn, that nigga doing it like that?" Unique could see the uneasiness on Strolla's face, so she switched gears and asked, "So, what's up with Fat Tee?"

"Nothin'. Still a big fat sucker, waiting to be licked. Now that you asked, you know I'm going to make sure that you a'ight as much as I can, but on the real, Nique . . . He could be the one to get you back on your feet."

"Damn, bitch, you know me too well."

"You know I do. We've been friends for how long?" Strolla asked.

"Not long enough."

"For real, we've had some good times. Even when I had gonorrhea and I couldn't fuck to get us no money, but you held us down."

"I know," Unique said. "What about the time when I ain't pay the insurance on the car and we went out and the car got shot up and was totaled?"

Strolla burst into laughter. "And you went and fucked the Arab dude and came back with a title and a car."

"Yup, the good old days," Unique cut her off. "So, why you say that ' bout Fat Tee?"

"He getting money like no tomorrow, plus you know he always wanted to fuck you. When you got locked up, he kept checking on you through me, but I was mad at you and wasn't fucking with you, so I never gave ' im any info. All you got to do is give that nigga the guilt trip and I know you could be in."

"What made you change your mind about me?" Unique asked.

"I don't know. I just knew I couldn't stay mad at you forever, and I know you're gonna go back to court, so I'll get the bond money back," Strolla said, and then she changed the subject. "So, you going after Big Tee or what?" she asked.

"I'm two steps ahead of you," Unique boasted.

"He got a house that he always bragging about, but no one has ever seen it. He stacking paper in piles knee high, from what I be hearing, and he be tricking with strippers. But I know for a fact you can knock them trick bitches out of the water on your worst day." Strolla threw in a bid for herself. "When you get that nigga to take you shopping, make sure you pick up yo' girl something like old times."

"You know I got you," Unique assured her. "But for real, you know it ain't about you. It's about my god-daughter now."

Strolla didn't miss the presumption and audacity that Unique displayed by appointing herself godmother, but she ignored it. "You know I never liked his ass from back in the day. I say use that nigga up."

"A'ight. Well, hurry up and gobble that food down so I can track his ass down like the feds," Unique said.

Once they were in the car, Unique was anxious to see Treniece. Strolla gave her a puzzled look and said, "Damn, girl, you never used to like kids."

"That was the old Unique. I've changed a lot since then," Unique said. "Now, make sure I get a picture of my niece."

"Don't worry, I got you."

"I want a few photos of her."

Strolla took Unique to her house to get all settled in. Unique was struck by how Strolla was living. Everything in the house was plush; nothing in Strolla's place was from Wal-Mart or Target, not even the shower curtain hooks. The home was a brick, three-story mini-mansion. The front yard alone was as big as a small city park, it seemed. The inside was designed and furnished in a modern décor. Unique was highly impressed and even more jealous.

Strolla brought out little Treniece from the nursery.

Unique gasped, "Oh my God, she is sooo beautiful! I love her sooo much!" She picked up Treniece and hugged her. As she played with Treniece, she asked Strolla the dreaded question they both knew was coming, but neither knew how to approach. "So, what's up with Took? You heard from him?" Unique always regretted not

228

playing fair with Took when he went away to prison. He was her first and only love.

"He good. I heard from him the other day. He's still the same old Took." She called out to the nanny, "Olga, it's time for Treniece's nap."

Funny how shit can change in a matter of three years. From rags to motherfuckin' riches, Unique thought as she looked over the house and Strolla. *Shit is about to switch up for me too around this motherfucker, believe that.*

Unique wanted to soak in the sunken bathtub for hours, but thirty minutes and a good douche would have to be good enough. When she came out of the bathroom adjacent to the guestroom, she noticed there were a few things on the bed: underclothes, three outfits and some personal hygiene items.

"Strolla!" she called out.

"Yes?" At first Unique didn't know where the voice came from; then she noticed the little intercom device on the wall.

"Come here," she shouted.

Strolla came running through the door. "What's wrong?"

"Nothing, I just want to thank you for the stuff. I really appreciate it."

"Girl, it ain't nothing. From one friend to another."

"Thanks anyway. Look, Strolla, I know that I've done some real shiesty and raunchy shit in my day to you. I lied on you and to you. I want to apologize for real from the bottom of my heart. I know to have a friend you have to be a friend, and I'm willing to play fair with you."

"Ahhh, that's sweet!" Strolla looked at Unique.

"I know it'll be hard for us to get to where we were before all the drama happened with me setting up Fat Tee to get robbed and never letting you know."

"I know. I couldn't believe it when Train told me that you had him rob the craps shooting party you had at your house."

"I know, and I'm sorry I didn't tell nobody but him."

"And you know to this day Fat Tee don't know that you set all that shit up. Fuck gold digging, you need to get a job acting in Hollywood," Strolla said, giving Unique her props for having the brains to pull off such a clever robbery.

"Thanks, girl. If you ever hear they hiring, let me know, because gaming niggas is a hard job. You never know where they're coming from. If it was another way for me to eat and get on my feet, I would." She confided in her once best friend, "I wish I could turn the time back and play fair by Took and hold him down like I should have. I would have never went to prison and we'd be together." She took a deep breath and let it out in a sigh. "Woulda, coulda, shoulda is always in hindsight, huh?"

"Girl, trust me. Everything is going to be all right. There are no chance encounters. Everything happens for a reason, and everything is always better the second go around. And that includes our friendship!" Strolla said with such sincerity that Unique had tears in her eyes.

"Thanks, Strolla." Unique gave her a hug. "I promise no back stabbing, nothing. We gonna keep it real as real can get. No lies or secrets whatsoever."

"Okay," Strolla agreed. "A promise is a promise."

"Yup, and that's my word," she swore. Then she asked, "So, do the computer and scanner in here work?"

"Yeah, it do."

Strolla showed Unique all the ins and outs of the new computer, but Unique wasn't a novice thanks to the prison computer courses that she mastered while behind bars.

"Okay, I got it. I'm good," Unique said.

Unique never realized that two hours had flown by while she was so diligently working on her get-money-quick scandal. All of a sudden, she heard a familiar voice.

"Damn, I don't remember that shit being tight like that."

It couldn't be. The voice alone made her shake a bit, while her stomach was in her panties and her heart skipped several beats. She almost didn't want to look up because she didn't want to be disappointed. After a second that seemed like an eternity, she looked toward the door. It was Took in the flesh. Although she was extremely distracted, she was quick enough on her feet to shut down the screen she was working on.

"Damn, baby," he said, walking over to her. As he got closer, her heart pounded with anxiety. He began touching her firm thighs. "Damn, baby, you look good as shit."

She regained her composure and said nonchalantly, "Yeah, a bitch been working out." She held her breath, not knowing what to expect from Took. Maybe a mean punch followed by a hellafied beat down. She would've deserved every lick of it.

"What's up, baby?" He looked into her eyes and said it the way he would have said it a few years ago when everything was all good between them, before he went to jail.

Just then, without another moment's hesitation, she jumped up and hugged Took. She would have never thought in a million years that their reunion would be so smooth after the way she carried him, spending all his money and leaving him for dead in the penitentiary, but he hadn't pulled out his gun yet. Judging by the way he embraced her and the bulge that began to rise in his pants, she knew, to her surprise, an ass whipping wasn't

231

in order for her. There was something significant about the hug. It was a warm, intense hug instead of a cold, impersonal one.

"So, I see you made it home safely, huh?" he said after pulling away from her and looking her over for the second time. She nodded with tears were in her eyes. He wiped the moisture away with his fingers and asked, "What's wrong, baby?" Unique shook her head, and as the tears flowed, he continued to wipe them away, taking her into his arms again. "Baby, its gon' be okay." He gave her some tissue from a box on the dresser.

"I just . . . I just," she sniffed, "I just feel so bad for the way I did you, but I didn't know no better." She grabbed the tissue from him and wiped her nose. For the first time in many years, she was actually genuine. The tears were authentic, not ones that she had contrived.

"I know, baby. It was partly my fault. I didn't train you how to survive on your own. I never wanted you to work or pay bills. I molded you to do what you did best, to be beautiful, to suck and fuck the shit out of me. That's all I required from you, so when I was locked up, you had no survival skills. What else was it for you to do?" He was trying to ease the pressure of her guilt.

She dried her tears and listened as he convinced her that she had been forgiven. He then changed the subject and asked, "So, how you and Strolla getting along?"

"It seems like everything is back like it was. I'm so proud of her, and I love her baby."

"Strolla good peeps, for real. When I called her and asked her to take the money to the courts and sign to bail you out, she ain't have no problem."

Unique went into shock for a minute. She had no idea that it was Took who put up the money to get her out. A lump developed in her throat; everything else he said to her became a blur for the next few minutes. She

232

was numb, but she managed to hear him say, "Look, hurry up and let's go. We need to get out of here for a li'l while."

"You ain't going to take me out to kill me, are you?" Unique asked with a skeptical look on her face.

"Hell naw. You crazy as shit." He patted her on the butt and laughed. "I'm taking you to the hotel so we can catch up and lay up. We can't do that shit in here. We two grown motherfuckers. What the fuck we look like laying up all in somebody else's shit?"

"Say no more," Unique said, putting her shoes on. The thought of getting some dick after two and a half years was a godsend, especially since it was Took's dick. Who'da thought that life back on the streets of Richmond was going to be so sweet?

Let's Do it

Took and Unique lay in each other's arms after hours of intense sex. "You ain't gonna hurt my feelings, are you?" she asked meekly.

"Stop bein' so fuckin' cynical. You know that's not how I get down."

"I hear you talking," she said before hopping up to go to the bathroom. When she came back out, she said, "I'm hungry. Can we go get something to eat?"

"It's gonna have to be somewhere cheap because I ain't got no real money. I used all the money to get you a real lawyer and pay that got damn bail."

"Fo' real?" She stuck her head out of the door.

"Fo' real." He nodded. "The first day I hit the streets, Train took me shopping and then gave me the money from the heist y'all did. He never touched one dime of it. I couldn't sleep knowing you were in the belly of the same beast that I was just released from." He was referring to the share of the money Train got from the robbery Unique orchestrated while Took was on lock. Train had so much love for Took, it was only right to hold the paper until he returned to the streets.

"Damn," she said as she walked back into the room and sat on the edge of the bed. Took's words were taking a toll on her. There was no doubt that she loved him with all her heart in spite of the shiesty stuff she did to him. And he never stopped loving her. However, she knew that things would never be the same. Talk about love enduring all pain.

"I'm a team player, and it won't nothing but some money. Plus I'd never leave you for dead. I'll kill a nigga to make sure you a'ight."

"I don't deserve you, Took." Unique really wanted to try to work things out again with Took. As soon as she thought that things could never be the same between them, he surprised her. Love conquers all. If she could get one more chance with him, she would jump, hook, line and sinker. "But I feel bad you had to use all that money to help me get out of that mess."

"Look, baby, stop tripping over the money. It ain't nothing but a thang, and we can get some more. They print that shit e'ry day."

"You right," she nodded her head, "and I like the sound of that."

He sat up in the bed. "It's obvious that we work better together than apart. Together, our life was perfect. It was when we were apart that shit started breaking down. Neither of us self destructed, but we both came damn near close to it. I couldn't keep from bustin' a nigga up in prison, and well, you know the road you chose to travel. You got good potential, but when you not focused and don't have the proper direction, you make fucked up choices. Bad decisions out of desperation."

"Okay, Mr. Analyst," she said and dropped her eyes, not wanting to face the reality.

"Thanks fo' the compliment," he said with a smile then changed the subject. "Look, I got some ideas on how we can get us some money, but we gonna have to work together."

"What do you have in mind, Daddy?" she whined like a little girl wanting to make her father happy.

"What you mean, what?" Took asked. "My thing has always been taking people's shit after they stack it. All we gotta do is pick off a couple of fat vics. After we get our weight up, we can leave up out of this raggedy-ass town. It's crystal clear that Richtown ain't got no love for us."

Unique nodded her head in agreement. She had been hoping to live life like the ghetto version of the Huxtables, but what the hell? Took had come through for her, and as long as they were working together, she would do anything—anything to keep her in Took's stable.

"So, you got any candidates that can be put at the top of the list?"

Unique was caught off guard by his question. She didn't know if he was testing her or what. She didn't know which way to answer, and Took could see it, too. He knew Unique really wanted things to be like they were when he was out in there in the streets getting the money and she was playing June Cleaver. But things were real shabby for them right now, and they had to eat.

"Look, baby, from here on out, it ain't no secrets between us. We the fucking new millennium Bonnie and Clyde. We gonna do this shit here together," he motioned by pointing to himself and to her, "for the betterment of us. Fuck the rest of the world. It's about us. Who we got but each other? Nobody. I mean, we got Train and Strolla, but at the end of the motherfuckin' day, in their eyes, it's about them, it ain't us. If it's them or us, then guess who they picking? We need to be on the same accord. Together, one, us, one, our and we. No one else. Just me and you!"

"True," she said with a smile, loving the idea. "I just don't want you thinking fucked up about me."

"Look, I don't give a fuck about your cunning and conniving ways, as long as it's for me and not against me. As a matter of fact, that's that shit that makes my dick hard. A woman that can think. I don't need a show bitch, right now, I need a go-hard bitch. I need a bitch that got heart, who ain't got no problem riding for her nigga, who can get down and dirty for ours."

236

"Where do I sign up? Knowing that you got my back, I'll put that bitch Bonnie to shame," Unique said with a laugh.

"A'ight, we'll see," he said and hit her with the pillow. She fell back on the bed, laughing, and then sat up.

"So, what part do you want me to play?"

"Come on, don't try to clown me like you don't know," Took said before popping a piece of gum in his mouth. "You meet them motherfuckers, bait them in and line them up for me to come in and leave them niggas' pockets, stash and cash on empty."

"A'ight, but how you want me to do it?"

"Do what you do."

She hesitantly asked, "What's the limits?"

"Look, it's like this." He looked into her eyes and gave her the run-down. "A good mechanic uses the right tools necessary to get the job done, meaning do what you gotta do, as long as you get the job done. Make them motherfuckers get lax and let their guards down."

"Well," Unique said slowly, "you said we were being honest with each other, right?"

"Right."

"I know I got a hell of a conversation piece, and for some niggas that's good enough, but the real money-getting niggas who is used to bitches by the dozen, the only way to get them niggas' attention and keep it is to give them some pussy. Are you—"

He cut her off. "Baby, that giving up pussy shit don't faze me. I don't give a fuck about a nigga getting some pussy. What I care about is your heart. A nigga steal that, that's when it's going to be some problems between us and some smoke in the city."

Unique paused for a minute with ambivalent feelings. In a way, she wished that Took would put up a fuss about her fucking another male. Then she realized that if she had a square for a man, then he would not be okay with it; but she was dealing with a real live gangsta nigga.

He interrupted her thoughts and went in for the kill. "While I was in jail, you was out here fucking and sucking and you didn't send me one iron dime, and I was a'ight. You know good and well I'm a'ight with the shit when it's gonna benefit us both."

She sat silently, eating up every word that Took dished out.

"So, you got any vics, Ms. Bonnie?" he asked as he pulled out some weed and a fresh Philly blunt.

"I got a couple in mind, but it's going to take a minute to manifest, plus they're out of town."

"Out of town is cool. But for starters, we gonna need some local shit to get us on the road."

"I been gone for two and a half years, so I need a few days to see who getting it and who faking it. You been out here. You ain't come across any sure things? I know you been thinking about this for a minute."

Took ran his hand down the length of her body and said, "Off the top of my head? What about that nigga Fat Tee?"

"Just say the word," Unique assured Took.

"Then Fat Tee it is," Took said. Unique looked at him for further instructions, but he only lit the blunt and took a pull.

Never Turn a Ho Into a Housewife

The next morning, Unique sat at the computer in Strolla's guest bedroom. Took had brought her back there the night before, saying it would be best for her to stay with her friend for another day or so while he took care of his business.

"Strolla," she called out.

"What?" Strolla asked, coming into the room.

"I need some old sweats and a T-shirt," Unique said.

"Okay, no problem, but what you need some old shit for?"

"I gotta catch a cab 'round where Fat Tee is. I don't want you to take me, because I don't want him to know we down in case I have to do some shiesty shit. I want to have some old shit on so he can see that nobody is fucking with me but him and take me shopping."

"He gon' be open, anyway, because you just came home."

"I know, but I'm leaving no room for error."

Unique got the cab to pull around the corner and instructed the driver to wait while she walked a block to her destination. She'd had two and half years to come up with this plan, and she was more than ready to put it into action. Before she knocked on the door, she checked to make sure the letter was in her bag. A dark-skinned, gray-haired elderly lady with no teeth in her mouth cracked the door. "Who are you?" she grumbled.

"I'm Unique Bryant, ma'am. I'm an ex-girlfriend of Baby Jon." Unique was as polite as she could be.

"And?" Baby Jon's grandmother put her hands on her hips.

"And his baby momma."

"Baby momma?" the surprised old lady said with a raised eyebrow. Unique nodded and lowered her head as the lady quickly opened up the door, closed her flowery housecoat and invited her in.

"I really don't mean to come here and disturb you, but I need your help. I'm sooo desperate. You have no idea." Unique wiped her eyes. She was putting on an Academy Award-winning performance as the tears rolled down her face.

"What's wrong, baby?" the woman asked as Unique kept sniffling. "Tell Momma Rawlings what's got you so upset."

"Momma Rawlings, I just . . . I just can't take it no mo'," Unique said and broke down in phony sobs.

"If you don't tell me what's goin' on, I can't help you," Momma Rawlings said, passing her a tissue.

Unique blew her nose and said, "I try all I can, and I can't never win."

"Baby, just take a deep breath and tell Momma Rawlings what's goin' on," she said, taking Unique into her arms. Unique had never actually had a mother figure show her love. Her own mother only used her hands to beat Unique when she was frustrated because she had no money to get high. The embrace touched her for a moment, but it didn't take her long to snap back into form and get back to the business at hand.

She looked dead into the woman's eyes. "Momma Rawlings, I just got out of jail for a crime I didn't commit. Once I was locked up, I found out that I was three months pregnant."

"Gracious, chile."

"I know, but I gave my baby the best nourishment that I could while I was in there. I never heard from Jon. E'ryday I would pray for Jon to contact me so he could take care of the baby for me until I got out." Unique looked away as tears poured down her face. She sniffed. "I gave birth to my baby and they let me hold her." Unique paused then began to wail as if she were in physical pain. "They . . . they only let me hold her for about ten seconds before they snatched her away and hauled her off to foster care," she managed to get out through the feigned hysterics. Then she pulled out the photo of Treniece as a newborn that Strolla had given her earlier. She showed it to Momma Rawlings.

"Aw, what a pretty little thing," Momma Rawlings said and took Unique into her arms again. "Baby, we gon' get her back, I promise you. I'm gon' get in touch with Baby Jon and let him know."

That comment made Unique want to jump up and down as if she had just hit the lotto. She had the grandmother's blessings. It was time to go in for the kill. She pulled out the authentic looking letter she had created on the computer. "When I got home from prison and contacted them, I got this letter."

Momma Rawlings took the letter and started to read it, but Unique blurted out its contents. "They say that a family is gonna adopt her. I have to get a lawyer fast."

"Don't worry, baby. Baby Jon will take care of all this. I promise you he's going to take care of it," the grandmother assured her. "When did you come home, chile?"

"Three days ago," Unique answered. "I've been trying to get my baby back ever since."

"Where you stayin' at?"

"With my girlfriend," she said meekly.

"Well, give me your number so I can have Jon call you and y'all can put your heads together."

"I don't usually get back to my girlfriend's house until late, because I be out all day looking for a job."

241

"Well, let me write down my number." Momma Rawlings got up and began looking for a pen. "Here, make sure you check in with me e'ry day, and if you need a place to stay, my door is always open."

"Thank you, Momma." They shared a hug and a moment together.

Just like that, she was in. She had Baby Jon's grandmother on her team. It was too bad that Momma Rawlings didn't know that she was actually teaming up with the enemy. Unique laughed as she walked out of the old lady's house. Actually, if Momma Rawlings knew that Unique had been framed for Baby Jon's crimes and he had left her to rot in the penitentiary while he was off, God knows where, spending all of her hard-earned money, Momma Rawlings would be on her side anyway.

On to my next vic . . . Unique thought as she hopped back into the waiting cab. As they headed to the next destination, she licked her lollipop and enjoyed the smell of the city air coming through the window.

Unique arrived in the hood where Fat Tee had been known to hang. She looked around, and the hood had not changed a bit. This wasn't a good thing. The buildings were still in desperate need of repair, the playground consisted of an old mattress and a tire swing, and baggy-pants-wearing young hustlers were out in full force, slinging their drugs. The crackheads were out trying to make a dollar out of fifteen cents any way they could. Either the folks on the city council didn't know what was going on in the hood or they just didn't care.

She rolled up as Fat Tee was getting out of his SUV. *Bingo.* She leaned out the window and said, "Some things don't never change."

"Hey, baby," he said with a smile as she got out of the cab and gave him a hug. He was so big that she couldn't even wrap her arms all the way around him. He

242

still looked the same except that he had gotten rounder and bigger. She acted like they were madly in love, although Fat Tee had never touched her in a sexual way.

Fat Tee and Unique went way back, when he was one of Took's workers. Took went to jail without collecting his cut from a job he put Fat Tee on. He got Unique to call Fat Tee on a three-way, and Fat Tee acted as if he had the money, telling Took to send Unique to pick it up. When Unique arrived, Fat Tee played hide and seek with her. He told his workers to say he had just stepped out, then he hid in one of his crack houses until Unique left. After this game happened a few times, Unique finally gave up on collecting the money from Fat Tee.

Fat Tee ended up turning a drug strip into an empire, but Unique never had any respect for him. She secretly held ill feelings. However, back then, she knew she couldn't beat him, so she basically joined him, stroking his ego, gaining his trust. Then she got him to agree to have a huge crap party at her house. It was one of the largest after-hours, open to the public crap games to ever hit their hood. At the height of the party, Unique had Train and his homeboys come into the party with ski masks. They laid everybody down and cleaned the whole party out. Nobody was excluded: men, women, or transvestites. And nothing was excluded, either. Money, drugs, guns, big trucks and the slum jewelry—everything worth anything got taken. The partygoers understood from the way the thugs came in and overpowered the entire party that if nobody moved, nobody would get hurt. So, there were no heroes that night. Train and his boys rode off into the night like the long riders while Unique continued to play her role, crying like a baby because she had been robbed. When Fat Tee saw her alligator tears, he was putty in her hands. He comforted her and gave her money to pay her bills, never letting the thought to cross his mind that she had concocted the whole scam.

Licking his lips, he asked, "Where you goin'?" He couldn't help but lust over Unique's body.

"With you." Unique reached into the cab and pulled out her brown paper bag. She set it on the hood of his Range Rover.

He smiled and reached in his pocket to pay the cab driver. The cab pulled off and Fat Tee looked her over in the tight sweatpants that revealed every single curve in her body. All of his silver teeth were glistening as he asked, "Where you was goin', fo' real?"

"Around here to find you."

"Stop bullshittin'." He studied her closely.

"I'm dead serious. Who else I got out here on these streets? All I did while I was in was think about you. But I ain't have no address or nothing to call you or write you. As much as I tried, I couldn't get you out of my mind. I hated the fact that you were in my mind like that."

"Why?"

"Because you left me for dead."

He tried to deny it with a *you know better than that* look. "I did ask Strolla, but she was trippin'." He knew that was no-win conversation, so he decided to focus on now instead of the past. "I'm here now, and I ain't going to never leave you for dead again." He gave her another hug, palming her ass with both of his hands. "Where you just comin' from?"

"The daggone bus station."

"Stop joking," he said.

"Yup. I came straight from jail lookin' for you. Tee, I want to get my shit together," she said with a sincere look, batting her eyelashes. "Doing that time made me think about a whole bunch of things. I want a real family, a nigga that's down for me no matter what. For real, I had a lot of time to think." She stood beside his car and kicked game to him as people passed by.

"What's up with you and dat nigga Took?" he asked. "You know he's home, right?"

"Fuck Took." She paused. "Of all people, you know good and well that nigga ain't fuckin' with me."

"I ain't knowed." He smiled. He was paranoid for a minute, looking all around. "Look, I don't be 'round here like that no mo'."

"Then I'm glad I found you when I did," Unique said, sliding up next to him.

"I be chilling now. My bank is too long to be out here," he bragged. "If a nigga run up on me, even on one of my bad days, shit, that nigga can retire from the dope game."

Unique never responded. She acted like she didn't care, but she was soaking up everything as he continued to let her in on how he was living.

"I just came 'round here to collect my paper. Here," he chirped the Rover to unlock the door, "get in and wait for me. I'll be right back. I'ma go in this do' right quick."

She did as she was instructed. When Tee came out of the house, he looked like a man who felt his life was finally coming together. His cheddar was long, and the girl he had always wanted was out of jail and about to be in his arms. He and Unique had a shady past, but there was something about the shade that attracted him to her. It was too bad he didn't know that lightning was about to strike twice. Unique had robbed him blind once and was about to do it again, but he never saw it coming—the last time or this time, either.

The splurging that Fat Tee poured on her for the next week was just what she needed; shopping, eating out and money in her pocket. At first Tee was a bit skeptical about Unique, but once she lip-boxed his dick and put that snapping coochie on him, just like a fisherman, she reeled him in. Although it was only a week, Fat Tee fell for her hard. At first they lay up in a hotel, but when he was sure that Unique had nobody else in her world, he wanted to truly lock her down. After one week, he moved her in with him in his spot, turning her into his housewife. No one from the hood, none of his workers or friends, had ever been to his house before now.

Unique knew the way to his heart was riding his dick, but once she got her foot in the door, she followed up through his stomach, cooking like a gourmet chef. Unique also gassed his head up selling him dreams about his sex game. She moaned like he was the best thing that had ever touched her. And if that wasn't enough, she would complain about how he'd put a hurting on her, saying she was sore from the way he laid pipe on her. He would say, "Damn, baby, I know my li'l dick can't do much damage."

"It ain't the size of the ship but the motion in the ocean," she would convince him, "and you damn sure know what to do with what you got." This alone had Fat Tee overconfident in Unique and their relationship.

Since Fat Tee had always wanted Unique, he went overboard, trying to impress her by spending, and sharing all of his business with her. He would make and take business phone calls and transactions around her, allowing her to go with him to drop off work and pick up money. She was so deep in his mind within a two-week period that he allowed Unique to count all the money and sit nearby as he weighed out the work.

Fat Tee wasn't new to the game; he had been hustling for years. He should have known better than to try to turn a ho into a housewife, and since he knew her background, Unique should have never been his June Cleaver. But it's always been said that Pussy Is Power!

$$$$$$$

Unique's court date finally came. Fat Tee came with her and waited outside while her attorney, Mr.Emerson, took about five minutes to convince the judge to grant them a continuance. After they left the courthouse, Fat Tee said he needed to take a trip to re-up, but Unique managed to persuade him to take her away to Atlantic City for the weekend.

"Baby, I been locked up all that time. I need to have me a little fun," she whined.

They caught a quick flight. Fat Tee left his re-up cash and all his stash money in their house while he and Unique lay up in the finest hotel in Atlantic City and dined on prime ribs and champagne.

Once they returned to the city, Fat Tee told Unique he had to go and take care of business as they drove home.

"Boo, I need to go to the mall today," Unique said.

He didn't want to say no to Unique, but he also knew he'd played enough this weekend and had to handle his business. Unique knew this too but she was looking at him like she didn't expect to hear him refuse. Fat Tee took a deep breath and came clean.

"Baby, I ain't got no time to run you to the mall. I done had niggas on hold for almost a week now."

"Well, I told you, you didn't have to go to court with me. You could have left the day before and been back after I came from court."

"Boo, you know I didn't want to miss your court date."

"I told you my lawyer said they were gonna continue it."

"But still, I am yo' man, and I wanted to be by your side."

"I appreciate it, boo." She leaned over and kissed his cheek.

"Well, work with me then."

"You know I don't want to hold you up, because I want you to hurry up and come home to me. So go on ahead and drop me off at my friend's house and I'll catch a ride to the mall and then home later."

There was no way she could be with him when he arrived back home. He was stupid, but at this point, Gomer Pyle would've known he'd been set up.

Fat Tee took her to the address she gave him. After going into the apartment building, she came out to wave and let him know that her friend had answered the door.

As soon as Fat Tee pulled off, she hauled tail. If anyone who saw her didn't know any better, she could have been mistaken for Marion Jones, as fast as she was running. She didn't stop sprinting until she got to the convenience store six blocks away. She was winded, but those prison aerobics had paid off. Unique called a cab from the pay phone and made a mental note to get a cell phone. The driver showed up, and she gave him her destination. Five minutes later, she was at Took's apartment.

She put her key in the door and let herself in. Upon entering the apartment, she couldn't believe what her eyes revealed. She did a double take to make sure she was in the right place. For a minute she thought she was hallucinating as she looked around the house and saw all of Fat Tee's furniture. She proceeded to the bedroom and saw Took in Fat Tee's bed, reading the Sunday comics.

"Took, I know you didn't. You took that nigga's furniture," Unique said in astonishment.

"I got your shit that was over there too. Check the closet. It's hung up just the way you left it."

"You funny as shit." Unique went over to the closet and saw all of the things that Fat Tee had bought her. Just like Took said, it was all in order.

"Oh yeah, either that nigga was about to propose to you or he was about to cheat on you, because I got a four-carat engagement ring that I found under all those size fifty-six boxers. That fat motherfucker may have a heart attack after this."

"But his furniture, Took?" Unique just laughed, still in awe that Took had cleaned out Fat Tee's apartment.

"Not only his furniture; but everything that nigga owns. You would have been proud of me. I made the motherfuckin' Grinch look like a choir boy." Took picked up one of Fat Tee's champagne glasses and took a sip from it.

Unique caught sight of the expensive decorative crystal. "Everything?" she asked, shaking her head with a devilish grin. "How were you able to pull it off?"

"It was the easiest shit I ever did, except one time I did think we were gonna get to'-off when a neighbor came over."

"What happened?" Unique asked.

"When they saw the moving truck and us in our uniforms, the lady next door came over. I guess she was just being nosy. I was sure she was gonna call the police. I was half done, but I was prepared to haul ass."

"So what happened?"

"We were jive messed up for a minute. Like I said, I thought she was gonna call the police, but she didn't. She brought over lemonade and asked us did we need any help. She said she would be happy to assist anyone who was getting her shady neighbor out of the community."

"No she didn't!"

"Once we knew the neighbor was cool, we took e'rything. We didn't even leave that fat fucker lunch meat for a sandwich."

"So, was he holding like I told you?" she inquired as her eyes turned into dollar signs.

"You did good, baby!" He nodded then patted her on the back. "He was holding sho' nuff! Between all the cash and the jewelry, it was a little over a half a mil in there."

Unique's pussy got wet when she heard the amount. "Half a million? For real?" Her eyes grew bigger, and so did the dollar signs.

"Not to mention all the furniture," Took said then changed the channel on Fat Tee's Phillips sixty-two-inch plasma TV. "The fat nigga do have good taste."

"But what made you take all that dude's stuff like that? His silverware, his towels, shower curtain, all that?"

"A man has a long time to get his thoughts clear when he's doing time." Took reached over to Fat Tee's bedside table and picked up the box of Philly blunts he'd just bought from the 7-Eleven. Then it dawned on him that Unique had just gotten out of prison herself. "But you know all about that. While I was down, it hit me that Fat Tee was the only one that could have gave the police the information they needed to convict me. If that ain't enough, then the pig nigga didn't pay the money that he owed me." Took looked as if he was thinking back to another time. "Then to top it off," Took paused to split the cigar down the middle with his fingernail, and then he looked her in the eyes, "the nigga tried to take my bitch. Three strikes and he got served. He got what he

250

was begging for, and he better count his blessings that he ain't dead."

Unique took off her clothes and lay down on the bed. "Well, come and take some of this pussy like you took all Fat Tee's shit."

He snickered as he rolled over to Unique to lay a little pipe.

The Show on the Road

"Hey, Momma Rawlings," Unique said softly through the receiver of the phone.

"Hey, baby," the sweet old lady responded.

"How are you doing?"

"I've been fine. Just really worried about you. I've been prayin' for you."

"Thank you. Lord knows I need it."

"We all do." Momma Rawlings sighed before giving Unique the good news. "I talked to Baby Jon, and he says no need to worry about nothing!"

"Really?" Unique exclaimed.

"Yes, baby. He wanted me to give you this number and said for you to call him."

Unique wanted to hang up as soon as the number rolled off Momma Rawlings's tongue, but she played it off with a little bit of small talk. As badly as Unique wanted to call Baby Jon, Took had instructed her not to. Thirty-five minutes after Unique hung up the phone, they were on their way to Greenville, South Carolina, but before they hit the highway, they stopped by Train and Strolla's house so Took could talk to Train.

While the guys talked outside on the deck, Strolla and Unique sat in the kitchen, drinking coffee. Strolla caught Unique up on the latest. "Girl, you know Fat Tee got an all points bulletin out for you!"

"I figured that, but as far as I'm concerned, fuuuuck that nigga."

"You know I know how you feel about him, but at the same time, we agreed to keep it real, so even though I know you could give a rabbit's ass, I had to tell you. That's what real friends do, right?" Strolla said.

"Yup." Unique nodded, touched by Strolla's last words. "That's what real friends do, keep each other on their toes," she said, but she was looking off in space as if something else was on her mind.

"What's wrong, girl? Where your mind at?" Strolla leaned forward.

"You know, Strolla, I just want you to know that I am so glad that we were able to move beyond the past and work on an even stronger relationship."

"I know, who'da thought, right?" Strolla said just as sincerely. "You know, Nique, when Took asked me to bail you out, I wasn't going to do it, but then Train asked me to, and that's why I did it. But now I'm actually glad I did. We have both matured so much, and you have become that missing relationship that I always longed for. I know it's only been a short while since you've been home, but I'm glad you're a part of my life again."

Unique had tears in her eyes. "Ohhh, thank you so much, Strolla. That means so much to me, for real."

"I know you're leaving, but I really wish you wasn't. But promise me you'll be careful," Strolla said.

"I will. I promise."

They were both silent for a while until Unique said, "You know, Strolla, I wasn't gonna say nothing, but since we're keeping it real with each other and we ain't gonna go out like we did before or fall out like most chicks . . ."

"Right," Strolla interrupted. "We can't be on that catty mess. We can't let nothing come between us."

"Well, I have to come clean with you about something, and this is only because I have to apologize to you. I had decided never to tell you, but I have to in order to keep my word in our relationship." Unique dropped her head to avoid eye contact, but then she looked at Strolla. "You know, for so long I've scammed on people and just looked at people for what I could get from them.

My word was nothing to me. I just said whatever words I needed to get what I wanted, but now it's different. I want to start being loyal to the folks I love, and that's you and Took. I want to be a loyal wife to him and be real with our friendship."

"I feel you," Strolla agreed. "I understand perfectly. I feel the same exact way."

"When I'm seventy-five years old, I want us to be wearing our little ugly hats, sitting on the porch, bragging on our grandkids together," Unique confided in Strolla.

"I agree," Strolla said with a smile. "I would love that for us."

"Well, to keep our slate clean and to be completely true to our friendship . . ."

"For sure."

"Now understand the truth hurts!"

"I know, but it is what it is, the truth. I would rather know the truth than live a lie," Strolla assured her friend.

"Let me cut straight to the chase," Unique said, taking a deep breath. "I hope we can still be friends and you won't hate me or be mad at me."

"Of course not," Strolla said, anxious to hear what Unique had to say.

"It's rough, but you know what, if you get mad, I understand. The bottom line is I have to get this off my chest."

Strolla put her arms around Unique as tears rolled down her face. "I feel so ashamed. I actually really feel bad about something I did in my past. It's only two things that I regret doing in my life. One of the them is leaving Took for dead while he was in jail." She covered her face and took another deep breath. "And . . ." She hesitated. "I don't know where to start."

"Just start from the beginning," Strolla urged her.

"Well, once the heist went down at that craps party . . . You remember that for a few days I just acted like I was so depressed and disappointed about the stick-up?"

"I remember," Strolla said, "because I cleaned the house and tried to get everything back in order."

"Well, after the dust settled, I went to meet Train to get my cut of the money."

"Right."

"Well, when I saw all that damn money that Train had and all the power he had from getting over like that, girl, you know my mind started racing, and dollar signs were registering through every bone in my body."

Strolla looked up at Unique as if she saw the knife coming toward her and there was nothing she could do.

"To make a long story short, I don't know what came over me. I just dropped to my knees and took control of Train's dick and gave him some head."

"What?" Strolla shouted.

Unique didn't know what to say, but she could see the frustration written all over Strolla's face. She reached to give Strolla a hug, but Strolla pulled away. "I'm sorry, Strolla. It didn't mean anything, and on top of that, he didn't even do it to me in my coochie. He did it to me in the butt if that makes you feel any better."

"Unique, you know what, I am really hurt. It's not event the fact that y'all had a sexual encounter, but the fact that Train claims he tells me everything and didn't tell me that."

"Girl, it didn't mean anything. And don't blame him. It's all in the past. Now I actually feel bad telling you, but I had to."

"No, Nique, I appreciate it."

Strolla took it under the chin, but Unique felt horrible on the inside. As they sat in total silence, their heart-to-heart chat was broken up by Took.

"Unique, come on. Saddle up and let's roll out."

Strolla looked as if she wanted to say something to Unique, but Took was standing at the door. "Come on, boo, we gotta go."

"A'ight." Unique looked at Took. "Just let me tell Strolla bye."

They embraced each other with a tight, secure hug. "I love you, girl. Take care of yo'self, hear?" Strolla said.

"I will." Unique let go of Strolla. "Kiss the baby for me."

"I will." Strolla promised Unique.

As Took and Unique went on the six-hour drive, Took had a friend get on the Internet to match an address to the phone number. Once they arrived in Greenville, they went straight to the address. Within ten minutes of watching the house, they saw Baby Jon leaving. Unique observed Baby Jon and thought, *Three years and this nigga still wearing his do-rag.*

Jon was still chocolate and handsome, though. His clothes were still very fashionable, and his whole package was up to par. He looked like money, and it made her mad that he had been living the life of luxury with her dough and never sent her a dime. Once Baby Jon was down the road, they put the plan into action.

"This nigga is so damn cheap, he ain't even got no dead bolt," Took said. Within a matter of seconds, Took had whipped out a credit card and they were in the house.

"You sure he ain't got no alarm?"

Took stopped in his tracks, looked at Unique and said, "This nigga is in the middle of the motherfucking boondocks. Who gonna hear it go off? And besides, he's comfortable as shit. He feel he don't need one. So he thinks, anyway."

Took ransacked the house from top to bottom; he even cut open the mattresses. Meanwhile, Unique kept a vigilant watch by the window. Took would've sworn that she didn't even blink.

After a long search, Took came up with nothing.

"This nigga might not even be ballin' no more," Took said impatiently, not thinking that Baby Jon was worth their time since he didn't have the money that Unique had imagined him to have. After all, it had been three years since Baby Jon escaped with Unique's money. Did he jerk the money off foolishly? Was the money long gone? Took didn't want to waste any more of his precious time on something that wasn't a sure lick.

Unique was annoyed with Took's whining. "Where a nigga that dropped out of school in the sixth grade get a new body style 745 from? He ballin'. Just be cool," she said, never taking her eyes off the window.

"Yeah, yeah." He plopped down in a chair and turned on Baby Jon's TV. "Look, we gon' give him until seven in the morning," Took said.

Morning came and went. Then 7 P.M. rolled around and brought darkness, and Baby Jon still had not come back home. Took dozed off and had several naps, but Unique never moved from the window. The desire for vengeance will do strange things to a person.

"Look, man, this nigga ain't coming back and he ain't ballin'. He living comfortably off of yo' money. It's time to go. We've been here for twenty-nine hours."

"Look, I can feel it. The nigga is coming back. If you got somewhere to go then you can go, but I'm staying. I can do this shit myself. But if you ever believed in me, ever, I need you to believe in me now." Her voice was sympathetic, but she never left the window. "Look, Took, this here is personal to me. That nigga took my money and left me on Gilligan's Island. All the shit was his. I'm

257

telling you, my woman's intuition tells me he's coming back."

"That nigga got you fucked up, don't he?" Took asked as if he couldn't believe it.

"Yup, but trust me, that joker is coming back." Just then, they heard Baby Jon roll up, and the car's headlights hit the house.

As soon as he opened the door, Took hit him so hard in the back of the head that Baby Jon was knocked unconscious. Took slipped on his ski mask. While Baby Jon was out cold, Took used duct tape to bind Baby Jon's hands behind his back and tape his ankles together. Baby Jon's eyes flickered open.

"Nigga, why the fuck you had me waiting two days for you?" Took hit Baby Jon upside the head again. Jon didn't respond. "Motherfucker, since you had us waiting for two days, you ain't got a whole bunch of time to bullshit us. I should kill you for wasting my time. You got sixty seconds to tell us where the hell the money is." Took placed the barrel of his pistol on Baby Jon's temple.

Without hesitation, Baby Jon submitted. "It's outside, under my dog's house." He recited the combination to the underground safe. Before Took left the room, he told Baby Jon, "You did the right thing. And it better be there."

Took went into the back yard with a silencer attached to his nine millimeter handgun. Before anyone knew it, both of the pit bull guard dogs were dead. He moved the doghouse, and just like Baby Jon said, there was a safe under it.

In the process of opening the safe, Took heard an agonizing cry. He pulled out his gun and ran back into the house. He couldn't believe his eyes; Unique was sodomizing Baby Jon with a broomstick. She had about five inches rammed up his ass. "I'm gonna fuck you with this broom one minute for every month I was locked down for your sorry ass." Unique paid no attention to the blood all over her hand. She just kept driving the stick home.

Took watched in horror. His stomach turned. There was no need for him to witness anybody getting raped of his manhood by a woman, so he ran back out to retrieve what he had come for. He made his way back out to the doghouse to gather up all the money while Baby Jon screamed like a banshee.

Once she was finished, Unique leaned on the counter, popped open a Pepsi and drank it, gulping it down. That was the moment Took realized that Unique wasn't as soft as he thought she was. She had heart, and would kill if she had to. She was perfect.

Big Time

On the ride to Atlanta, Took sat in the passenger seat, looking at fashion magazines. He tore out the pages with Li'l Kim, Foxy, Beyonce, Naomi and a few other models. He studied the pictures and put them straight in his pocket.

After arriving in Atlanta, it was taking them a little longer to catch up with Big Time than it did with Baby Jon. Although Unique had stolen the address out of Kitty's phone book before she left, they discovered that the address was a boogey. But the pictures of him that she had also taken weren't. So she knew what he looked like, but better than that, his name was a dead giveaway.

One night, after they had searched the strip clubs with no luck, they headed back to their hotel, both silently wondering if they'd ever find him. Just as they were pulling up to valet, a commercial came on the radio:

"Big Time Entertainment presents a get crunk party . . ."

That was all they needed to hear.

The next day, Took sent Unique over to Lenox Mall, instructing her to recreate some of the foxy pictures he had torn out of the magazine. He needed Unique to look like money so she could play her position. She had to look the part. And if a person in Atlanta wanted high fashion, then Lenox Mall was the place.

While Unique was in Saks trying on some shoes, she began a general conversation with another girl who she could tell was a diva.

"Those are so cute," Unique lied about some shoes the girl was trying on. Unique wouldn't have worn them to a dog show.

260

"You think so?"

"Yeah, girl, they are. Wonder if they have these in a size six." Unique picked up a pair of Chanel sandals.

The girl looked in the mirror. "I wonder if these are going to look right with what I'm trying to do."

"What you trying to do?" Unique asked.

"I'm supposed to be going to this party tonight."

"Oh, for real?"

"Yeah, I'm trying to catch me a baller," she whispered.

"Shoot, me too," Unique replied, making the girl feel more comfortable so she would loosen up.

"Well, damn, you need to come with me then."

"Where?"

"This guy name Big Time is having a party tonight." Unique didn't respond. She only listened. "And chile, that dude got so much freaking money, he makes your pussy get wet if you're in a five feet radius of him."

Unique laughed. "Girl, that's the shit I like."

"I'm Nek-qua." Unique extended her hand, giving the girl her alias.

"We done got to be best friends and don't even know each other's names," the girl said with a laugh. "I'm Missy."

Unique knew Missy was just the type of girl she needed in her corner in Atlanta. She could tell this girl made sure that her shit was in order to catch a baller. Unique looked her over; she had all the ingredients to wheel in a money-getting man. Her healthy-looking blond hair was in place in a spiked short haircut. Her nails and feet were done. She had a shape that looked like she had just stepped out of Bally's gym. Her makeup was flawless.

"Chile, you need to go with me to the party tonight," Missy repeated. "Maybe you can hook Big Time. I had

261

met one of his li'l workers, but the workers is getting money out of control too. His boy supposed to be leaving my name at the door," she said in an excited tone.

"Oh, okay," Unique agreed. "You just gotta give me your number and stuff. You might even have to pick me up because I'm not from here, and I don't know my way around here really good."

"That's cool. Now, you ain't gonna to stand me up, are you?"

"Naw, I'm going fo' real."

They continued to shop together, and Missy was impressed with Unique's sense of style. But Unique didn't overplay her hand and show off, because she didn't want to make Missy jealous. She knew how women could be.

That day flew past, and around 7:30, they both went their separate ways to get dressed. After they parted, they stayed on the phone.

While they were shopping, Took had gone to test drive a drop-top 635 BMW and convinced the dealer to allow him to keep it for a few days while he made his decision. He somehow got them to put thirty-day tags on it.

When they met up in the hotel room, Took gave Unique specific instructions about the rules of the night. He presented her with basically every scenario he could think of to prepare her for the takeover of Big Time. Handing her the keys to the 635 B'mer, he gave Unique a kiss then sent her off to hook up with Missy.

Unique met Missy at a restaurant near the hotel, where she instructed her to park her Toyota Solara and hop in the BMW. They were flossing like no tomorrow with the top down on the B'mer as they valet parked. They walked past the line wrapped around the building, straight to the front of the club to the VIP entrance, like Missy's friend had instructed them.

A girl with a twisted face stood at the door with a clipboard. "Yes?" she said nastily, after looking them both over from head to toe when they approached.

Missy spoke up. "Missy Johnson. My name should be on the list. Me and a guest."

"Nope, it's not," the girl said, not even looking at the clipboard.

"Ty was supposed to leave my name here. I just talked to him." Missy pulled out her cell phone to call Ty, but she didn't get an answer. She left a message on his phone.

"Well, the bottom line is you need to either pay or move to the side," the girl told them.

Missy looked as if she wanted to disappear right then and there.

"How much is it?" Unique interjected to try to repair the damage that was already done to her newfound friend's ego.

The girl rolled her eyes but then put a smile on her face. "It's a hundred and fifty dollars." She paused for just a second then stressed, "Each."

Unique went into her Hermes bag and pulled out three hundred-dollar bills. "Here you go," she said, peeling off the money as if it was nothing, pushing it to the employee. "Let's go, Missy." Unique looked at the girl with an expression on her face that said, *You ain't said shit, bitch.*

"Nope." The employee handed Unique her money. "The end of the line is back there for regular people. This line is for VIP guests only," she stressed.

As they were about to walk off, some guy walking past with an entourage stopped, looked both of them up and down and said, "Yo, they with me. Come on, ladies."

He smiled and they followed past the velvet ropes into the club. With the club jam-packed and the dude rolling with so many in his entourage, somehow they got separated from the guy who got them in.

"Girl, I don't see him," Missy said.

"Chile, it doesn't matter. As long as he got us in here."

They went straight to the bathroom and could barely hear the music. As they stood in line for a stall to come available, Unique put her hand up to share a word or two with Missy. "Two things I hate," Unique confided. "A: When a motherfucker stunt on me about having my name on the VIP list, and B: for a bitch's pussy to get wet about it."

"I feel you." Missy smiled and gave her a big high five. They both used the bathroom, checked their makeup and exited.

The club was unlike anything Unique had ever seen before. She was used to being the greatest hoochie of all times when she wanted to be, but the chicks in the club had her beat. The Ying Yang Twins' song, "Whistle While You Twirk" started playing, and the women went wild. Unique looked around the room, trying to make eye contact with a baller who could get them in the VIP room, but when "A Tip Drill" by Nelly blazed through the club's speakers, any prospects she might've had were not paying any attention to her. Maybe it was because she didn't have all of her female attributes hanging out.

She poked out her lips, mad at Took for not having her dressed half naked. Took wanted her to dress sexy and sophisticated. Evidently, he didn't know that he had the dress code for the night completely wrong. He knew that the club would be filled with tons of woman trying to emulate the video chicks, and he had wanted Unique to stand out in the crowd. The Just Cavalli beaded jeans with the halter top to match would have been a huge hit somewhere else, but that night, the ballers were looking for trashy, not classy.

Just as the thought crossed Unique's mind, Missy got the bouncer at VIP to let them in. When they got in, they saw that the raunchy, exotic dances going on behind the access-granted VIP were out of control. On a normal night, Unique would have been able to fit in, but this night, she was on a mission for something different, and under Took's tight orders.

As they stood around watching the girls, they turned to each other with a look that said, *These bitches are fierce.*

Unique decided to take matters into her own hands. "Money talks, right?"

Missy nodded. "Yup. You want to put up and buy a bottle, that's good, but we gotta sit down because my feet is killin' me."

"Not the new shoes," Unique quipped as they made their way over to a table near the back of the VIP.

They were seated for less than two minutes before a cocktail waitress came over. "These seats are reserved for Cristal bottle buyers," the server informed them with an attitude.

Missy glanced at Unique then looked at the waitress like she was about to go ghetto and smack the taste out her mouth. Unique smiled and said, "Then bring us two, and every time we pop the second bottle, bring another." The waitress's lip hit the floor. She wasn't used to women balling out of control like that with no man around. "Oh yeah, don't worry. We some classy chicks. We got you on the tip, momma."

"I didn't mean any disrespect. I'll be right back." The waitress disappeared into the crowd.

About five minutes later, Unique noticed the waitress making her way back over to them with her hands full. Unique leaned over to Missy and said, "Look, this is the deal. We about to be some balling broads. Mark my words and watch how these jokers flock to us. Don't even make any eye contact with them. Don't dance or offer conversation. Men always want what they think they can't have."

"Girl, I got it," Missy concurred.

They toasted, and like Unique predicted, the men paused when the bottles started popping. They all wanted to know who the two women were. When Unique brought the glass up to her mouth to take a sip of the champagne, she noticed Took watching her from over in the corner of the VIP. She was so stunned, she almost choked on her drink. Took lifted his glass from across the room.

The Cristal even pulled Ty over to the table. He gave Missy some lie about why he ain't hear his phone and how her name should have been on the VIP list. Missy just looked the other way and began favoring another guy with her attentions, letting Ty know good and well that she didn't want to hear that bull.

After about an hour of balling, Missy whispered in Unique's ear, "Here come Big Time, the dude whose party this is. He look like he's coming over here. The one in the yellow-and-white button-up shirt."

Big Time was indeed a cutie pie. The pictures that Kitty had did him no justice at all. He was a big dude, but he carried his weight well. Light-skinned with braids, he had a mean swagger. He was so clean-cut and cool.

Big Time walked up to their table. "Baby, your money is no longer any good in this club."

"What?" Unique questioned.

"From this point on, your tab is on me. That is, if you don't mind."

"I don't mind at all. I'm just trying to have a good time in this town."

"Well, you're talkin' to the right person then. I owns this town."

"Show me, because I don't believe you," Unique said, taking a sip of her drink. "Besides, I always heard that this was Jermaine Dupri's town."

"No problem, I'll do just that," he answered.

"How you gon' do that?" Unique asked in her most seductive voice. She had to put her mouth up to Big Time's ear to even be heard over the loud music.

He smiled because he liked Unique's style. He turned his head back and responded, "How about you be my special guest for my after party?"

"Where at?" She could tell by the look in his eyes what he was going to say next.

He leaned in to test the waters. "At my hotel suite."

"Oh." She knew she was in there. Once in his bed, it would be all she wrote. "But I think maybe we need to get to know each other a bit first."

For the rest of the night, he latched onto Unique like a duck takes to water, never going far from her. He took her around and began introducing her as his "baby." The other girls in the club were jealous, and Unique worked that moment for all that it was worth. She played her part to the tee. She purred when she spoke to him, and to all who were watching, it looked as though they had been together for years instead of a couple of hours.

When the party at the club was over, Big Time got Ty to drop Missy off, and Unique followed Big Time to the hotel. On the way there, he wanted to stop for gas. While he gassed up both cars, she told him she was going next door to the IHOP to use the restroom.

She ran into the restaurant to call Took on her cell phone. "Hey, boo," she greeted Took.

"Hey, baby," he returned.

"You ain't going to believe it. I reeled that clown in," she said, all excited. "He bit! Can you believe it?"

"Of course I can. I knew you would. I got faith in you, baby. Don't forget to wash your hands when you come out the restroom."

"Where are you?" she asked.

"Don't worry about it. I'm always close," Took teased. "Look, baby, listen up. I'm watching you every step of the way. You hear me? If something ever look shady, the most I'll ever be is a phone call away." Unique was silent as Took continued. "I was gonna surprise you, but I'll go ahead and tell you now. This is our last sting for a while. I made reservations for two weeks from now to take you on a romantic vacation. We can be back right before you have to go to court. With us working so hard, we barely had a chance to enjoy each other."

Then he laid on the charm. "I need you to spend some time with this joker. Baby, we got ten days. Try to get him to take you to where he keeps his money and product. I need you to lay down your best work, and only make contact with me when it's a hundred percent safe."

"Okay," she agreed, feeling slightly apprehensive.

"And you know what, baby? After ten days if nothing is popping, don't worry about it, because I don't want a thing to delay our vacation together. It's gonna be special. I got us a couple of passports and e'rything."

"Boo, I'm gonna make this clown eat out the palm of my hand." She smirked as she painted on the MAC lipstick.

"I know you will. Just keep me posted."

"Just watch my back," she shot back.

268

"Look, baby, that nigga is in the restaurant walking to the bathroom," he quickly warned Unique. "I'm gone."

"You that close to me?" she asked, surprised but happy.

"Always, and I'm gone before you get caught. I love you."

"Me too." She pressed the end button and opened up the door. Big Time was about five feet away.

"I was coming to check on you."

"I was trying to make sure I was all powdered up for you."

"You don't need no makeup, baby. You're America's next top model," he beamed, making sure she knew that in his eyes, she was a dime piece.

She smiled and thanked him, while discreetly scoping out the area to see if she could find Took. She didn't.

It didn't take long for Unique to pussy-whip Big Time. As a matter of fact, it was easier than she thought. He was a sucker for red bones, especially one equipped with good coochie, a cute face, and an out-of-this-world head game. It only took a few days to find out that when it came to his business, he was more comfortable trusting women than men. That's why he and Kitty were so close.

Watching the amount of weight he moved, Unique had to switch up her game. There were only a few days left before her and Took would be on some romantic island. She had to pick up the pace by overpowering him with her sex game day and night while he moved a bunch of weight in between.

While they were having a room service dinner eight days after they first met, Unique told him that she was about to leave in a day or so.

"Why?" he asked. "We got something nice here, and we need to be together. Whatever it is that you do in Memphis, I can see to it that you do it bigger and better in Atlanta." He took her hand. "I want you to get a place here with me. We gotta work out something."

"Well, first off, I gotta come clean with you."

He looked disappointed as he asked, "You got a nigga back home, don't you?"

"Naw." She put up her hand to calm him down. "Just hold tight."

"What is it then?"

"Look, if you let me finish then I can tell you."

"A'ight, I'm listening."

"My business back home," she started, "it's, shall we say, in the pharmaceutical sector." This took Big Time by surprise, and Unique knew there was no turning back now. "I came down here on a fishing expedition to try to find a new supplier."

"I see," Big Time said. "So, exactly what, uh, pharmaceutical do you specialize in?"

"Most of my clients are bisexual," she said. She used the code word for people who were both cocaine and heroin users. "I got fifty grand I need to invest, drive back to Memphis, see my distributors, and I can be back in your arms in about a week. Wait here a minute." Unique went outside to the car and got the Gucci knapsack filled with money. Took had just put it in the trunk that morning. She came back in and emptied the contents on the table in front of Big Time.

He looked at the stacks of money for a moment and thought about the past eight days he'd spent with her. No way an FBI agent could give head like that, and if she wasn't a fed, how much harm could a girl with fifty Gs be? He made up his mind. "Look no further." He smiled at Unique. "You found your new supplier."

Unique smiled. *This was too easy.*

"For now, get dressed. I gotta take you somewhere," Big Time instructed her.

He took her to the stash house, which was on the ninth floor of a very nice condominium building in downtown Atlanta. The living room was totally furnished, but it had an unlived-in feel to it. The apartment had two bedrooms and two bathrooms. In one of the bedrooms was a full-sized bed and nothing else. In the back bedroom, there was a large glass table with two chairs, one on each side, and an electric scale. To the left of the table was a walk-in closet behind two sliding wooden doors.

Big Time walked to the back room while Unique excused herself to use the bathroom before joining him. While in the other room, Unique made a phone call and said only two words: Apartment 527.

When Unique returned, Big Time pointed to one of the chairs and said, "Have a seat." She did as she was told. He pulled the sliding door to the left and stepped into the closet. Once inside, he switched on a light. From where Unique was sitting, she could see computer boxes stacked practically to the ceiling.

Unique wished Took was there right then. When Big Time stepped out of the closet with the large box in his hand, Unique greeted him with a .40-caliber handgun with a silencer.

"Put the box down and lay on your stomach. Now!" Unique shouted.

Big Time stopped in his tracks, eyes as big as saucers. He had known his dick would get him in real trouble one of these days, but he didn't think it would be this much trouble, and he surely didn't think it would be this day.

"Stop bullshitting," he said. He swore to himself at that moment that if he got out of this alive, he would hunt Unique down 'til his dying day.

Speaking clearly and firmly, Unique said, "I said get on the floor. And I mean it."

"Come on. You can't be serious." Big Time tried his hand.

The sound from the gun was like the wind escaping from the doorjamb of a Mercedes when it slammed shut.

"Aaaaaggh!" Big Time screamed and fell to the floor, holding his knee.

Within ten seconds, Took and Train were coming through the door, masked and with guns drawn. "Nigga, you know what's up. You can do this our way or you can take the highway."

Unique interrupted, "The highway to hell, that is."

Train handcuffed Big Time's ankles and hands while Took checked to be sure Unique was okay.

"It's in the closet," she informed them.

Took and Train hurried to the closet. When they looked inside, they couldn't believe their eyes. There were over two hundred kilos of cocaine and one hundred kilos of heroin in front of them.

Train glanced over at Big Time as he gathered all the drugs out of the closet. "Homey, you fell fo' the banana in the tailpipe."

"Never let your emotions override your intellect. You should have known better," Took said with a lopsided smile behind his mask.

"Li'l Time was thinking for Big Time, that's what's up," Unique added. "By the way, Kitty says to tell you hi. So much for that fish-pussy bitch! And by the way, she gives better head than you do!" Although Big Time could eat a hell of a pussy, Unique had to hit him with one below the belt.

About forty minutes later, after cleaning out Big Time's stash house, they were on the way out of the door. Unique smiled as she thought about all the money they could get for all the drugs they'd loaded into the rented SUV. She and Took were going to be set for life.

In Belize

The soft breeze creeping into the room through the open balcony doors woke Unique. When she opened her eyes, she briefly scanned the room then turned her head to her left and saw him lying there, sleeping as if he were dreaming. Unique thought she had been dreaming as well, but now she had confirmation that none of this was a dream. It was real.

She smiled when she realized that at least one minute had gone by and she was still watching Took sleep. *This is crazy,* she thought. *I'm sitting here watching a grown man sleep.* She leaned over and softly kissed his bare shoulder then slowly got out of the bed, trying not to wake him. Her bare feet hit the cold hardwood floors and it felt good. She stood there for a minute watching the sheer white curtains on the balcony door dance to the wind's rhythm. She started toward the breeze.

Unique didn't even bother moving the sheer pieces of silk cloth out of her way. She walked right through them, allowing the material to caress her face until she was out on the balcony. Once she was outside, the soft ocean breeze took over, its fingertips gently fondling her entire body.

She focused on the ocean's waves smacking the shore. This was the only sound she could hear. She didn't even hear Took get out of bed and make his way to join her on the balcony. He stood there next to her for several minutes, bare butt naked, as she remained focused on the waves.

"I ain't never seen the ocean before," Took said as he handed her a drink. "Or maybe I just ain't never paid attention before."

"Me either," Unique said, taking a sip of her drink. She looked up at Took, who really seemed to be taking note of the ocean, the enormity of it. It was bigger than the two of them ever would be.

Unique set down the drink, walked behind Took and put her arms around him so that her hands rested on his chest. She laid her face against his back. After a moment or two, she began placing little pecks all over his back. Took turned around and returned the favor by placing succulent kisses all over Unique's face. She rolled her head back as he began planting them all over her neck. The next thing she knew, he was attempting to carry her back into the room.

"No," Unique said, almost in a whisper. "Right here."

Took pushed her against the railing. Unique stood there for a moment, admiring his nakedness. Really admiring it. Took watched as she lifted her skimpy negligee over her head and let it drop at her feet. He began to knead her breasts with his hands; his tongue then followed suit, licking every inch of her breasts, taking each nipple in turn to rest between his lips.

"Oh, Took," Unique moaned. Her body was feeling warm and sensitive to his every touch.

He took Unique by the waist and leaned her up against the balcony. They kissed passionately for what seemed like forever before Unique could no longer take his dick simply rubbing against her. She needed it inside of her, so she took her hand and placed Took in. There the two stood on the balcony, their bodies in sync, pleasing one another.

"Oh, shit, you feel so good," Took said. "It's never felt like this before."

Took's slow strokes all of a sudden turned into quick, deep ones as Unique's titties began to dance with each thrust. He lifted Unique by her butt and she wrapped her legs around his waist, burying her nails into his back. Both their bodies tightened as they reached their climax together. They stood on the balcony, holding their position. Neither said a word. Not only was it the first time either had ever really witnessed the ocean, it was the first time they had truly made love since their reunion from prison.

By the time they went back inside, the Ecstasy and heroin mix that Took had dissolved in Unique's drink was now really taking effect. Took lay back in the king-sized bed while Unique's head bobbed up and down on his penis. She had taken her world famous, state-of-the-art blow job to another level.

When she came up for air and wiped her mouth with the back of her hand, Took's eyes were glazed over with lust. As she was about to go back down on him, he said, "Hold up. I need you to lay on your side." Unique did as she was told. Took raised her top leg as far as it would go and pushed his dick inside her with one thrust.

"Whose pussy is this?" he asked. He had never been so rough with her, but she loved it.

"Yours," she answered in a heavy voice, enjoying every minute of the action. Took pulled his Johnson straight back out of Unique's womb. He slid it down the crack of her ass and started to work its large head back and forth in her butthole. He used his hands to spread her cheeks so that he could explore a little deeper.

Unique raised her head with an expression of pure pain as she tried to shake off her drug-induced haze. Took shoved two fingers into her open pussy and started making circles with them like he was stirring a mixed drink. Her facial features transformed from pain to pleasure instantaneously. "Don't stop," she begged. "Please don't stop." Unique started to chew on her bottom lip, and it wasn't long before she was moving her ass in rhythm with Took. They went on for hours with wild, uninhibited sex, and then finally the drugs took over Unique's body and she fell into a deep, coma-like sleep.

She was awakened by a loud knock at the door. "Abre! Abre la puerta! Abre la puerta, puta! Es hora de hacer dinero! Es hora de trabajar! Tengo clientes esperando." The knocks turned into bangs.

When she opened her eyes, she sat up in the bed, trying to focus on where she was. She wasn't in the same tropical honeymoon spot where she fell asleep in Took's arms. This place, a dirty little room with crumbling walls and a concrete floor, was the lowest of the low. A horrible smell hit her in face; then she saw a huge bug crawling on a letter on the small, dingy pillow beside her. She grabbed the letter and opened it. It read:

It's been fun, but it's time for us to go our separate ways. I know you ain't surprised, are you? In the back of your mind, you never thought that this shit was real, did you? Well, let me put you down with what's really real. I spent my last money to get you out, which was the best investment that I ever made. I knew I would get my money back, but I never thought that I'd get a multimillion-dollar return in a matter of three months. But never underestimate the power of the pussy, especially attached to a conniving bitch.

We had a good thing going, no doubt, and for a minute I had convinced myself that the sky was the limit. But then I had a flashback of how I sat on the cell block, drinking Mountain Dew, waiting on mail call. Not only did I get clowned by the fellow inmates, but I was so disappointed when no letters came . . . because you were

*busy running around the city, drinking cum for pennies. A
nigga just can't forget that.*

*As of now, you are the property of Jose Villa. I sold
you to him for two chickens, a mule and a key of coke. The
mule because you played me for an ass, and the chicken
cuz you's a chicken head bitch. The coke was a bonus
that he threw in—which I gave to Train. Don't worry. They
gonna let you work off the debt for twenty dollars a trick.
They say the average bitch can work it off in five years,
but you ain't average. With that head game you got, I
know you can do it twice as fast. Oh, and I got your
passport, but I know you can get another. Strolla sends
her best and said 'what goes around comes around.'*

I know you'll be the wetbacks' favorite!

Just then, the door burst open and a large, sweaty
Hispanic man stumbled inside with some pesos in his
hand. Took had gotten over like a fat rat. He had stolen
her heart, her money and her passport. He saw to it that
she was a wanted woman, not only by the courts but by
all of her vics. Every single time they robbed someone,
Took's face was covered, but never hers. She was sure
that all three of the men had put a price on her head.

Taking in all that had happened, Unique wished
momentarily that she were back in prison with Kitty's
fishy pussy in her face. Then she thought again.
Although her heart ached immensely, she realized there
was no point in crying over spilled milk now. And for the
first time in her life, she realized that what goes around
actually does come back around . . . in double doses.
What you give life is what life gives you back!

She'd just have to put on her best game face and get
all she could get out of this situation, waiting for the day
when it would be her turn for payback. *They haven't*

seen the last of me, she said to herself. *On e'erything I love, I swear I'll be back.*

She balled up the note, looked at the sweaty man, licked her lips and said in her sexiest voice, "Hola, senor."